The Last Eligible BACHELOR

SEASONS OF CHANGE SERIES

ASHTYN NEWBOLD

THREE LEAF
PUBLISHING

Edited by Jenny Proctor

Three Leaf Publishing, LLC

www.ashtynnewbold.com

 Created with Vellum

CHAPTER 1

The duty of a lady's maid was, first and foremost, to offer a listening ear to her mistress. She was to be smart, informed, and sophisticated when it came to current fashions, as well as have a proficient knowledge of her mistress's complexion and which colors best suited it. Her arsenal was to include creams, combs, a sewing kit, and a touch of rose salve.

But with a mistress like Miss Sophia Sedgwick, I was required to keep more than just her complexion in perfect condition. I was required to keep her secrets.

"My mother refused my trip to Hampden Park again." Sophia slumped into the chair in front of me, letting out a long sigh. "She says I must go to Bibury instead. An invitation has come from some distant relative of mine, but I have no wish to meet her or endure her intentions for my visit." Sophia met my eyes in the mirror. "This old woman claims she has a handsome young gentleman to match me with, should I like to have the opportunity. There are four other ladies coming to meet him." She cast her gaze upward. "I don't care to beg and compete for attention from a gentleman who is likely not even handsome or rich. At any rate, I have no wish to be married yet, so why should I be forced to go?"

Sophia had already spent much of the day arguing with her mother over her expected trip to Bibury. Mrs. Sedgwick had not been willing to concede, and Sophia was expected to leave in less than a week. If she did happen to marry this mysterious gentleman, I could only hope she would take me with her as her lady's maid in her new household. She was quite fond of me when I listened silently to her prattle. Although, keeping Sophia unmarried would allow me to stay in the same household as my mother, who currently served as Mrs. Sedgwick's maid.

I began running my comb through her blonde hair. I opened my mouth to speak, but she raised her hand to shush me. "Oh, I do not care what you think. You are only a maid. How pathetic and sad that you are the only female I have to converse with." Her upper lip curled with disgust and she leaned closer to the mirror. She traced her cheek with her finger, sitting back with a scowl. Had she found something wrong? As I saw it, Sophia's appearance was as perfect as a lady could ever wish for. Porcelain skin, blue eyes, long, curved lashes, a natural flush to her cheeks...not a blemish in sight.

"If I went to Hampden Park for the spring instead, I could be with my dearest friend, Anne," Sophia continued. "I have been dreaming of seeing her grand home for years. Mama has never allowed me to go because she despises Anne's mother. She married the man Mama intended to wed, and their friendship has been shattered ever since."

If I were a gossip, I would have loads of secrets to spread below stairs. But I was raised a lady, and so would behave like one. There was also the unsettling fact that I could be released from my position in an instant if I was found gossiping. There had been a time Sophia had listened to *me*, but that was before I became her maid. All she cared now was that I conducted myself in a manner befitting my new station. So I continued combing in silence, a task which took several minutes, what with the length and thickness of her hair. My ears remained peeled, should she like to deposit any more secrets within them.

"But that does not mean I cannot be friends with Anne!" Sophia continued in a whine. "Perhaps in visiting Hampden Park, I might aid in reconciling our mothers. If I go to this matchmaking woman now, I will surely be pursued by the gentleman and have no choice but to accept his offer. I will have no opportunity for adventure again." She gave an anguished sigh. "How will I bear it?" True to form, she didn't really expect an answer. Her blue eyes caught on her reflection again. "I ought not to frown so much. I will have wrinkles like yours."

I examined my reflection. What wrinkles I had were

not caused by aging. I was just three days over two and twenty, after all. Regardless, their origin was not a mystery. I could think of the many times in my life I had chosen to frown when I might have smiled. If I had known to cherish what I once had, I might not have acquired such creases in my face, faint as they were. But Sophia missed nothing, especially when it came to the flaws of others.

"I should like a warm bath drawn in the morning."

I nodded, making a mental note.

"I have tea with my mother and Lady Dinah in the afternoon. Which dress do you suggest for my present complexion?" Sophia framed her face with her hands, looking up at me expectantly.

"I would suggest blue, perhaps the silk gown you purchased two weeks ago. Lady Dinah hasn't yet seen that one."

Sophia pursed her lips. "I will consider it." She turned back to face the mirror, and I quickly worked her hair into a braid for sleep before tightening the rags around her face.

She released a long yawn, pulling her night jacket over her chemise. "You may go now, Sherbrooke." She stood and climbed into bed. I curtsied before blowing out the candles around the room, taking the last one with me, the small light guiding me to the door and out into the dark hall of Sedgwick Manor.

Sherbrooke. I missed being called Tillie or Matilda. I would have even liked *Miss* Sherbrooke. Pinching my shoulder blades together, I corrected my thoughts. My life would never be what it once was. The Sedgwick family had been exceedingly kind in taking me on as Sophia's maid after the ruination my father brought upon my mother and me. I should be grateful. Content. Relieved. The words pounded into my skull as I made my way downstairs, trying to stir up real emotions inside me. Perhaps soon I would feel them.

My bed was a welcome sight, and I curled atop the blanket for a moment before readying myself for sleep. Tucking my chin onto my arm, I waited for my eyes to fully adjust to the dimness before reaching for the letter I kept under my pillow.

My dearest Tillie, it began. That first line was my favorite.

Papa's gruff and gentle voice floated up through the letter, entering my comprehension through my thoughts rather than my ears like I wished it would. It had been too long since I had heard him speak. Tears stung my eyes as I folded the letter closed again, each fold delicate and slow. I bit back my emotion, fighting the longing in my heart.

My life had changed. That was all. It had changed, but it was not over. There was always some good to be seen in every circumstance. My life was far more comfortable than Papa's life at the moment. I closed my eyes against the image of what he might be enduring now, after spending the last three months imprisoned in Canterbury Gaol.

And I was helpless, *entirely helpless* to save him.

I studied the letter again, my heavy exhales causing my candle flame to flicker in and out. The words had begun to fade on the creases, and soon the paper would tear. But I still couldn't stop myself from reading it every night. It was a wasteful thing to do, for I had already memorized each word.

My head pounded as I slipped the worn paper under my pillow, my body aching from the events of the day. Without bothering to change, I blew out the candle and my eyes drifted closed. It seemed I had only slept for a few hours before a thick hand grasped my upper arm.

My eyes shot open, heart pounding. Had I slept too long? I had accustomed myself to the new schedule, but the unforgiving face of the housekeeper, Mrs. Brisbane, stared down at me. Her square jaw and wide-set eyes looked rather masculine in the dimness.

"Mistress Sophia 'as taken ill," she said.

I rubbed my eyes, staggering to my feet. A sharp pain drove into my skull, and I blinked hard in an attempt to clear it. I chided myself for feeling disappointed in the sleep I would lose. Sophia's health was a much greater priority.

"With what?" I pulled my loose hairs together into a knot at the base of my neck, covering it once again with my ruffled cap. "Has the physician already been called for?"

"No. She claims it be a mild ailment."

I hurried past Mrs. Brisbane and made my way to Sophia's room. There were times when her 'ailments' were less illness and more nightmare related. The dark corridors had formed a map in my head over the last year, especially the path from my room below stairs to Sophia's grand bedchamber. When I opened the door, Sophia bolted upright in her bed, her blonde hair sticking out at strange angles where it had escaped the braid. More unsettling, however, was the eager smile on her face.

"Sherbrooke, I could not sleep." She bounced in her covers. "I have had the most clever idea."

I walked closer, doing all I could to maintain an even expression. She had pulled me out of bed to tell me her idea? Could she not have waited until morning? I took in her appearance, searching for any sign of illness. Aside from the strange smile on her face, she seemed to be perfectly ordinary. "I was told you were ill."

Her eyes rounded. "Not *ill*. I am *unwell*. There is a difference, you know. I am unwell because I cannot sleep for fear of forgetting my clever idea."

"I see." I held in my sigh as I approached, hands clasped behind my back. I did not need to encourage her to share the idea—she appeared to be near to bursting for withholding it as long as she already had.

She brought her knees to her chest, resting her chin atop them with a broad smile. "As you know, I have no wish to go to Bibury, and my parents intend to force me into it."

I nodded.

"Hampden Park is *on the way* to Bibury."

"Indeed."

"As I have never met this strange, matchmaking woman before, she would be none the wiser as to what my appearance and conduct are like." She brushed an errant strand of hair away from her face. "If I were to somehow convince Papa not to accompany me to Bibury and to allow you to be my sole chaperone on the trip, then my idea will be quite plausible indeed." She seemed to be thinking aloud now, tapping her knee with her fingertips. "Yes, it could certainly be as clever as I think it is."

As her maid, I was expected to keep quiet and patient and simply listen, but I was tempted to ask for further explanation. I still had at least an hour before dawn, and if Sophia wasn't truly ill, then I could go back to sleep.

Her eyes lit up as she studied me up and down. "I suppose you have not been a maid for long. Surely you have not forgotten all of your social graces yet. With a little training you could be taught to remember them, and behave as I, or any lady of high breeding, would."

What did she mean? I squinted against the ache in my head, blinking hard to bring moisture to my dry, stinging eyes.

"I'm afraid I'm a bit confused, miss." I raised my eyebrows subtly.

Sophia let out a quiet laugh, one that slowly progressed into a shrill giggle. "Now, if I am to confide in you, you mustn't tell anyone of my plan. But of course, I have no choice but to confide in you because you are such an integral part of the whole of it. Do you promise me your absolute confidence?"

"As always, miss." An unsettling feeling entered my stomach, and my curiosity heightened. What could I possibly have to do with this strange idea that had caused her to summon me in the middle of the night?

She giggled again, hiding her face in her blankets before regarding me seriously. "*I* will not be going to Bibury to meet this mysterious gentleman, Sherbrooke. You will."

CHAPTER 2

"*P*ardon me?" I raised both eyebrows at her, my stomach plummeting.

Sophia simply continued her staring, her smile growing ever more mischievous. "I spoke quite plainly. You will be going to Bibury in my place."

I took a step closer. She must have actually been ill to have suggested such a thing. "I—"

Sophia held up a hand, rotating on her bed until she faced me. "If I can manage to convince my father to allow you to come as my only chaperone, then we will stop at Hampden Park on the way to Bibury, where I will stay for the entirety of the trip. You will assume my identity in Bibury and fulfill the demands of my parents."

My head spun with a sudden lightness. She could not be serious.

"The woman there has never met me," Sophia continued. "She will not know the difference. You already know more about me than anyone else, so it should not be difficult for you to answer any questions about my life that may be directed at you. I know you were raised a lady, and I have heard you even had a season in London, so I have no doubt you are capable of behaving properly, even if you have adopted unladylike habits." Her eyes took me in with a hint of disdain. "It is the perfect plan, really. You could never draw the attention of any gentleman even if you threw yourself at his feet. In this case, you must do all you can to avoid his notice and return home with me at the end of the spring, at which time we will inform my parents that the noted gentleman simply selected a different lady from among the party."

I shook my head, hardly aware of the small movement. My feet were rooted to the floor, my heart hammering. With a hard swallow, I found my voice. "I am employed by your parents, miss. Please understand that I cannot do something so defiant as that, even with your guidance."

Sophia's face colored, her nostrils flaring. "You are *my* maid. You must be loyal to me and obey all of my wishes."

I took a step closer, lifting my hands in front of me in an attempt to calm her. "The consequences would be dire for both of us if the scheme was discovered. Even if it was not, you shouldn't trust that my behavior will reflect well on your name. I—I am not a lady any longer." I tried to keep my voice even, but it did not seem to be working to dissuade her. My courage slipped a little faster at the frustration that overtook her expression with new force.

"Our plan will not be discovered." She leveled me with

her gaze. "You are entirely capable of acting the part of a proper lady. I knew you before. I watched you. I am confident you will have no problem at all once you are dressed in something less dull and have a proper hair arrangement."

When had it become *our* plan? And when had Sophia shown any confidence in me before? She was three years younger than me, and we had lived in the same neighborhood our entire lives, but I had never known her to notice anything I said or did until I became her maid. I took a deep breath. "I still don't think it's wise, miss."

Her eyes flashed. I had spoken too frankly. I bit my lip, wringing my hands together behind my back. "It is a clever idea, indeed, but—but I'm not certain it's possible to execute without mishap."

Sophia's face shifted, a calmness washing over her features that only unnerved me further. "My parents trust me entirely. They will trust when I say I am staying with this matchmaking woman in Bibury, and they will trust when I say I did not attract the gentleman's eye. They would also trust if I told them that you had spread rumors about me below stairs, or that you had stolen some of my possessions and sold them in town." Her eyebrows lowered. "Do you value your position at Sedgwick Manor?"

My jaw hung slack for a moment, and my heart sickened with dread. "Yes." My voice was a strangled whisper, not nearly as confident as I had wanted it to be.

"Then you will do as I say." Sophia had never demonstrated such manipulation before. She had always been rather rude and condescending, but I had wondered if that was simply my new perspective, speaking to a lady as her maid rather than her equal, that had given me that opinion. But there was no questioning the threat that gleamed in her eyes. "I will train you over the next week to ensure you are up to the task. You will go to Bibury and fill my place until I am expected at home. I will enjoy my long-awaited visit to Hampden Park, and Mama and Papa will be none the wiser. Nor will this matchmaker, and nor will Mr. Hill."

My face blanched—my pulse thrumming against my ears. "Mr. Hill?"

"Indeed." Sophia scowled.

"Do you know anything about this Mr. Hill?"

"I know that if he comes recommended by this strange woman, then I have no interest in courting him. I would much rather enjoy time with Anne at Hampden Park. I have always dreamed of visiting, you know, and I refuse to let my one chance be stolen away by the ridiculous conspiring of this unknown relative of mine and my parents."

I certainly did know that she wanted to visit Hampden Park—it was all she ever spoke about.

I shook myself of my worries, calming myself with a deep breath. I wasn't actually going to go along with this ridiculous plot. However, Sophia's threat still hung in the air. Would her parents truly believe her if she accused me of things that weren't true? I stood in silence, trying to gather my thoughts into words that might dissuade her.

"You will not change my mind," Sophia said in a

chilling voice before I could speak. "I am quite determined." She raised her chin. "If you do not help me, I will ensure you lose your position here, and I will find a different maid who will do as I ask. Your mother will be forced to leave as well. So, will you do this for me, Sherbrooke?"

I closed my eyes against the force of her words, my stomach heaving. Neither of us could afford to lose our positions at Sedgwick Manor. My mother and I had come with no previous experience and no references; the Sedgwick family—having been acquainted with my parents before our fall from society—had taken pity on us. They had overlooked our reputations and offered to give us the work that we so desperately needed.

Defying Sophia could jeopardize all of that. Without the compassion of the Sedgwicks, we would have nowhere to live or work. As panic coursed through my limbs, my forehead beaded with perspiration. As far as Mr. and Mrs. Sedgwick knew, Sophia was akin to an angel. She had fooled them well. She had even fooled me, at times, with her sweet smiles and pretty face. They would never take my word over hers, so my mother and I would be on the streets before we knew it. Telling anyone of her scheme would be futile. And if Sophia accused me of theft, I could be faced with a fate much like Papa's.

I had no choice.

"Yes, miss."

Sophia's eyes lit up, flickering with delight. "Perfect. We shall begin your tutelage later this morning. I will write up a timeline of all the events of my life for you to study, perchance Mrs. Ollerton, your hostess, has been told anything about me by my parents. Additionally, I will write you a list of all my preferences from foods to colors to fashions, though these are less important. I will never meet these people again, so you may guess at some things while you are impersonating me. So long as you are elegant, but not *too* elegant so as to draw Mr. Hill's attention, all will be well." She clapped her hands together. "Oh, I feel so daring!"

All I felt was ill.

My thoughts blurred together into incomprehensible streaks, making my vision splotchy. I held one palm against my stomach, taking a long breath through my nostrils. Sophia's room had always smelled strongly of rose perfume, but tonight it seemed to be suffocating me. "I must advise you again—"

She held up a hand. "You are only a maid, Sherbrooke. You cannot pretend to be wiser than me. We will carry out this plan, and you will not speak a word of it to anyone or your days at Sedgwick Manor are over. Do you understand?"

Only a maid. Over the last several months, I had been shrinking into this small shell of expectation. A maid was not expected to be intelligent or to have any respectable ideas of her own. A maid was not meant to speak, or lead —but to listen, obey, and follow. Orders were received, never given. Respect was the opposite—given, but never received.

So I kept my mouth closed, giving a weak nod in place of my words. I had never thought the day would come that I would ever act the part of a lady again. I had put that life far behind me, using all my might not to yearn for it. It had taken so much focus and discipline to feel grateful for my circumstances. If I remembered what it felt like to be truly seen and listened to again, I would surely begin wishing for a life I could never really have. Dread pounded through my chest, my feet still rooted to the floorboards.

Sophia slid back under her blankets, nestling into her pillow, her golden curls forming a halo around her head. "I should like to actually get a bit of sleep tonight, but I fear I am far too excited now. Hampden Park," she said amid a sigh. "We shall commence our planning in the morning. You may leave, Sherbrooke."

I hurried out of her room, stopping outside the door. I pressed my back against the cool wall, and a shiver rolled through my body. Did Sophia not understand the pitfalls of this plan? How could I properly impersonate her for an entire month? There was still so little I knew of this entire ordeal. As Sophia had explained it, there seemed to be a female relative of hers who was intent on securing a match for this Mr. Hill, so she had invited several young ladies to come visit to see if he might select his wife from among them. It was strange, to say the least.

But Sophia was right. It would not be difficult for me to escape the gentleman's notice among four other young ladies, if my first season in London was any indication. I had never been any man's first choice. I squared my shoulders, taking a deep breath. If Sophia's threats were true, then I could not tell anyone about her plan, not even Mama. Perhaps Mr. Sedgwick would see sense and not allow his daughter to travel so far with only her maid as a chaperone.

But all it would take was a flutter of Sophia's lashes and her father would succumb. He always did. The most charming people were the most dangerous, and Sophia could charm her way to any place she wanted to go. Even the illustrious Hampden Park.

CHAPTER 3

*M*ama's arms wrapped around me like the climbing vines on the garden archway. "I'll miss you, dear Tillie." She pressed a kiss against my cheek before stepping back. Mama stood just an inch or two shorter than me, with the same dark hair and dark eyes. Her brow creased with worry, even more so than usual. It was easy to guess what was worrying her now. She was likely worried that Sophia would marry this Mr. Hill, and that I would be kept as her maid and moved to Bibury forever.

I closed my mouth against the truth I so wished I could tell. Sophia would not be competing for Mr. Hill's attention, I would. In fact, I would be doing quite the opposite —avoiding his attention at all costs. If Sophia's confidence in me was well placed in any regard, it was in my ability to be invisible.

"I will miss you too, Mama." I squeezed her hand.

Letters would be too expensive to send and would take too long to arrive in Bibury. If Mama had any news about Papa, I wouldn't receive them until I returned. My anxiety rose at the realization that much could happen in one month. Papa had been awaiting trial for three months, but that could change in an instant.

"Take great care in Mistress Sophia's appearance," Mama said in a firm voice. "You know how eager her parents are to see her succeed."

"I will." I gave a weak smile, ignoring the way my insides tossed and turned. I had only a few minutes to spare before it was time for my departure with Sophia. We had spent the last week rehearsing my manners and talents, most of which felt strangely unfamiliar. I was certainly out of practice. But after a few days, the skills returned to me as if they had never left. Since becoming Sophia's maid, I had been doing all I could to present her in a way that involved coiffing and dressing and styling. But for the next month, I would be presenting her in a way I never thought I would. Every word I spoke would be hers, every movement, every mistake. To the guests in Bibury, I would *be* Miss Sophia Sedgwick.

Yet the two of us could not be more different. Sophia was blonde, blue-eyed, with porcelain skin. My hair was a dark coffee brown, my eyes the same, my skin marked with freckles. I had never carried myself with the poise and confidence of Sophia, nor had I spoken with as much rehearsed elegance while in social situations. Sophia assured me that all the guests were unfamiliar with the appearance or conduct of the Sedgwicks' only daughter, but the fear persisted that I would be discovered immediately upon my arrival.

Mama pulled me in for one last hug before sending me toward the house. The carriage was already waiting, and I still had to help Sophia finish packing her final belongings. We had already packed her second trunk full of dresses for my use while in Bibury, most of which were dresses she had already planned to give me anyway, as I often wore her second-hand clothing. Her father had taken a great deal of convincing from Sophia to allow her the trip with only myself as a chaperone, but he had eventually agreed, requiring a second maid, Jessie, to accompany us. It had worked to our favor, for it wouldn't suit for me to arrive in Bibury unaccompanied if I were charading as Sophia, so Jessie would stay there with me.

I found Sophia in her room. After folding the last of her dresses, we made our way downstairs, where the footmen began loading our trunks and valises onto the coach.

Mr. and Mrs. Sedgwick watched their daughter with proud smiles, Mrs. Sedgwick holding a handkerchief to her nose. "I cannot believe my daughter is off to meet Mr. Hill," she whimpered to her neighbor, a short, plump woman who had come to visit for tea an hour earlier. "Mrs. Ollerton has all praise for the man and seems to think Sophia will suit him. I believe the town of Bibury will be quite attractive as well, for I have heard it is lovely in the spring." She gave another wave as Sophia climbed happily into the coach. "The next time I see her she could be engaged!" Mrs. Sedgwick looked near to dissolving into tears of pride.

I followed after Sophia into the carriage. The other maid, Jessie, entered after me. Jessie hadn't spoken to me much since my arrival at Sedgwick Manor, nor had several of the other servants. As the lady's maid, I was not to be trusted. Any gossip they wished to share below stairs was shushed at the sight of me, a trusted confidant of the family. Even now, Jessie watched me with a hint of worry, but it was also accompanied by pity. She knew the task I was to accomplish. At least I would have a friend to confide in during the ordeal.

The moment Sophia's mother was out of sight, her sweet smile transformed to one of mischief, and she ducked away from the carriage window. "I believe we have fooled them all."

I stared at the passing scenery as Sedgwick Manor grew smaller in the distance, disappearing entirely as we moved down the slope of the path.

I exchanged a quick glance with Jessie, her brown eyes filled with a similar measure of misgiving.

Mrs. Ollerton, I had learned, was the name of the matchmaking woman Sophia had spoken about. She was Sophia's mother's cousin, a woman she had never met, and whom Mrs. Sedgwick had only shared one greeting in her entire life. As unfamiliar as Mrs. Ollerton was with Sophia and her parents, it was even more surprising that she had written to invite Sophia to come to her house in Bibury.

According to Sophia, Mrs. Ollerton had learned that she was of marriageable age and considered a beauty. That had been enough to earn Sophia an invitation.

Jessie knew much less than I did about the situation, and it showed in the deep creases on her brow. "How'll we fool the guests in Bibury? I daresay that'll be much more difficult than foolin' your family."

"I don't believe it will be," Sophia said with a sigh. "If Mrs. Ollerton is daft enough to think herself a talented matchmaker, and if a gentleman is daft enough to allow himself to be thrown into an event such as this, then they will have no problem believing Sherbrooke's impersonation of me."

The nature of this visit was still quite puzzling, and Jessie's concerns echoed my own. Why was this Mr. Hill allowing Mrs. Ollerton to seek a wife for him? As Sophia had explained in greater detail that week, Mrs. Ollerton had intentionally sought out some of her distant relatives, young women, to come for this specific purpose. She intended to find a wife for Mr. Hill by the end of the spring, and he had agreed to it all. What sort of man would agree to choose his wife from among a total of five young ladies? There was a great chance he could find little to admire in all of them. All of *us*. Mr. Hill's task sounded even more difficult than my own. All I had to do was ensure I was the *least* admirable of the five.

"I have no doubt Sherbrooke will pass easily to the bottom of his notice," Sophia said in an offhand voice. "My mother learned that at least two of the ladies in attendance are considered quite beautiful and accomplished in London. They were unsuccessful in their first seasons, however, and so their parents agreed to allow Mrs. Ollerton to attempt a match for them with Mr. Hill. He is quite eager to be married, I have heard. All the events of this house party will be entirely proper, and in an area far removed from Town, there will be no need for reputations to suffer if he appears to be courting multiple women at once." Sophia laughed. "I am glad to have no part of that." She took one of her golden curls between her fingers, gazing contentedly at the passing countryside.

I exchanged another glance with Jessie, not bothering to hide my dismay. My pulse had not been normal for days, it seemed, always racing with anticipation or dread. I could hardly believe that soon I would be wearing elegant gowns, dancing and conversing and living like a lady all over again. I squeezed my eyes closed to calm the surge of nervousness that clenched my stomach. How could I do this?

Do not be too elegant, Sophia had warned me on multiple occasions. *Men are drawn to elegance, and you mustn't give Mr. Hill anything that might draw his eye to you for even a moment.*

That would not be difficult. Even before becoming a maid, I had never been very elegant. I swallowed hard as I recalled my great failure of a Season. I would have to simply replicate that as I tried to evade Mr. Hill's attention.

The journey to Hampden Park was expected to take three days. After leaving Sophia there, Jessie and I would stop at the inn between Hampden Park and Bibury, where

Jessie would help me change into one of Sophia's gowns and arrange my hair. The rest of the journey would take less than a day, and then I would be welcomed in and introduced to Mrs. Ollerton as Miss Sophia Sedgwick.

"One last pin," Jessie said in a quiet voice. The pin scraped my scalp, and I found that I had grown much more sensitive to the pricks than I had once been. I grimaced as the metal scraped across my head and settled into place among all the others. She held up a small looking glass to my face. The style was one I often used on Sophia, and I had explained it to Jessie as best I could. She had very limited experience with the duties of a lady's maid, but she had arranged my hair with surprising accuracy.

"You do look like a lady." Jessie blinked fast when she circled to face me. "Perhaps Mistress Sophia was correct about your ability to succeed."

I rubbed my hands over my skirts before pulling on Sophia's old kid gloves. I flexed my fingers. "When my success rests on being unnoticed, I share her confidence. The area of my concern is in whether or not I will be able to behave properly for the entire trip." I bit my lip.

"I'll be sure to correct you if I see anything amiss." Jessie smiled, letting out a long puff of air. "But I be nervous."

"*You* are nervous?" I scoffed. "Perhaps you should be

the one in this soft muslin gown and kid gloves. I feel like an imposter."

Jessie laughed. "That's because you are one."

Right. An imposter. What would happen if that was discovered? Never mind the fact that I could tarnish Sophia's name, but I would lose my position at Sedgwick Manor for certain, as would Mama. I could not ruin this. With luck, Mr. Hill would make his choice within the first week of my visit, and then the rest of my time in Bibury could be spent in peace.

When we stepped outside the inn, the air was cold. I wrapped my arms around myself, squinting up at the sky. I had thought winter had been left in the past, but small flecks of white floated in the air above, particles of snow. Thankfully, Sophia had sent me with a thick wool spencer. Jessie, however, shivered as we embarked on the final stretch of the journey. I offered her both blankets in the carriage, keeping warm enough with my fingers enrobed in leather and the thick, wool jacket. Despite the chill in the air, flowers had begun bursting among the grasses outside the window, growing more and more numerous as we rode closer to Bibury.

Sophia hadn't been able to tell me very much concerning the house I would be living at for the next month, only that it was called Winslow House, and had only been described as charming by its owner, which gave her every reason to believe it was not *actually* charming.

At least not as charming as Hampden Park.

I focused on the passing countryside rather than the

nerves spinning in my stomach. Sophia was expected to arrive last by Mrs. Sedgwick's design—a grand finale, of sorts. I rather hoped my arrival felt more like an afterthought. Hopefully by the time I arrived Mr. Hill would have already selected his favorite from among the other young ladies. I comforted myself with that thought.

"That's the village of Bibury." Jessie's quiet voice drifted toward me. I followed her gaze to the quaint village ahead, where rows of stone cottages sat huddled together, trailing along a garden path. The stone was the color of freshly baked bread, golden and bright in the afternoon sunlight. Small purple and white flowers dotted the surrounding bushes. The earth seemed to be drawing a deep and satisfying breath, as if it had been holding it in anticipation of this beauty for all the winter months. I clung my hands together in my lap, trying to replace my anxiety with excitement. No matter the circumstances, at least I would get to spend the next month near such a beautiful village.

Winslow house was just one mile away, and we arrived much quicker than I had hoped. I took a deep, quaking breath, and Jessie rested her hand on my arm. "You've nothing to dread, Tillie. You look the part of a lady. No one'll suspect you of anything."

It was *acting* the part that terrified me. Winslow House came into clear view out the window, fashioned out of similar stone to the cottages in the village, but much larger, nestled among newly awakened gardens, the colors bright and vibrant. Only a few branches were still bare, reaching toward the house like slender fingers.

As the carriage came to a stop, two footmen walked out the front doors, followed closely by a woman in an extravagant gown, her pale curls pinned atop her head. A minuscule, polite smile pulled on her lips.

I tried to imitate the expression, clutching handfuls of my skirts as the doors opened. *Don't be too elegant. Men are drawn to elegance, and you mustn't give Mr. Hill anything that might draw his eye to you for even a moment.* Sophia's words coursed through my mind again as I stepped down onto the drive. The house appeared much larger now that it loomed directly in front of me, and the approaching woman appeared much more intimidating.

"Miss Sedgwick, is it?" Her chin lifted as she surveyed me, her slightly upturned nose pointing directly at the carriage as she glanced inside, a furrow overtaking her brow as Jessie stepped out. She peeked dramatically to both sides of the carriage interior. "Have you made this entire journey with only your maid?"

"Indeed, ma'am." I attempted a note of confidence in my voice, but it still came out quiet.

Her lips pursed, but she didn't make further comment on the subject. Instead, she led me over the narrow path that led to the front doors. The path was flanked with bushes and shrubs, the tips of the leaves covered in droplets of moisture, as well as three stone sculptures. My legs felt as if *they* had been turned to stone for how heavy they were, dragging me along behind Mrs. Ollerton. I corrected my posture when I noticed myself slumping. *Elegant, but not too elegant.*

"You have arrived just in time for tea," Mrs. Ollerton said. "If you would prefer to rest from your journey first, you may, but otherwise, we will welcome you into the drawing room to meet the other young ladies, as well as Mr. Hill." Her face lit up when she spoke his name, a hint of whimsy in her voice.

What was it about this man that could so easily lift the disdain off Mrs. Ollerton's face in an instant? Though I supposed it wasn't all that surprising. I had learned that women tended to pour out their judgements readily on other women but found far less to dislike in men.

"Which would you prefer?" Mrs. Ollerton asked when I didn't reply.

It would likely be better for my goals to meet Mr. Hill now, rather than worry over it for another few hours. After all, he was sure to find less to admire about me at this moment, with my hair slipping from Jessie's coiffure and smelling like the inside of a stuffy carriage. "I feel rested enough, thank you. I should be glad to meet the guests." For the sake of my health, I could not allow my stomach to twist and my heart to pound for much longer.

Mrs. Ollerton gave me a knowing smile. "You have every reason to be eager, my dear." She still wore her wistful expression as she led me toward the drawing room door. "Mr. Hill is a most handsome and amiable gentleman."

"So I have heard," I muttered to myself.

"Speak up, Miss Sedgwick. Men cannot abide mumbling. You must do all you can to make a favorable impression on him." She turned to face me, her thin brows arching, as if to convey the seriousness of this situation. Little did she know that I had every wish to *not* make a favorable impression. I was to be invisible. Silent. Unnoticed.

"I will try." I gave a weak smile, one that Mrs. Ollerton studied for a long moment before giving a huffed breath and turning toward the footman. She nodded, and he opened the door, revealing the quaint and heavily decorated drawing room. From the doorway, the entire room was visible. The floral wall papers, multiple vases and flowers, a large pianoforte, the small brown dog beneath it, and the five people who sat on an assortment of red sofas and gilded chairs surrounding the empty tea table.

Two young ladies flanked both sides of a gentleman, who could only have been the infamous Mr. Hill.

He was much younger than I had expected. Considering the desperation he seemed to have to be married off by Mrs. Ollerton, I had expected a man with at least a bit of grey in his hair, or perhaps a slight hunch to his shoulders. Instead, the man sitting at the center of the room couldn't have even yet been thirty. Between his broad, squared shoulders and firm jaw, he immediately struck me as handsome. He glanced up at my entrance, and even from across the room I could see that his eyes were blue. Sharp, inquisitive, and framed with dark brows and lashes. His golden hair was combed neatly, contrary to most styles I had seen among fashionable men in London. It gave him a striking appearance, one that breathed with all the confidence and assurance that I lacked.

My feet stopped, and I was suddenly tempted to hide behind Mrs. Ollerton.

Her full skirts would hide me quite nicely if I crouched.

The ladies in the room seemed every bit as entranced with Mr. Hill as I was. I shook myself, feeling a slight flush on my cheeks for staring at him for so long. His gaze only lingered on me for a brief moment before flitting back to the young lady beside him, with whom I seemed to have interrupted a conversation. He finished with a few short words, unintelligible from where I stood, before rising. He walked closer, and thankfully, Mrs. Ollerton spoke.

"Mr. Hill, may I present my final guest, Miss Sophia Sedgwick."

He offered a bow, and I curtsied, wobbling a bit with the motion. It was somewhat of a relief that Mr. Hill seemed so refined and handsome. Sophia was right. It was highly unlikely for any man to take notice of me, and certainly not a man the likes of Mr. Hill.

I met his gaze. The color of his eyes was even more piercing from a closer proximity, a deep blue streaked with multiple tones of grey, like the blurred connection between the sky and an unsettled sea.

"It is a pleasure to meet you, Miss Sedgwick." Mr. Hill's voice wrapped around me like a melody, giving a weight-lessness to my feet that was both unfamiliar and terrifying. Even though he had only spoken a few words, the other four ladies watched from behind his tall frame, looking me over with hints of warning in their gazes. All four ladies had very different appearances: two blonde, one brunette, and one auburn haired. But I had already found one commonality among them. They all watched me in the same competitive manner, as if to say, *Mr. Hill is mine.*

I swallowed, turning my attention back to his much-too-handsome face. How easy would it be to blend into the background among such eager participants, and how entertaining would it be to watch them fight over him? A slight smile pulled on the edge of my mouth, and my nerves almost entirely vanished. I corrected my expression and regarded Mr. Hill in as timid a manner as possible. "It is a pleasure to meet you as well, Mr. Hill." I looked away from his face, doing all I could to be forgettable and meek. It was not difficult to feign shyness around him, and I was quite proud of my performance.

With another wobbling curtsy, I moved aside to allow Mrs. Ollerton room to address him. Amid my thoughts, I had not heard the drawing room door open, nor had I heard the maid sneaking past me with the tea tray. As I came out of my curtsy and stepped abruptly to the right, I collided with something solid.

A slight shriek met my ears as a young maid stumbled over my foot, catching hold of my sleeve to steady herself as the tea tray tipped forward, sending a bowl of jam and tray of tartlets to make a solid impact with Mr. Hill's jacket. One tart made a sound splat against his *firm jaw.* Only once I had gathered my senses did I notice the tea pot that had shattered and spilled its contents all over his boots and Mrs. Ollerton's Turkish rug.

"Oh, Miss Sedgwick!" Mrs. Ollerton's voice came out,

high-pitched and enraged as she took in the scene. My jaw hung loose, and I quickly scrambled to the ground, scooping up as many of the spilled tartlets as possible, the raspberry jam oozing between my fingers and causing further dripping onto the carpet. The maid I had caused to trip was already doing all she could to clean as well, and only when I noticed her look of alarm did I realize that a lady would *never* have been crawling across the ground to gather up tarts.

I straightened quickly and came to my feet. My face burned hot, no doubt redder than the jam that was smeared on the right side of Mr. Hill's face.

The other four ladies in the room watched me as if I were a foreign species of animal that had meandered my way from the Indian jungle right into the drawing room of Winslow House. I *had* been crawling across the ground, after all.

I wiped my hands on my skirts before realizing it.

Elegant, Tillie. Very elegant indeed.

CHAPTER 4

*T*he walls of the drawing room seemed to be closing in on all sides, and I wished they would. It might have been a much-needed distraction from the disaster I had just created.

Mr. Hill calmly withdrew his handkerchief. I thought he would raise it to his own face to wipe off the jam, but instead he extended it to me, half his mouth lifting in a smile. "I must say, raspberry jam is my favorite, but I prefer eating it over applying it to my complexion. Is that what you ladies do to achieve such a flush to your cheeks?" He winked, much to my dismay, before setting the clean white linen in my hand.

My dripping, sticky hand.

A new surge of heat engulfed my cheeks as I cleaned between my fingers as best I could. Had he just smiled? After I had ruined his clean clothing and embarrassed him in front of the entire party? I must have been imagining it.

I hurried as quickly as I could to clean my hands before looking up at Mrs. Ollerton, who still wore an obvious expression of dismay.

"Miss Sedgwick mustn't be allowed near the tea tray on future occasions," she said between deep breaths. I noticed a tartlet near Mr. Hill's shoe, but before I could point it out, he stepped forward, crushing it further into the carpet. I cringed.

His stare bore down on my face. Could I have possibly made a greater mistake? I had made myself anything but invisible. Thankfully, though, I had shown myself in an inelegant, disagreeable light; if this was Mr. Hill's first impression of me, it was sure to keep him far away. Sophia would be mortified if she knew how I had represented her, crawling along the ground gathering up tartlets. I grimaced before reluctantly meeting Mr. Hill's gaze.

Before he could speak, a tall young woman spoke up from behind him. "So we see that the charms of Mr. Hill affect even the most stoic of women. I cannot imagine a single lady would not be inclined to humiliate herself to gain his attention."

The other three ladies laughed, a myriad of intonations from rasped and quiet to shrill and loud.

I handed the dirtied handkerchief to the maid, who was still busy cleaning off the floor. "I—I did not intentionally...no." I laughed, a weak means of defending myself. "You must see I was not attempting to win his attention." I did not want his attention, nor would I ever have it again.

The ladies exchanged smiles amongst themselves before the tall one cast me a look of pity.

I looked down at the floor, trying to imagine myself any place but here. There would be no victory to tell Jessie of. She and Sophia had both been wrong to put their faith in me. When I glanced up, Mr. Hill's piercing blue eyes were still fixed on me. His voice, deep and soft, met my ears. "You have won my attention, nonetheless." He winked again, and this time I was sure I had not imagined it.

He turned away in one swift motion, facing Mrs. Ollerton. "Please excuse me."

"Oh, yes, of course." Mrs. Ollerton fluttered her hands about herself as if unsure whether to allow him to leave or not, before giving a resolute nod. With so much jam and tea all over his clothing, he must have been eager to change.

And eager to escape me.

The moment Mr. Hill left the room, Mrs. Ollerton's exhale turned to something of a groan. "Miss Sedgwick…" she began in a reprimanding voice.

I squeezed my eyes closed, shaking my head at the floor. "Forgive me, Mrs. Ollerton. Perhaps I am a bit tired from my journey, after all." I put a hand to my head, hoping the gesture would add credibility to my claim. A familiar pounding headache had started creeping up my temples again, but this one had surely been brought on by embarrassment. Mr. Hill's sharp gaze still lived in my mind. What had he meant when he said I had won his attention? That had been the very last thing I had hoped to do.

"It may be wise for you to spend the rest of the day relaxing in your bedchamber." Mrs. Ollerton's thin lips were pressed together, her brows drawn down. "Perhaps tomorrow you will awaken with a bit more elegance and grace."

I drew a heavy breath, nodding my agreement. "I do become quite ungainly when I am tired."

Mrs. Ollerton's eyes rounded. "Do you? Oh, I am quite glad to hear that behavior like this will not be a common tragedy."

Was this her idea of a tragedy? A pot of spilled tea and a few tartlets? I had seen far more tragedy in the form of poverty and desperation, lives destroyed and lost, loved ones cast away to prisons where they had little hope of escape, and every expectation of execution or starvation. My heart ached, the sting spreading over my arms and tingling into my fingertips. I dropped a curtsy. "I thank you for understanding, Mrs. Ollerton." I kept my voice meek and reserved.

"I will have a tray sent to your room for dinner, and you may spend the rest of the evening to yourself. I will give your excuses to Mr. Hill, though your absence at dinner may come as something of a relief to him after the events of this afternoon." She spoke casually, but the other four women in the room erupted in quiet laughter.

Mrs. Ollerton seemed to remember they were still there, for she turned around in a quick swish of her stiff taffeta skirts. "In the chaos, I'm afraid I neglected to intro-duce you to my other guests," she said in a methodical tone. "Allow me to present Miss Joanna Benham." Mrs. Ollerton gestured to the brunette woman, who was the shortest of the four, and the most extravagantly dressed. She then introduced Miss Lydia Coppins, who was petite with honey-blonde hair, and seemed to possess a great deal of energy. The next was Miss Mary Taplow, the woman with the deep auburn hair, the quietest of the four, and then Miss Caroline Downsfield, the tall blonde who had made the remark about my desire for attention. She gave me a polite smile with Mrs. Ollerton watching, but as soon as the woman's back was turned, her expression transformed to one of disdain and condescension.

After the introductions were complete, Mrs. Ollerton dismissed me to my bedchamber, enlisting the maid who I had caused to trip to lead me there. She did not seem very pleased with me, and understandably so.

Thankfully Jessie was inside my room to greet me, finishing unpacking my trunk.

"You did not have to do that for me." I shook my head, dropping to my knees to help her.

Jessie shook her head, swatting my hand away. "'Tis my duty. How did it go? Tell me everything."

I sat back on my heels, hiding my face in my sticky hands. Mr. Hill's handkerchief hadn't managed to clean them completely. "I made a complete fool of myself. Or rather, of Sophia." I cringed.

Jessie chewed her lower lip. "How so?"

I explained everything, from the spilled tea tray to the scrambling around on my knees to clean it up. "I was not thinking clearly!" I sighed, gritting my teeth. "How could I have been so daft?"

Jessie paused for a short moment, studying my face. "Was the gentleman handsome?"

"Well, yes," I said in a blunt voice. "There is no questioning that."

"Then I know exactly why you be actin' all foolish." She wiggled her eyebrows.

"No, Jessie. No." I held up a hand. "You are wrong. I would have done the same thing no matter how blue his eyes were."

Jessie giggled, eyeing me with no small amount of suspicion.

"I was simply nervous to be meeting so many new people under Sophia's...pretenses." I rubbed one side of my face before remembering the jam on my fingers. The substance stuck on the tiny hairs near my ear. I groaned. "Did I mention Mr. Hill had to remove himself from the party to wash himself because I soiled his clothing and his face?"

Jessie laughed again, throwing her head back. "'Twill take a great deal of timidity to make him forget you now."

"It doesn't matter if he remembers me for what happened today," I said in a confident voice, though I didn't feel it. "If he comes to think of me as the 'clumsy, odd, ridiculous lady' of the five, then I will consider that a success. All Sophia asked of me was that I do not draw his eye toward me as a potential choice of wife. He will choose one of the other ladies, I am sure of it."

Jessie gave a slow nod, pursing her lips before a laugh burst out. "I believe you've done the trick."

I joined her laughter, holding one hand against my side before pulling it away fast. I needed to stop touching things with my jam covered fingers. "I think you are right. Perhaps now all that remains for us to do is enjoy our time away from Sedgwick Manor. I wish we could explore Bibury this afternoon. Mrs. Ollerton has condemned me to this room to rest until tomorrow morning." I turned toward the window, where a clear view of the gardens showed through the glass.

"Perhaps if you arise early enough tomorrow, you'll have an opportunity to see the grounds before the rest of the guests demand your time."

I smiled, letting the sun warm my cheeks as I stepped closer to the window. "That sounds like a wonderful plan."

Arising before the sun had become a habit of mine, so I was surprised to find the peach glow of dawn seeping through the drapes when I awoke the next morning. I tossed the blankets off as quickly as I could before remembering that I was not at Sedgwick Manor; I was at Winslow House. I did not have to attend to Sophia, or anyone else today. I could take a leisurely walk through the gardens instead.

I stretched my back, unable to stop the wide smile on my cheeks.

When I stepped outside, the faint trill of birdsong

carried across the peach and pale grey sky. The grass was damp, as if it had rained overnight. My boots made a suctioning sound as I marched over the grass that led to the stone path. The path seemed to lead straight through the gardens behind the house, so I followed it, ducking under the slightly overgrown trees. The branches were only partially clothed in leaves, large gaps still remaining from the winter months. What flowers the bushes did bear were small and pink, white, and purple, bursting out in tiny buds.

I filled my lungs with the chilled air, wrapping my arms around myself. Perhaps I should have waited for the sun to rise completely before setting out on my exploration, but I had been too excited. Winslow House was lovely, and I could only imagine how it would look a month from now, when spring had fully emerged among the bushes and trees. Two robins were perched on the lowest branch of a nearby tree, chirping to one another, as if making commentary on my impertinence to be interrupting their quiet morning routine.

I stopped under a stone archway, examining the vines that climbed up the sides, much like the ones in the gardens at Sedgwick Manor where Mama had bid me farewell. I closed my eyes, breathing in the earthy smell of rain and the faint scent of sweet flowers. I sang a tune under my breath. Mama had warned me against ever singing in front of anyone, as my pitch was 'the worst she had ever heard,' but had encouraged me to sing to my heart's content when I was alone, for singing was the only way to truly free the soul. I sang in a quiet voice at first, letting my soft, shaking voice join the birds in the trees.

O'er mountain, o'er valley, o'er rolling green hill
 Little Anne goes riding
 O'er stream, o'er woods, with a lone quadrille
 A man she soon be finding

My voice grew louder as I began the second verse, and I spun in a circle beneath the archway, closing my eyes as faint droplets of rain fell on my cheeks.

"Good morning, Miss Sedgwick."

I staggered back at the voice that came from behind me, pressing a hand against my chest. My heart beat more wildly than the wings of the robins in the nearby tree as they took desperate flight away from the sound of a gentleman's voice.

If only I had wings too.

My stomach plummeted. Had he heard me singing? I did not have to face him to know who it was. That melodic, deep voice was not easy to forget. *Elegant, but not too elegant*, flashed through my mind again, and I realized just how far from elegant I was in this moment. I had left my hair in a braid over my shoulder, rather than a neat, more acceptable coiffure. I hadn't expected to encounter anyone this early in the morning, and especially not Mr. Hill.

Perhaps I was mistaken. It could have been a groundskeeper or some other man who somehow knew my name. Or rather, *Sophia's* name. I turned around with as much timid indifference as I could manage. My heart continued its wild pounding as my hopes crashed down around me.

It was not a groundskeeper.

"Mr. Hill," I choked, dropping a quick curtsy. In my mind, I had foolishly expected to see him with jam still smeared on his cheek. But instead, he didn't have anything on his cheek but faint stubble and a deep dimple from his lopsided smile. Drat. What had I done to make him smile now? And why did it do such strange things to my stomach? I swallowed, searching for my voice, which had somehow deserted me after my loud and horrific singing. "F-forgive me. I did not expect to see anyone this early." I stared at a pebble near my boot.

"What is there to forgive?" he asked, a smile still evident in his voice. "It was a privilege to hear your…lovely singing."

I glanced up, stepping a pace backward at the same time. "You must forgive me for subjecting you to such a horrendous sound." I paused. "Additionally…you must forgive me for the tarts I assailed you with yesterday. It seems I have now trespassed on what is likely your daily routine, for which I should also apologize and excuse myself at once." I took another step back, but he filled the space I made, tipping his head to one side. I leaned against one edge of the archway, crossing my arms awkwardly in front of me.

A deep chuckle escaped him. "This is not my daily routine, but if it becomes yours then I might have to make it mine, as well."

My heart leaped. "I, well, I have no intention of exploring the gardens this early again. The weather is still a bit cold, you see, and I have never been one to abide cold weather."

"You seemed to have been enjoying yourself immensely before you saw me."

I remembered the way I had been standing, eyes closed, singing with deep content. I *had* been enjoying myself. But now it seemed Mr. Hill was enjoying *himself* far too much. What else could I do to repel him? I searched my mind for an idea, but nothing came. Surely he was simply accustomed to flirting with any lady he conversed with; this couldn't possibly be out of the ordinary for him. But then, the fact that he was voluntarily conversing with me at all was unsettling. "I was quite content, if you must know," I said. "I much prefer being alone than speaking with others at this hour of the day. I am not at all amiable until at least ten o'clock, and not fully amiable until the afternoon." I put on a scowl, hoping it would frighten or jar him at least a little.

His smile only grew, and those blasted dimples appeared again. "I see. You did seem quite amiable yesterday afternoon when you spilled the tea tray." One of his dark eyebrows arched, and a teasing glint entered his eyes. "You helped me escape an unwelcome gathering in the drawing room."

"Unwelcome?" I cursed my tongue for questioning him. It would only prolong this conversation that should not have even been occurring.

He studied my face for a long moment before letting out a quiet sigh. "It is no matter. Let it be sufficient that I am grateful for your well-timed interference." Another deep chuckle came from him, and I scolded myself for allowing the flutter it caused in my stomach. Why should a man like Mr. Hill need Mrs. Ollerton to help him find a match? He could have had his pick of any young lady, but instead he was resigned to picking between five. Well, four, since I was not to be included.

"How can you be grateful? I soiled your clothing and spilled tea on your shoes..." my voice trailed off. I did not care to relive that dreadful experience.

His lips curled into a playful grin. "I was most grateful to see your blush as a result, and I must say I find it quite becoming."

As much as I willed them not to, my cheeks burst into flames at his words, burning hot at the centers. "It is not charming," I blurted as fear caught up to me. What was I saying? Trying to convince him of my shortcomings seemed the only way to erase that smile on his face. "I daresay I look very much like a lobster."

Mr. Hill chuckled. "You must allow me to contradict you, Miss Sedgwick. I have never seen such a pretty lobster."

Where were those robins? If only they could each take hold of one of my sleeves and fly me up into the air where Mr. Hill could not see the increasing dismay and color on my face. Completely bereft of a response, I did what I could to drive my claim that I was not amiable in the morning: I shot him my most cutting glare before turning on my heel and marching toward the doors I had escaped from that morning. My heart pounded as I hurried away.

Mr. Hill's boots scuffed distantly over the path behind me, but I didn't turn around, desperate as I was to escape the sound of his chuckling.

"Mrs. Ollerton has planned a trip into Bibury this afternoon," he called, stopping me. "I look forward to finding you in your most amiable state."

I bit my lip, debating whether or not to turn around. Deciding it would be better to pretend I had not heard him, I hurried inside the doors.

I pressed a hand to my chest, feeling the quick beating of my heart against my palm. Willing myself to relax was proving a difficult task. Did Mr. Hill flirt so shamelessly with all the ladies here? I could easily envision the tall, blonde woman, Miss Downsfield, flirting back and enjoying every moment of it. Was Mr. Hill simply testing me, to see if I were just as eager to win his attention as Miss Downsfield? He seemed to delight in the attention.

Well, he would be getting none of it from me.

I took a deep breath, hastening back to my room before Mrs. Ollerton could find me.

Or Mr. Hill, for that matter.

CHAPTER 5

$\mathcal{I}$ walked into the village beside Miss Coppins, who, much like me, seemed to prefer keeping a distance between herself and the most eager ladies who flocked around Mr. Hill. Miss Downsfield had been the one to claim his arm, and the other two ladies seemed fit to send her sprawling across the hills if given the chance. They trailed behind, parasols and baskets in hand.

Mrs. Ollerton had mentioned at breakfast that there were a number of poor families surrounding Bibury, and the ladies had been quick to offer their goodwill toward them. They had busied themselves organizing baskets of food and now walked into town with the baskets hooked proudly on their elbows.

"I am not accustomed to so much walking," Miss Coppins said in a nervous voice. I glanced toward her to find a deep crease in her brow. She pushed a damp blonde curl from her forehead. "I feel as though my heart might burst at any moment."

I touched her arm, confused by her sudden alarm. "Do you need to rest? I will wait with you."

She gave a quiet laugh, shaking her head in quick, small twitches. "No, Miss Sedgwick, you are too kind. I say that simply because my uncle met such a fate. He was not accustomed to exercise of any sort, and when he began, he suffered a failing of his heart much like I just described." Her eyes rounded as she looked at me, two large, hazel spheres. "That is why I am quite resolved never to begin exercising. If I do, I should likely have the same thing occur to my heart."

I gave a slow nod, steadying her arm as her breathing became faster. "Please accept my condolences for your uncle," I said. "But...I do not think you are in danger."

Miss Coppins cast me a hesitant glance. "We might take our pace down to a leisurely stroll. The other ladies are walking quite quickly, even Mrs. Ollerton. I worry over her, especially." Her voice squeaked. "One as aged as she has a much greater chance of ailment."

I watched Mrs. Ollerton as she led the group forward, a satisfied smile on her face as she examined Miss Downsfield on Mr. Hill's arm. She was not as old as Miss Coppins seemed to believe. "Indeed," I said, "but she seems quite spry."

"My uncle seemed spry."

I met Miss Coppins's panicked eyes quickly before

looking away. "Oh. Well...let us pray Mrs. Ollerton survives our trip to Bibury."

Miss Coppins gave a solemn nod, casting her gaze heavenward for a long moment—long enough for me to realize she was indeed praying at that very moment. A smile lifted her serious expression moments later, and she took a deep breath. "Spring air is best for the constitution, you know, aside from seaside air."

"I did not know that."

"It is a very important fact to know, so I am glad to have enlightened you."

Despite her oddities, Miss Coppins was still my favorite of the ladies I had met. She did not seem quite as competitive, and had even spared me a smile, which was far more than the other women had done. We walked in silence for several minutes before I noticed a sly smile on Miss Coppins's face. "Do you know what else may cause my heart to burst?"

I shook my head, examining her for any sign that she was fatigued by the walk. Her gaze was situated straight ahead, and I guessed her words before she spoke them. "Mr. Frederick Hill. He is the most handsome man I have ever met. Do you agree? Of course, I have no expectation that he will choose me." She laughed. "Certainly not with a lady like Miss Downsfield nearby. But I will not complain to be in his company for the next month."

I had been doing all I could not to think of Mr. Hill at all, especially after our early-morning interaction. "I agree with you, Miss Coppins, on the fact that he is handsome. But that is not enough to recommend a man in my opinion. I do not know enough of Mr. Hill yet to entertain any thoughts of ever becoming his wife. I don't consider it a possibility. I too think he will choose Miss Downsfield."

Miss Coppins stared at me as if I were mad. "A gentleman with such a generous income who is as handsome as Mr. Hill is more rare than a flower sprouting out of a pile of snow." She let out a giggle, covering her mouth with her glove. "Any woman would be a fool not to hope to marry him."

"Then I must be a fool." I smiled. The more ladies who knew that I was not eager to connect myself with the gentleman, the better. Then they might stop glaring at me and allow me to be their friend.

"Then why did you come?" Miss Coppins's brow scrunched, her pale eyebrows disappearing in the shade of her bonnet.

"My parents forced me to." I shrugged, searching for something to say that would suit Sophia's situation. "I have come only for an adventure. My parents would be far too happy if I happened to make a match while I am here, so I have every intention of avoiding Mr. Hill as much as I am able."

Miss Coppins smiled, brushing aside her hair again. She seemed to have forgotten her fears about her exercise, walking with increased energy over the hills. "Oh, Miss Downsfield will be quite pleased to hear that."

I frowned. "Why?"

"She saw you with Mr. Hill out her window this morning. She was quite furious."

I nearly stopped walking. So I had not been imagining her increased animosity toward me. She could not possibly view me as a threat, could she? It seemed Mr. Hill was already partial toward her. I watched as they walked arm in arm, her coy smile tipped up toward him. He appeared to be speaking to her, but I couldn't hear the specifics of the conversation from where Miss Coppins and I walked several feet behind.

"She has no reason to be furious," I said in a quick voice. "It was a chance encounter, and I have no intention of taking my walk at that hour again."

"You should not take a daily walk at all, Miss Sedgwick." Miss Coppins cast me a look of reprimand. "Do not forget my uncle."

I held back my grimace. I hardly knew what to say to this Miss Coppins and her strange ideas. She was quite pretty, and I could imagine that must have been the reason Mrs. Ollerton selected her as one of her guests. Behind her pretty exterior, however, she seemed to be a bit odd and lacked the confidence that Mr. Hill would ever notice her. That gave me even more hope. If he had indeed already set his sights on Miss Downsfield, it would be much easier to relax for the rest of the trip.

But Mr. Hill's words to me that morning in the gardens refused to desert me, even as much as I tried to pretend they had not happened. He was flirtatious *by nature*, I assured myself. That was all.

When at last the stone cottages of Bibury came into view, Miss Coppins and I reached the rest of the group, walking at a much quicker pace than we had been before. Mrs. Ollerton cast me a smile. My unblemished behavior at breakfast seemed to have forgiven the events of the previous day, at least enough to evade any more of her reprimanding scowls.

As I approached, Mr. Hill glanced over his shoulder, meeting my gaze with a smile of his own. I did as I had done at breakfast—focused my attention on anything but his face. My palms began to perspire inside my gloves as I felt his continued gaze burning on my cheek. Thankfully, here in Bibury there was much more to capture my interest than a plate of eggs.

The steep, slanted rooftops of the identical cottages were dotted with birds who seemed to be overlooking the village with as much admiration as I felt. It was truly beautiful. Beyond the small houses, Mrs. Ollerton had explained, there was a market center with several shops, as well as additional apartments and homes of those less fortunate people—the ones the ladies had come to deliver their baskets to.

Miss Coppins skipped forward, stopping beside Miss Taplow. She whispered in her ear before both ladies glanced back at me. I shifted uncomfortably, pretending I didn't notice that I was likely the subject of their whispered conversation. I could only hope Miss Coppins was simply telling Miss Taplow how I was not interested in courting Mr. Hill.

Mrs. Ollerton called for our attention. "We should not like to overwhelm the poor families with too many of us at each residence. Those who have prepared baskets will have to split into two groups. Mr. Hill knows this area quite well, so he might guide half of you to the homes in most need, and I will guide the other half. Shall we meet again near the shops when we are finished?"

The group nodded their assent, and I crossed my arms in front of me. I did not have a basket to give. The other ladies had been eager to shine in front of Mr. Hill with their generosity, so they had not told me of their plan to give them to the poor in town. Though they likely viewed it as sabotage, it would work to my advantage if he viewed me as less generous and thoughtful than the rest.

Before becoming Sophia's maid, I had often walked into our nearby town with my mother, where we gave as much as we could afford to one family with whom we were closely acquainted. But it was not always food or money. Sometimes we would simply sit in the cramped parlor and enjoy conversation with the mother of the home while I played with the children. The memory filled me with warmth and longing at once, and I tightened my hands at my sides to combat it. After having been on the receiving side of such generosity from the Sedgwicks after my father was sent to prison, our rent unable to be paid, I had wished and wished for another opportunity to serve and give something again.

"Well, then, who should like to come with me?" Mrs. Ollerton asked, raising her thin eyebrows expectantly.

The insects had never buzzed so loudly. Miss Downsfield feigned a yawn, and Miss Taplow and Miss Benham both seemed to have become extremely interested in the wicker handles on their baskets.

"I will." I approached Mrs. Ollerton, who welcomed me with a warm smile.

"And I will receive you even more gladly knowing you have sacrificed time with Mr. Hill to join me." Mrs. Ollerton cast me a knowing glance.

"It is no great sacrifice," I said in a quiet voice. "I enjoy your company just as much."

Mrs. Ollerton let out a loud laugh. "I could never claim to be half as charming as Mr. Hill, and you know it. There is no need to attempt to win my favor by lies, Miss Sedgwick." Her voice took on a scolding tone.

I refrained from protesting again. My gaze accidentally jumped to Mr. Hill, who watched me with his half-smile. I lowered my brows into a scowl before returning my attention to the ground.

"Who else would like to join us?" Mrs. Ollerton said. "Miss Sedgwick, it seems, did not have the patience to assemble a basket, so I will need one of you ladies to join us, so we have something to give besides our company."

Several seconds passed in silence before Mrs. Ollerton let out a quiet grumble. "If no one will volunteer, then I choose…Miss Taplow. Join us, if you will."

Her lips pursed and she trudged forward, away from Mr. Hill's free arm, which she had seemed quite poised to snatch. She put on a smile, but it was obviously all for display, like a perfectly trimmed bonnet resting in a shop window.

Miss Downsfield didn't hide her victorious smirk as she watched Miss Taplow walk away from her prize. How did Mr. Hill feel to have so many ladies vying for him? Surely his pride did not need the bolstering it was receiving. He must have known how attractive he was and reveled in the attention. Perhaps he never intended to marry at all, and he was a rake, simply feeding his own pride and toying with as many hearts as possible to entertain himself.

Compiling as long a list as possible of Mr. Hill's potential pitfalls would make my task of avoiding him even easier.

"Let us be on our way, then." Mrs. Ollerton started down the path toward the cottages, a bright smile on her face. Mr. Hill began walking in the same direction before following the opposite curve in the path toward a different area of the village. Miss Taplow watched him go, a gleam of longing in her eyes.

The farther down the path we walked, the busier the town seemed to become. There were many people on the streets who seemed like they could benefit from our basket, but Mrs. Ollerton appeared to have a specific family in mind. The path curved around the last of the stone cottages, leading to a row of narrow houses that were much smaller and less sturdy. If the wind were strong enough, it might have knocked them down. Perhaps that was why they were built in such proximity, as if to huddle together and rely on the strength of the others.

Mrs. Ollerton knocked thrice on the door of the first one, waiting for a long moment before a woman answered. Her dark hair hung loose around her face, and she held a baby on one hip. Her thin face broke into a smile when she saw Mrs. Ollerton, and she welcomed us inside. Miss Taplow walked carefully, a slight grimace on her face as she slid through the narrow doorway.

"Mrs. Ollerton," the woman said, "am I glad to see you." She hoisted the child up higher on her hip, taking the hand of another young child inside. "My husband's been workin' hard, but we love the bread from Winslow House the most." Her son beamed up at the basket in Miss Taplow's hand, a glint of excitement in his eyes. The woman smiled down at the boy. "That'll suit our stew quite nicely this evenin', won't it? Can you thank Mrs. Ollerton and her friends?"

The boy offered a whisper of gratitude before backing away, a shy smile on his lips.

"It is our pleasure, Mrs. Roberts." Mrs. Ollerton introduced Miss Taplow first, then me to the woman before casting her gaze about the room. She gave a quiet gasp. "Who is this young girl?"

I followed her gaze to the corner, where a young boy and girl sat with a bilbocatch, laughing as they tried to land the ball on the peg. They fell silent when they noticed the attention on them. The little girl's smile faded.

"This be the daughter of a tenant of a nearby property," Mrs. Roberts said. "Her father be quite ill, so she's stayin' with us for a time. Her mother died last year, so with her father ill, no one be there to look after her. Her father has the physician lookin' after him, but he don't dare risk her fallin' ill too."

"How tragic." Mrs. Ollerton smiled at the girl, who tucked her chin, hiding her face away.

"Will she be away from home for long?" I asked, my heart aching over the uncertainty and fear the girl must have been feeling.

"'Tis difficult to say." The woman shrugged. "If any family has need of generosity, it be hers. I do much appreciate your baskets, and I'll share all I can with her father."

I studied the girl again, noting her slumped shoulders and narrow frame. Even my life as a maid was much easier than hers. I knew I could expect a meal three times each day and a steady and comfortable place to sleep. But I sympathized with her over the uncertainty she must have felt over her father. Would he recover? Would my father be hung for the accusations placed upon him? I pressed down the fear and pain that rose in my heart at the thought.

After exchanging a few short words with Mrs. Roberts, we went on our way, meeting the other group outside the modiste. Sophia had sent me with all her saved pin money over the last several weeks, as it would only be realistic for a woman of her breeding to have funds of her own to spend. She had entrusted me to *use it well*. Surely, she had meant for me to use it on purchasing her some new accessories, but after visiting Mrs. Roberts, I had a better idea of where to put that money. Sophia had a dowry awaiting her, so she did not treasure or value a few pounds like I did, or like the family of that poor girl would.

While all the ladies perused the shop, I kept my reticule held tightly closed, my heart pounding with excitement over my plan. But that did not stop me from admiring the row of pretty ribbons in the modiste. I had often shopped with Sophia, and out of habit, I examined the ribbons with her complexion and eye color in mind. Her skin was much paler than mine, as well as her eyes and hair, so I found myself drawn toward the various shades of blue and pink. As an added bonus, in this quiet corner of the shop, I did not have to hear Miss Benham go into raptures again over a certain fabric that had caught her eye. I enjoyed my moment of peace, touching the end of a satin ribbon. The silky fabric cascaded over my fingertips.

A deep baritone voice came from my left. "An excellent choice."

I nearly tugged the ribbon off the spool. Mr. Hill's chuckle quickly followed, far too close to my ear. "Forgive me for startling you yet again."

I gathered my wits, keeping my gaze fixed firmly on the ribbon I still clutched between my fingers. "I take it as your revenge for my spilling tea on your boots?"

He chuckled again, though I hadn't meant to make him laugh. Drat. I bit my lower lip. Had he already grown bored with the company of the other ladies? Perhaps they were too enthralled with the fabrics across the room to notice him for once.

"Are you considering that one?" he asked, bending

slightly to examine the ribbon I held more closely. "It would suit you quite well."

My heart lifted without permission at his compliment. It hadn't seemed overly flirtatious, but simply sincere. Did he really think such a pretty ribbon would suit me? I shook myself. It didn't matter what he thought.

His gloved hand took the ribbon end from my grasp, turning it over in his palm. He was standing close enough for me to smell the scent of leather and soap he carried. It took me a moment to remember that he had asked me a question. "I don't plan to purchase any ribbons today," I said.

I dared a glance up at his face. His blue eyes met mine, a shade or two darker than the ribbon he held. The sincerity I had imagined to see on his face was masked by a teasing glint, one I recalled seeing early that morning in the gardens. "Why not? It does seem to be the most beautiful of the choices before you."

"Indeed." I swallowed, tearing my gaze away from his face. "I must agree. But I am simply admiring it."

"I have never found a great deal to admire in a modiste shop before." Mr. Hill's voice still carried the teasing tone. "But today I find there is much to admire."

"I have never known a gentleman to find pleasure in admiring a row of ribbons." I cast him a look of disbelief before focusing on the ribbons again. Surely Miss Downsfield had noticed our conversation by now; could she not attempt to interrupt it? I cast a quick look over my shoulder, disappointed to find all four ladies with their backs turned to me as they leaned close to a piece of beadwork.

"I did not come over here to admire the *ribbons*, Miss Sedgwick."

Oh. My face burned, and I reminded myself that he had been flirting with all the other ladies too. Hadn't he? I had not been close enough to overhear his conversation on the walk with Miss Downsfield, but all the flirtatious smiles she had been giving him must have been encouraged.

His smile curved upward on one edge when I glanced up, and I cast him a scowl. I cleared my throat, pointing up at the row that rested just above the ribbons. "Oh, I see. You must mean the lace," I stammered. "I must agree that it is quite lovely as well. I see why you would have come to admire it instead." I kept my expression as even as possible before dropping the blue ribbon and turning toward the other ladies.

In a similar fashion to that morning, he chuckled as I scurried away.

Would any of the other women deny that he had been flirting with them too? Surely I was not the only one. But it was also true that the other ladies were likely much less entertaining to flirt with, as they knew how to properly react to comments like the ones Mr. Hill had just made. He seemed to find great pleasure in seeing me squirm with discomfort and blush redder than the sofas in the drawing room at Winslow House.

Searching for an escape, I came to stop behind Miss

Coppins. I tapped her arm, and she turned to face me with a smile.

"Would you like to go to the millinery with me?" I asked. "I saw a lovely bonnet in the window on our way here."

"Was it the straw bonnet with the lavender ribbons?"

In truth, I had not noticed a bonnet at all. Mr. Hill was simply far too close for me to be comfortable in the modiste's for another moment. "Yes, that one."

"Yes, let us go see it right now." Miss Coppins looped her arm through mine, leaning close to my ear. "The fabric Miss Benham has been admiring for ages is not even very pretty."

I would have to be careful around Miss Coppins. Her loyalty seemed to shift quite quickly. Or perhaps she enjoyed whispering and gossiping about everyone in turn. Either way, she was the closest thing to a friend I could claim at Winslow House besides Jessie. If only Jessie could have disguised herself as a lady too, then I would not be alone in my tricks.

What would Mr. Hill think if he knew I was a maid? The idea set my heart pounding. He would regret ever admiring me at all.

CHAPTER 6

Since Mr. Hill was the only gentleman at Winslow House, he was the only one to linger in the drawing room for port after dinner. It had been my first night attending dinner at the house, and it had taken all my concentration to remember the manners I had grown up learning. I was glad Sophia had taken the time to remind me where to place my serviette, as that had been the first thing to slip my mind. After an uneventful but delicious four course dinner, I was quite proud of myself for not spilling any food or doing anything that might draw Mr. Hill's attention toward me.

I had successfully avoided his gaze for the entire meal, in fact, only glancing up when I was spoken to by Mrs. Ollerton, who had seemed somewhat frustrated by my persistent silence throughout the meal. I had not been trying to be rude, but the concentration my manners required was all I could focus on. And the concentration required *not* to look up at Mr. Hill when I felt his gaze on the side of my face.

I had been seated next to Miss Benham at dinner, and she had proved to be much more amiable than I had previously expected. And now, sitting in the drawing room among just the other ladies, she seemed even more at ease while not in the company of Mr. Hill.

"And what is your favorite color combination in a ballgown?" Miss Benham raised one dark eyebrow in my direction. "Do you prefer one shade, or multiple hues and embellishments?"

I could certainly guess what Miss Benham preferred. She was always dressed in pleated, beaded, and lace-covered gowns with multiple layers of fabric in a great variety. Being so petite and short in frame, the gowns seemed to swallow her.

"I prefer a more simple sort of gown, usually with one shade." I smiled as I answered, hoping she would not judge me too harshly. "Although, that is simply my own preference. There are many women like yourself who look lovely with embellishments."

Miss Benham appeared satisfied with that response, glancing down at her bodice. "It took my modiste three weeks to complete the embroidery on the sleeves and bodice alone." She raised her chin. "I would never have the patience for such work."

"Nor would I." It was what Sophia would have said, though I disagreed. In my time as Sophia's maid, I had learned far more about sewing than I had ever thought would be necessary, and I found I actually enjoyed it. I had been taught to embroider before, but never to mend or even construct simple gowns. Sophia had given me several of her old dresses to wear when I had come to work as her maid, and I had learned to make minor alterations so they would fit me correctly.

Miss Downsfield sat forward in her chair, casting an inquisitive glance about the room. The height of her blonde curls only made her figure appear even more tall and slender. "Where do you suppose Mr. Hill will choose to sit when he returns from the dining room?"

The seat beside her was empty, as well as the seats on both sides of Miss Coppins and one to the right of Miss Taplow. Mrs. Ollerton sat on the other side of her. Miss Benham did not have a seat beside her, but I did. I swallowed. My seat was farthest from the door, thank the heavens, so I had nothing to worry about. I faced Miss Downsfield with a smile. "After the attention he paid you today in the village, I assume he would choose a seat beside you." It was obviously the answer she had been hunting for, as it caused a sly smile to curl her lips.

"I think you might be correct, Miss Sedgwick."

"No, I don't think so." Miss Taplow frowned, tapping her slipper on the rug. "Mr. Hill seems intent to distribute his time evenly between all of us until he is certain about his choice. If he already spent a great deal of time conversing with you today, Miss Downsfield, then I suspect he should like to choose a different lady to sit by this evening."

"Perhaps he already has made his choice but is simply keeping it a secret." Miss Downsfield rubbed her gloved fingers together nonchalantly, the twist of her lips persisting.

"How could he have already made his choice after two days?" Miss Coppins crossed her arms. "You and Miss Benham and Miss Taplow are all so beautiful."

I ignored the sting that struck me as my name failed to be mentioned on that list. It was true, Miss Coppins and I were certainly less elegant and beautiful as the other three ladies, at least by the standard of beauty society upheld at the moment. Miss Coppins's freckles and my tanned skin had much to do with it. I sat forward, debating over whether or not to indulge my curiosity. "Have you all had many interactions with Mr. Hill? I must confess he is still quite mysterious to me." I held my breath, hoping to hear that he had said similar, flirtatious things to all of them. If he had, wouldn't they be boasting of it? Each woman trying to prove that he preferred her over everyone else?

Silence reigned for far too long before Miss Downsfield spoke in a boastful voice. "Well, he did walk with me all the way to town today."

"Did you see the purchase he made at the modiste's?" Miss Taplow interrupted. "He was quite secretive about it." She wiggled her eyebrows, the motion causing her auburn ringlets to shift on her temples. "What do you suppose it was?"

"I told him repeatedly of the lace I wanted to add to

the neckline of my ball gown," Miss Benham said, squaring her shoulders. "It could only have been a piece of that."

Miss Taplow bit her lip. "Yes, I suppose he did endure your commentary on it for so long that he might have purchased it just to stop your prattling."

Miss Benham scowled, her jaw tightening.

"What is his conversation like?" Miss Coppins asked, an edge of longing in her voice.

I hid my curiosity as best I could, feigning deep interest in my gloves as Miss Downsfield spoke.

"It can be quite shocking, actually." She gave a small laugh. "He is a shameless flirt if I have ever met one."

Miss Taplow scowled at the ground. It seemed she had not received the same treatment that Miss Downsfield, and even *I*, had. Miss Benham sat up straighter. "Yes, yes, I have experienced the same while conversing with Mr. Hill." Her voice was quick. "He is quite incorrigible." She gave a broad smile, staring at Miss Downsfield as if she were challenging her to question her words.

Miss Downsfield accepted that challenge with an upward tip of her chin. "What has he said to you, Miss Benham?"

Miss Benham cleared her throat, a high-pitched sound. "Well, just this morning as I left the breakfast room, he— he told me he thought I looked quite lovely." She narrowed her eyes. "What has he said to you?"

Miss Downsfield laughed, sharing a glance with Mrs. Ollerton, who had been watching the exchange with deep interest. "Oh, that is quite tame compared to what he has said to me."

My stomach clenched. What had Mr. Hill said to Miss Downsfield? I silently prayed it was more audacious than what he had said to me. My heart pounded. At least by this conversation I could assume that he was indeed a flirt, not simply trying to win *my* favor with his comments and winks.

"Well, what did he say to you?" Miss Benham's cheeks had turned red in the centers, whether by shame or anger, I couldn't tell.

Miss Downsfield opened her mouth to speak just as the drawing room door opened. Her mouth snapped closed.

Mr. Hill entered, and from the corner of my eye, I caught every spine in the room straighten. All expressions of accusation and vexation melted into pleasant smiles of greeting and grace. My brow knit together as I tried to understand all that I had just heard, my expression quite different from the pleasant smiles all the other ladies wore.

Sweeping his gaze over the room, Mr. Hill took one step, then another, a slight smile curling his lips. He was walking in Miss Downsfield's direction, which did not come as a surprise to me. He did seem quite partial to her, and even more so now after what she had just revealed about his flirtations with her. But when he reached the center of the room near where Miss Downsfield sat, he continued walking...past Miss Taplow and Miss Coppins, and all the way to the farthest corner of the room where I sat with Miss Benham. I barely caught Miss Downsfield's dejected expression before Mr. Hill blocked her from my view.

With a contented sigh, he sunk down into the chair beside mine, not a care for his own posture. He turned his head toward me and smiled. "Miss Sedgwick."

"Mr. Hill." My voice came out with more air than sound.

My eyes met Mrs. Ollerton's across the room, whose nose crinkled slightly as she offered a discreet pat of comfort to Miss Downsfield's wrist. Her mouth moved, and I read her lips. *He pities her.* Another comforting pat. *He is a gentleman, after all.*

Understanding dawned on Miss Downsfield's face, and her smile returned.

Hopefully Mrs. Ollerton was right. It made much more sense than the fears that had begun to take root inside me: that he might have genuinely found something to admire in me. *Don't be ridiculous, Tillie.* No man had ever found anything to admire in me. I had spent much of my Season on the outskirts of the ballroom, only invited to dance when I was, just as Mrs. Ollerton had said, *pitied.*

"How would you all like to be entertained this evening?" Mrs. Ollerton asked. "Perhaps we might recite a bit of poetry? I rarely have the opportunity to be surrounded by so many young and intelligent people with whom to discuss the deeper meanings behind verse."

Mr. Hill leaned against the armrest of his chair—the one closer to me. "I am quite fond of poetry."

"Especially when it is read by pretty young ladies?" Miss Downsfield raised one eyebrow with a coy smile.

"That does increase my fondness of any poem." He gave a charming smile, and I had to refrain from groaning. That comment alone would give Miss Downsfield far too much pleasure. As I expected, Miss Downsfield sat back with a satisfied smile aimed in Miss Benham's direction.

"Poems recited from memory are even more impressive," Mr. Hill said. "I will be quite eager to hear if any of you have one to share."

A look of panic stole over Miss Downsfield's features before they smoothed over once again. If only I could share my arsenal with her. I had dozens of poems memorized from the days my governess had encouraged extensive reading. I had not been required to memorize them, but I had wanted to, so I would never forget the beautiful words and messages. Papa valued poetry, and he had taught me to regard it as a deep, meaningful form of art—words forged in the heart. Tonight, of course, knowing that Mr. Hill liked poetry, I would voice opinions quite to the contrary.

"Who would like to stand first?" Mrs. Ollerton's eyes gleamed with excitement in the candlelight. "Perhaps Mr. Hill might call on each lady to rise and share a poem? And I would be quite loath if Mr. Hill did not also recite his favorite poem for our enjoyment."

"I would be glad to." Mr. Hill chuckled. He turned toward me. "Miss Sedgwick, do you have a poem to recite?"

I met his gaze, maintaining eye contact so he could not

decipher my lies. "I'm afraid not. I have never seen fit to memorize a poem. I do not enjoy poetry in the slightest."

His eyebrows rose, causing two long creases to appear in his forehead. Even with that expression he was unjustly handsome. "Will it be torturous for you to endure this evening of poetry, then?" That teasing glint was still in his eyes.

"No, I shall endure it, but I will not contribute to something I so thoroughly dislike." I put on a grimace. I may have been doing it too brown, but my points had failed to come across boldly enough in the past. Mr. Hill often took my words as jest when they were not.

Mr. Hill studied my face for a long moment. "That is a shame. I was looking forward to your recitation." His mouth curved upward on one corner, the teasing grin I had come to recognize. "So I should like to hear you sing for us instead."

CHAPTER 7

"Oh, Miss Sedgwick, I did not know you were an accomplished singer." Mrs. Ollerton sat on the edge of her chair, her eyes round with excitement.

I would have glared at Mr. Hill, but everyone in the room was now watching me. He had heard my horrendous singing in the gardens. Why would he ever think that asking me to sing was a good idea?

By the sly grin on his lips, I could tell that he had only suggested it to embarrass me. He likely wanted to watch me blush and stammer and avoid singing for the crowd. So I would do precisely the opposite.

Although my heart pounded furiously in my chest, I maintained an even expression.

Mrs. Ollerton continued, "Well, we would be privileged to hear a song from Miss Sedgwick in the place of poetry, wouldn't we, Mr. Hill?" She did not have any qualms about offering flirtatious smiles of her own toward

Mr. Hill, and he did not even flinch, as accustomed as he was to making women into fools.

I gritted my teeth, keeping a pleasant smile on my lips to cover it.

"Indeed," Mr. Hill said in an enthusiastic voice.

I caught Miss Downsfield's gaze, her eyes narrowed with accusation. Miss Coppins had told me that Miss Downsfield had seen me in the gardens with Mr. Hill. She must have known it was purely coincidental, but the spite in her gaze spoke otherwise.

"Let us save it for last," Mr. Hill continued. "It shall be our grand finale."

My quiet exhale came out in something of a growl, and I slid my gaze discreetly toward him. He still wore his victorious smile, sitting back as if he were about to enjoy my awkward stammering of excuses.

Well, he was mistaken. I sat up straighter. "Oh, yes, Mrs. Ollerton. It is actually the only admirable accomplishment I can own up to. I will ensure it is as grand a finale as you all are hoping for."

Mr. Hill's smile faltered, his head tipping as he regarded me with deep curiosity. Good. I had surprised him. If he thought I was predictable and entertaining, he was wrong. I would prove to him that he could never dare consider courting me if he hoped not to be laughed out of any party. I could burst into song at any moment, off-key and loud.

"Shall we start here with Miss Taplow?" Mrs. Ollerton asked. "She has informed me that she has a poem she would like to recite."

Mr. Hill gave a nod; breathing felt much easier with his gaze focused on someone else. "Yes, of course."

Miss Taplow stood and recited a poem from Shakespeare, her voice quick and soft. Mr. Hill applauded as she reclaimed her seat. Miss Benham volunteered next, then Miss Coppins, both of whom recited poems I had also memorized, and I was able to catch the words which they accidentally omitted. Miss Coppins had even missed an entire line. Mr. Hill's gaze reflected deep thought as he listened, and I even caught a slight tip of his head at Miss Coppins's omission. Did he have all these memorized too?

When it came time for Miss Downsfield's poem, she shook her head softly. "Unfortunately I do not have a very strong memory when it comes to words on a page. I adore poetry though, likely just as much as you do, Mr. Hill." She gave a sweet smile. "I have enjoyed listening to these poems very much, and it is my dearest wish that I had something to contribute…" Her eyes darted toward the pianoforte, and she turned her body slightly in that direction. Was she hoping Mr. Hill would invite her to sing as well?

"There is no need to lament," Mr. Hill said. "There will be other opportunities for you to showcase the talents you do have." He offered her a polite smile, and I couldn't help but notice the difference between that smile and the others I had seen on his face. Why did he save the flirtatious, teasing grins for me? My lungs felt heavy, and I could hardly draw a breath. It was nearly my turn to sing. What had I been thinking? I had already made a spectacle of myself when I spilled the tea tray, and now here I was preparing to sing a horrendous song for all the guests. Sophia had specifically told me to be invisible. To remain unnoticed.

"Now, Mr. Hill, would you treat us with your favorite poem before we hear from Miss Sedgwick?" Mrs. Ollerton said. "Or perhaps your poem should be our finale instead?"

Panic clenched in my muscles. That would mean my performance was next. My palms began sweating profusely inside my gloves.

"No, no, I mustn't follow a performance like Miss Sedgwick's. Her song absolutely must be the finale." Mr. Hill's false humility was grating. Did he realize that all this praise directed at me would only embarrass him once everyone heard how dreadful my singing really was?

He stood, glancing down at me as he did, a mischievous smile on his lips. He cleared his throat. "I will recite my favorite from Wordsworth. It is brief, but I connect deeply with the words."

All the ladies in the room watched him eagerly, as if ready to drink up this insight into his soul. My heart rapped against my chest, a brief moment of calm before I would be forced to ruin it all with my singing.

Mr. Hill's voice was gentle and strong as he spoke, and it filled the room.

My heart leaps up when I behold
A rainbow in the sky

. . .

Those first lines sent my stomach fluttering. This was the poem Papa had loved the most. Every time it rained, he had held me up to the window, or led me to the window by the hand once I was too large to hold. Together we would search for a rainbow in the sky. Most of the time, we found one from that vantage point, but other times we walked outside on the wet grass to expand our search. My heart yearned for those moments, and I held my breath as Mr. Hill continued on.

So was it when my life began;
So is it now I am a man;
So be it when I shall grow old,
Or let me die!
The Child is father of the Man;
And I could wish my days to be
Bound each to each by natural piety.

The moment he finished, the breath I had been holding slipped out of my lungs, and my heart ached. Did Mr. Hill share my sense of wonder with nature? If he valued that poem as much as he said he did, then he must.

Hearing that poem again reminded me of what I had lost. How much I had changed. I had tried to hold onto that sense of wonder in seeing a rainbow across a spring sky, but since becoming Sophia's maid it had faded away. I had become less observant of the beautiful things the world had to offer. Everything had become grey. The sky, the rainbows, the flowers, even my heart had lost its brightness and joy. Nothing could ever be as colorful and marvelous in a world where Papa was trapped in a cage. Birds did not sing with as much perfection anymore, and rainbows didn't exist. Only rain.

Mr. Hill sat down, and I realized too late that I hadn't applauded. Without permission, my gaze traveled to his face, searching every inch of it for something familiar, for the things I felt within myself. Mr. Hill's blue eyes were filled with more than a teasing glint. They went far deeper than that. They were not a puddle or a shallow pond. His eyes held a sea of emotions and experiences. Even without the various shades of blue and grey, I would have been unable to see past the surface. He seemed determined to hide those depths from me and everyone else.

The question assailed me again: what was he doing here at Winslow House?

"I believe it is your turn, Miss Sedgwick," he said in a quiet voice.

His words jarred me back to the present. At that moment, he was here to tease me. To humiliate me. To entertain himself at my expense.

With a deep breath, I came to my feet. I felt Mr. Hill's gaze on my back as I walked to the pianoforte. I had never played well, but I had been taught a few easy songs that could be used if ever I was forced to perform at a party. Much like tonight. There was one song in particular that

Mama had advised me never to perform, unless I wished to appear like an *unrefined child* as she had phrased it.

The song I had sung that morning in the gardens was short enough to spare the guests the prolonged agony of hearing me sing, but just strange enough to shock them all. I had learned it from a servant in my household as a child by the name of Anne. She had sung it each morning as she worked outside my window. I had not understood the meaning until I had grown older and realized she had been singing about her preference for freedom and nature over marriage. The irony of singing it here was too exciting to resist.

My hands shook as I sat down at the pianoforte. I had to do it, if only to ensure Mr. Hill never, ever considered me. I plunked out the first few notes before beginning in my shaking voice.

O'er mountain, o'er valley, o'er rolling green hill
  Little Anne goes riding
  O'er stream, o'er woods, with a lone quadrille
  A man she soon be finding

Hark! A bird sings in the trees
  A tune made just for Little Anne
  She feels a light and calming breeze
  Without the coming gentleman

. . .

O'er mountain, O'er valley, O'er rolling green hill
  Little Anne goes riding
  O'er stream, O'er woods, with a lone quadrille
  From the man she soon be hiding

Hark! A bird sings in the trees
  A tune made just for Little Anne
  She feels a light and calming breeze
  Without the coming gentleman

I heard every crack, every mismatched tune. I was not deaf to my inability to sing, but I acted as if I believed my talent to be unmatched, swaying with the music. When my last note rang through the air, I stood in one swift motion, offering a curtsy with a modest smile.

I quickly searched for Mr. Hill's gaze, but I couldn't find it. His head was tipped down and turned away, toward the wall. A sense of triumph nearly lifted me to my toes.

I had frightened him. He could not even look at me.

The other ladies, however, did not seem afraid to. I took in their expressions of disdain and shock, pretending not to notice. I focused instead on Mr. Hill's perfect reaction. With his head tipped down, I couldn't see any of his features. Was he grimacing in disgust? I frowned as I noticed his shoulders shaking slightly.

Had I brought him to agonized tears?

I had known I lacked talent, but not enough to bring a

grown man such distress. It was even better than I had hoped.

"Thank you, Miss Sedgwick," Mrs. Ollerton said finally, her voice hollow. "That was…certainly a grand finale. Please do have a seat."

On my way back to my chair, I studied Mr. Hill again. When I was just a few feet away, he sat up straighter, and I could finally see his expression.

He was laughing.

And he seemed to have been laughing for a prolonged moment, as his eyes brimmed with tears and his smile was broad and filled with amusement.

My heart sank.

"That was brilliant," he whispered as I took my seat. "I didn't think you would do it." The twinkle of mirth in his eyes transformed as he stared at me. It was unfamiliar and strange, and it took me a long moment to realize it was admiration. My stomach twisted as he leaned closer, hiding his smile from the rest of the room. "You have certainly shocked Mrs. Ollerton."

I took a deep breath to calm my sudden nerves, glancing up at the woman. She smoothed her hands over her skirts repeatedly, a stern wrinkle in her brow. She looked as if she were on the verge of storming out of the drawing room to compose herself. I almost laughed but held it inside. I would have to feign innocence.

"Why didn't you think I would sing?" I furrowed my brow in confusion to appear more convincing. "I do try to showcase my talents as often as I am able. I am most grateful that you encouraged me to perform."

He shook his head, his smile only growing. I watched that smile, a deep flutter erupting in my stomach. It took all my energy not to smile myself. How could the expression be so contagious? I had just humiliated myself in order to secure his dismay but had failed. I should not have *any* reason to smile.

"The other guests appear to be envious of your accomplishments," he whispered.

"How could they be envious of my singing?" I glanced across the room, where all the ladies watched with narrowed eyes, not even listening to Mrs. Ollerton's explanation of the plans for the next day. I could hardly listen either, not with Mr. Hill whispering so close to my ear.

"It is not your singing they are envious of." His voice grew even more quiet. "I suppose they are most envious that I asked you to sing at all...that you have accomplished the task they all came here to achieve."

My heart pounded hard against my chest. "What task is that?"

His breath brushed against my cheek as he spoke, the smile in his voice sending a thrill through my chest. "To capture my undivided attention."

Had I heard him correctly? I couldn't breathe as I dared a glance at his eyes. The teasing glint still lingered there, giving me hope that perhaps he was not serious. How had I captured his undivided attention? Yes, I had certainly drawn attention to myself tonight, but I had intended for it to be *negative* attention. How could Mr. Hill find a single thing I had done intriguing? I had made a fool of myself again and again.

Darting my gaze around the room, I slumped in relief. No one seemed to have overheard his words. But Mr. Hill still watched me, as if waiting for my reply.

I felt suddenly shy, fear climbing up my spine at an alarming rate. "That—that was not my intention, sir." My words were sharper than I intended.

His brow furrowed, and confusion flooded his features. "Then why did you come here?"

"I—" My voice stopped. How could I explain it? Mr. Hill knew that all of us had come for a chance at marrying him. He was well aware of his own charms and wealth. "I came because I was forced to." My voice barely carried over Mrs. Ollerton's prattle, but Mr. Hill seemed to have heard me, if his concerned frown was any indication.

It wasn't a lie. Sophia would have been forced to come to Bibury if she had not forced me to come in her place. "My—er—my parents did not give me a choice in the matter." I glanced up at him, growing increasingly uncomfortable with the growing scrutiny from the other ladies and their indiscreet attempts at eavesdropping. Miss Downsfield sat on the very edge of her chair, her head turned slightly toward us, and I could only imagine Miss Benham had heard at least a few of our words from her place on my other side.

Mr. Hill watched me for a long moment, until my face burned hot and my lungs tightened. Finally he spoke, a slight smile of understanding pulling up one edge of his lips. "We have that in common, then. I was forced to come as well."

It was my turn to be confused. I scowled as I watched him turn in his chair toward the group, obviously noticing the eavesdropping that was becoming less and less discreet. There was so much I didn't know about Mr. Hill. I had been tempted to ask Mrs. Ollerton why he had required her assistance to make a match, but since she had not already explained it, I worried it wasn't a subject she would be willing to discuss. Had he really been forced to come?

My questions would have to remain unanswered. After this evening, I was fairly certain my efforts had failed entirely. Speaking with him again with any level of attentiveness was not an option.

He could have been teasing about the things he said, but there had been too much sincerity behind his voice when he had told me how I had captured his attention— precisely the opposite of what I had come here to achieve. The other ladies had given him all their attention, and I hadn't.

Is that what had drawn him to me?

An idea formed in the back of my mind, and my heart pounded. If I chose to behave more like the other ladies— fawning over him, flirting, following his every move...then would he change his opinion of me? Perhaps in avoiding him I was giving him a challenge that he could not resist. I would have to take a lesson from Miss Downsfield if I hoped to drive him away for good.

I had been going about it all wrong.

I had *stood out* with my antics.

What I needed to do to be truly invisible was *fit in* among the elegant, eager, and dramatic ways of the other four guests.

It would be difficult, but it could be done. I could prattle on and on about fashion like Miss Benham if I wanted, and I could certainly fabricate some worries about my health like those Miss Coppins had told me about. Miss Taplow was quiet, but very elegant and polite, and I knew from my tutelage in my youth that I could effect that demeanor with a bit of focus. My confidence faltered as I considered Miss Downsfield. Could I be the first to clutch Mr. Hill's arm on a walk, or cast him flirtatious smiles with every word he spoke?

I spent the rest of the evening in deep thought, hardly hearing any of the conversation in the room. If this was going to be my new plan, then I would need to wait until the next day to put it into effect, after carefully planning the details with Jessie and ensuring it wasn't a ridiculous idea.

When it was finally time to retire for the evening, I hurried out the door and away from Mr. Hill's watchful gaze. Once I was safely inside my bedchamber, I rang for Jessie. We had much to discuss.

CHAPTER 8

*J*essie turned me toward the mirror again, tugging on my shoulders when I resisted. "Tillie," she grumbled. "It's not perfect yet."

I complied with her prodding, turning toward my reflection with a sigh. Jessie had been fussing over my hair arrangement for over an hour, determined to make it as intricate and detailed as Miss Benham's. Perhaps even more so. Sophia had sent me with an assortment of decorative pins, combs, wraps, and ribbons that could be used in my hair, and Jessie had enjoyed herself far too much in selecting which ones she wanted to test on me. After attempting two different coiffures, she seemed to finally be content with this one, aside from one pesky curl.

She straightened the pearl pins around the crown of my head, twisting the curls on each side of my face around her finger to shape them correctly.

"Need I remind you that Mrs. Ollerton has planned

several activities out of doors today?" I said with a teasing smile. "I don't think that curl will stay exactly as you have arranged it."

Jessie huffed a breath, casting me a teasing frown in the mirror. "Yes, but what matters most is your first impression on the ladies. If you walk down to the breakfast room with limp curls, they'll not be envious of you, will they?"

"The point is not to make the other ladies envious," I said with a sigh. "It is to *become* like the other ladies. I must fit in, so Mr. Hill finds nothing unique about me to entertain himself with."

"Yes, I suppose you be right, but I still want him to find you pretty."

I jerked my head away from her twisting fingers. "No. We must ensure he finds me quite the opposite. This hair arrangement is meant to be extreme, not attractive." I looked in the mirror again, smiling at the way my curls piled several inches off my head. "I look very much like Miss Benham. You have done well, Jessie."

She gave a modest smile, stepping away and studying her work. "I do think I've improved. Now, your gown." She walked to the wardrobe and removed the most detailed of the dresses Sophia had sent, which was still not nearly as intricate as Miss Benham's wardrobe. It was a pale pink with a second layer of sheer chiffon over the skirts. It looked more like a ball gown than a morning dress, but it was something Miss Benham would wear simply because she wished to. Her confidence was fashionable in itself, and that was exactly what I needed to emulate. Miss Downs-field's confidence was unmatched as well.

Until today.

I planned to exceed it if I could. If I added a few ridiculous comments to my conversation, I could demonstrate a similarity to Miss Coppins, and if I held myself with elegant posture at all times, Miss Taplow would find her equal in me as well. Mr. Hill would not recognize me at all.

Squaring my shoulders, I studied the glint of determination in my eyes in the mirror. This would undo the damage I had done. It had to. My heart threw itself against my ribs, pounding so hard I could hear my own pulse. I was not even a real lady! I was a lady's *maid*. It had been difficult enough to act the part of a timid, submissive lady. How could I be a flirtatious, competitive, fashionable one?

Jessie must have sensed my worry, for she stepped forward, threading her arm around my shoulders. "You'll behave perfectly."

I smiled. "If you can call Miss Downfield's behavior perfect, then yes, I will."

Jessie laughed, covering her lips with her fingers.

After dressing in the pink gown, I made my way downstairs, focusing on each step. Keeping my shoulders back, I practiced my smug, disdainful expression. Miss Downsfield wore such an expression at least half the time. The other half, she wore one of infatuation as she stared at Mr. Hill. That was the part that scared me the most. Would flirting with him have the opposite effect of what I intended? I had even practiced my shrill laughter, and Jessie had said it was astonishingly similar to Sophia's laugh.

When I reached the door to the breakfast room, I gathered my wits about me. Mrs. Ollerton's voice carried into the hallway, followed by a much deeper tone that could only have been Mr. Hill. His voice was too quiet from my place in the hall to decipher his words, but Mrs. Ollerton said something about delicious eggs.

With a deep breath, I walked inside, putting on my practiced expression. It faltered when I saw that it was just Mr. Hill and Mrs. Ollerton in the room so far. I had expected to see all the women surrounding him already, but I had come too early. If I was the only young lady in the room, I was still bound to stand out. Drat it all. How late was fashionable? I would have expected Miss Downsfield to be here early to ensure she had the chair next to him at the table.

Mr. Hill looked up from his plate and stood, his gaze steady as he watched me enter, a light smile on his lips. Had he even noticed the extravagance of my appearance? I curtsied, forgetting my practiced flirtatious smile. It was much more difficult offering it to Mr. Hill rather than my own reflection. *Focus, Tillie,* I demanded inwardly before walking to the sidebar to fill my plate. I hardly noticed what I chose to eat. All I could think of was the greeting I had tried to pluck up the courage to give him. Before I could lose my nerve, I turned and chose the chair directly beside Mr. Hill.

He did seem surprised.

But *pleasantly* surprised.

I took a deep breath, hoping he couldn't hear the nervous tremor behind it. Putting on my most flirtatious smile, I rotated toward him.

"Good morning, Mr. Hill. I cannot believe my good fortune to have been the first lady to come to breakfast this morning. I wouldn't have possibly been able to secure a place next to you at the table if I hadn't been." I batted my eyelashes slowly as I had seen Miss Downsfield do, tipping my head to one side with a demure smile. "Even if I hadn't been this fortunate, I would have fought the other women for a precious moment to speak with you."

His surprise persisted, mingled with a hint of confusion. My gaze flitted to Mrs. Ollerton, who watched me with wide eyes, her serviette hovering over her lips.

Mr. Hill sat back in his chair, studying me with his intent gaze. "What is this important matter you wish to speak with me about?"

I gave my most shrill laugh, leaning closer to him— close enough to catch his scent again. I met his eyes, realizing that I had leaned close enough to see the deep green lines that marked the blue of his irises. I cleared my throat, sitting back slightly. I forgot to smile. "Oh, it is not an important *matter*. It is simply the privilege of speaking with you at all that is precious to me." I fluttered my eyelids again before realizing that I may have been doing that more often than Miss Downsfield had. It was no wonder my Season had been a disaster. I could not flirt in the slightest.

My efforts did appear to be working somewhat. I

consoled myself with the look of growing confusion on Mr. Hill's face as he watched me.

Mrs. Ollerton cleared her throat, a slight squeak in the sound. "You seem quite different this morning, Miss Sedgwick," she said, her voice slow and careful. "Did you sleep well? Are you ill?"

"Is there something in your eye?" Mr. Hill added in a voice of mock concern, a smile curling one edge of his mouth.

So I *had* taken my eyelash fluttering to an extreme. I addressed Mrs. Ollerton first. "Yes, in fact, I awoke today feeling much more refreshed than I have been in days. I daresay I am finally feeling like myself. I am quite dull and quiet when I am suffering from exhaustion as I have been lately. But today, I awoke with a clear sense of all my ambitions." I turned my gaze to Mr. Hill with a coy grin. I felt ill for letting a single one of those words escape me, and for even attempting such outrageous behavior.

Mr. Hill continued to stare at me with a furrowed brow, but there was an edge of amusement behind his eyes, a curiosity that I didn't understand. Was I not convincing enough?

"And no, Mr. Hill," I said, picking up my fork, "I have nothing in my eye, although I find it most thoughtful that you would inquire." I stabbed at my plate while smiling up at him, missing my eggs entirely.

"Well," Mrs. Ollerton said, "I am quite glad you are so...refreshed." She gave a pained smile, taking another bite from her plate, swallowing it quickly.

A pang of guilt struck me as I realized how much distress I had caused Mrs. Ollerton in such a short time. Surely she regretted ever inviting Sophia Sedgwick to her matchmaking party. Is that what this gathering was called? I hardly knew. My thoughts wandered back to Mr. Hill's words the night before, that he too had been forced to come. What did that mean? My curiosity had been tugging at me ever since.

Refocusing my attention on the task at hand, I smiled at Mrs. Ollerton. "I daresay I have never felt so refreshed in my entire life. Although, I cannot owe it all to the quality of my sleep. I must owe a great deal of it to Mr. Hill, as a lady cannot feel anything but alert and renewed when in the presence of such an agreeable, handsome gentleman."

Mr. Hill choked on his water, setting down his cup and coughing. He cleared his throat. "I did not know I had such an effect on you, Miss Sedgwick."

I touched a hand to my collarbone, addressing Mrs. Ollerton with an adoring smile. "Not only is he agreeable and handsome, but he is also humble."

She agreed with an emphatic nod. "Indeed, he is."

Turning back toward Mr. Hill, I made sure he caught sight of my broad smile. My cheeks ached. I hadn't smiled this much in a very long time. His demeanor seemed to change slightly, as if he were beginning to believe my act. He turned his attention back to his plate, a deep furrow on his brow. Good. Let him be confused. Let him be disappointed in me. It would not be long before I drove his attention away for good. For a strange reason, something inside me resisted the idea. As much as I hated to admit it, I had been flattered by his attention, as uncalled for as it was. No man had ever found me so fascinating before.

Don't be ridiculous, I scolded myself. He did not find me fascinating. He found me entertaining and unique.

Well, that all would change today.

Mr. Hill ate in silence for several minutes. I had run out of things to say to him, so I took to conversing with Mrs. Ollerton instead, directing the conversation to topics that I was sure would bore Mr. Hill. We spoke of fabric and bonnets and all matters of fashion. Mrs. Ollerton complimented my hair, and I told her just how long Jessie had agonized over it. As discreetly as possible, I checked Mr. Hill's expression throughout the conversation, noting the lack of a flirtatious smile. He looked simply confused. And surprised. But not *pleasantly* surprised any longer.

My nerves had begun to dissolve, and I played my new role with more confidence. Eventually, the other ladies entered the room, and I sat up straighter. Now was my chance to blend in.

The moment she walked through the door, Miss Downsfield fixed me with a hard stare, her blonde curls spilling over her forehead and hiding the scowl I knew pinched on her pale brows. Her vexation was surely tied to the fact that I was seated next to Mr. Hill, but it also could have something to do with the fact that I returned her challenging stare this time. If I were to be like her, I would also have to be competitive.

She sat down on the other side of Mrs. Ollerton, and the other three ladies filled the empty chairs.

"Good morning, Miss Sedgwick," Miss Benham said as she took the chair on my other side.

"Good morning," I said. "*Mr. Hill* has been such a pleasant companion for breakfast, as well as Mrs. Ollerton, of course."

All the ladies seemed to glance at my plate, then Mr. Hill's, in perfect synchrony, likely noting that both our plates were nearly empty.

"Yes, we've had a lengthy and diverting conversation." I brushed a curl from my forehead as I had seen Miss Downsfield do, but the motion released a loose hair, and it tangled in my lashes, brushing against my eye. I blinked rapidly, my eye flooding with moisture as the loose hair irritated it. I blinked hard again, but it didn't dispel the hair. I picked at my lashes, trying to catch the hair that was tangled in them.

"Are you unwell, Miss Sedgwick?" Miss Coppins grew pale as she watched me from across the table. "Shall we call for the physician?"

"No, no." I held up a hand, my rapid blinking continuing as a tear balanced on the edge of my eyelid.

"Good heavens, what is the matter?" Behind the blur of my vision, I saw the outline of Mrs. Ollerton's dismayed features.

Around a sigh, I finally succumbed. "There is something in my eye."

As expected, Mr. Hill leaned slightly closer. "I suspected so."

Between my forefinger and thumb, I finally caught hold of the culprit, a short, thin hair that had fallen out of my hairline, likely from all of Jessie's combing and tugging from that morning. Once my eye was clear, I blinked away the moisture. Could I not act without embarrassing myself for one day? I reminded myself that Mr. Hill reveled in my reactions of shame and shyness. I would have to change that.

"Oh, Mr. Hill, of course you were right." I gave a shrill laugh. "You are always right, I daresay. I cannot imagine how a man as intelligent and respected as yourself could ever be wrong." I glanced at the other women at the table, who nodded their agreement.

Mr. Hill's eyes narrowed with suspicion as he watched me, and I quickly stammered for a new subject. "There, my eye is now healed. There will be no need for a physician today, Miss Coppins."

The worry on her face didn't seem to have lessened. Her large eyes remained as round as saucers. "Are you certain? You may have given your eye a dreadful scratch, and I should hate to have you awaken tomorrow without your vision."

"Oh...well, I believe I will be just fine." I spoke in a reassuring voice. "I don't believe I will lose my vision on account of a small hair in my eye."

"Well, we could all lose much more today than our vision with Mrs. Ollerton's planned activity." Miss Coppins had not seemed very eager to participate when our hostess had announced that we would be practicing archery that day. "Imagine if an arrow were to fly in the wrong direction?" She wrung her hands together. "I cannot comprehend the horror of seeing one of you, my dear friends, struck by an arrow."

Mrs. Ollerton gaped at her. "Miss Coppins, we will exercise every necessary safety precaution. Not to worry."

"There is no greater precaution than staying inside," she said in an offhand voice, crossing her arms.

CHAPTER 9

After all the ladies finished eating, we walked outside together, where two tables had been set up with an assortment of small desserts and pitchers of lemonade. It wasn't quite warm enough yet to go out of doors without a spencer jacket, so I wore the one that Sophia had sent me with—a dark blue with detailed sleeves and brass buttons. The moment we reached the tables, Miss Coppins chose a chair, still uninterested in practicing any shooting.

The back property of Winslow House didn't include a wide or expansive lawn. It was covered with garden paths and trees, but Mrs. Ollerton had designated a small section for archery, tucked far beyond the flowering bushes, just before the treeline. Six targets had been set up, three across from one another. We would shoot at one set until our arrows ran out before crossing the lawn and shooting at the other set.

I could only recall shooting a bow once, and it had not been a great skill of mine. In my life, I had come to accept that my skills, or accomplishments, were not the common or expected ones. After my first season in London, I had determined that I had no accomplishments or skills at all, but since then, I had learned that my talents were simply of a different sort. I was quite skilled at listening, arranging hair, and choosing accessories for Sophia. I did all I could to be loyal, kind, and honest. Those were accomplishments I would prefer over singing and shooting and playing the pianoforte.

If I could manage to be as loyal, kind, and honest as Mama, then I would be content. If every person in the world prioritized such qualities over frivolous pursuits, there would not be so many ill feelings among people. Papa would not have made his mistake, at least, and he would not have been sent to prison for it.

I stood near the tables by Miss Coppins, observing the other members of the party. Of all the ladies, Miss Taplow seemed the most eager to pick up a bow. This activity had been her idea in the first place. She stood in front of the far left target, her features serious as she examined the target from all angles. When Mrs. Ollerton gave permission to begin, Miss Taplow snatched up her bow, checking to see if Mr. Hill was watching before positioning the arrow.

In one swift motion, she raised the bow, took her aim, and released the arrow. It landed slightly to the right of the center of the target. Her eyes narrowed in frustration. How did she think that was inadequate? If I could shoot with accuracy like hers, I would be quite pleased with myself. She glanced at Mr. Hill, who appeared impressed with her skill.

Good. Perhaps he had decided that Miss Taplow was now the best choice. Hope began rising inside me as he walked toward her, offering his compliments.

With his back turned, I moved toward one of the targets, picking up the bow. It looked slightly different from the one I had used years before, but I remembered how to hold it at least. The target hadn't seemed so distant before, but now that I held the bow, it seemed very small and very far from where I stood. I really did need help and asking Mr. Hill in a flirtatious way would accomplish more than one of my goals.

"Mr. Hill?" I made my voice loud and shrill like Miss Downsfield's.

He turned toward me immediately, one eyebrow raised.

"It seems I have forgotten how to shoot." I laughed, pausing to smooth the curls on my brow. "I wondered if you might teach me?" My gaze flickered to Miss Taplow's flirtatious smile as she said something unintelligible to Mr. Hill. I replicated that smile, beckoning him closer. He seemed reluctant to leave Miss Taplow's side, and I counted that as a victory. Had my plan begun working already? Jessie would be so proud. My smile was not even entirely fake by the time Mr. Hill reached me. As exhausting as this act was, at least it was not all for nothing.

In the sunlight, Mr. Hill's eyes appeared even more blue.

It took a great deal of focus to turn my attention back to the target. *Should I* have been looking in his eyes? Eye contact was essential to flirting, at least in my limited experience, but I found speaking difficult with his penetrating gaze fixed on mine. I felt as if he could see me for who I truly was: a maid. A maid pretending to be a confident, flirtatious lady. If he looked closely enough, he would see that this was all an act, and that I found him far more attractive than I should have.

"When was the last time you shot a bow, Miss Sedgwick?" Mr. Hill gave his usual half-smile.

"Oh, it has been several years." I pursed my lips into a coy grin. "I haven't the slightest idea of what to do." I held out the bow, shrugging one shoulder with a sigh. "Will you please help me?" My voice was sugary and sweet, and I almost cringed.

The other ladies still watched, but Mr. Hill's whisper must have been carried on the breeze that rifled through my curls, reaching my right ear only. "I will help you if you stop with your charade."

My heart leaped, then picked up speed. I glanced up at him, meeting his deep blue eyes and the mischief that shone in them. "My charade?" I kept my voice even and calm, though I could hardly breathe. Surely he didn't mean my charade of pretending to be Sophia. How could he have known? He must have meant the drastic changes in my behavior. All I could do was feign confusion.

"Yes, your charade." He turned toward the target. "I have never seen such a drastic change in a woman simply because she slept well the night before." He raised an eyebrow at me.

To combat the suspicion on his face, I laughed. "Oh, Mr. Hill, you are too droll. I assure you, I feel quite refreshed. I was not truly myself until today. What you saw in me before can be the only thing worthy of being called a charade." At the sound of my laughter, all the ladies, even the focused Miss Taplow began watching us.

Mr. Hill did not appear to believe my words, a hint of frustration rising on his brow.

"I suppose you are now unwilling to teach me to shoot," I said with a sigh. "Unwilling to even be near me, perhaps. Miss Benham seems to be eager for your assistance; you might go help her—"

He shook his head, taking a step closer. "I will teach you, Miss Sedgwick. I am not one to leave a lady in distress."

A lady. Would he leave a *maid* in distress?

He drew closer, tipping his head toward the bow I held. "Take it in your left hand."

I obeyed, my pulse suddenly quicker than it had been a moment before. He leaned toward me, guiding my hand to the correct place on the bow. Even through my gloves, my skin tingled as his fingers covered mine. I could feel the tangible stares of all the other ladies like needles against my back.

Mr. Hill moved behind me, leaning his head toward the target from behind my shoulder. When he spoke, his voice was deep and musical and quite close to my ear. "Keep your arm straight."

What had been the breeze rustling my hair before was now his breath, sending yet another string of shivers over my neck and shoulders. What had I been thinking asking him for this? I hadn't expected it to affect me, but I could hardly think and breathe with him standing so close. His fingers shifted away from mine, sliding up my arm to straighten my elbow. "Turn your body so you are standing perpendicular to the target."

Before he could take me by the waist and straighten me himself, I obeyed. All my planned giggles and flirting had entirely slipped my mind.

"Precisely," he said. "Now, the arrow." He set the arrow in my right hand, guiding it into place.

His arms surrounded me, one straightening my grip on the bow, and the other on the arrow. When his hand moved to my back to adjust my posture, my breath caught in my chest. Did he realize the effect he was having on me? Did it amuse him? I had been determined to pretend his assistance delighted me, but it unsettled me more than anything else. I should not have felt anything for Mr. Hill but dread at the thought of him being near me, smiling and speaking close to my ear.

"Have you taken your aim?" he asked.

I almost nodded but worried I would lose my posture.

"Then release."

I let go of the arrow, keeping my bow upright until the arrow sank into the second ring of the target. I gasped.

How had I managed to shoot almost as accurately as Miss Taplow? A broad smile pulled on my cheeks as I turned toward Mr. Hill. "Look!" I pointed at the arrow, still unable to believe it was mine. My genuine delight had been a mistake. Mr. Hill smiled down at me, his eyes warm and gentle.

"Er—Oh, Mr. Hill, you are a most talented instructor." I batted my lashes, drawing one step closer to him with a laugh. "I could not have possibly hit the target without your expert touch."

His smile faded and he lifted one eyebrow. "I believe there was a condition to my assistance."

My own smile fell, and he walked away without another word. Just that simple raise of one eyebrow told me my charade had not fooled him as I had hoped. It had left him confused, to be sure, but that was all.

Over the course of the hour, Miss Taplow became increasingly less skilled with her bow, eventually asking Mr. Hill for assistance just like I had received. I had tried my very best not to be envious when Mr. Hill touched Miss Downsfield's hand like he had touched mine, but I couldn't help it. What was wrong with me?

If Mr. Hill had not been fooled yet, he would be. If I persisted for long enough, he might begin to believe that he had been wrong about me.

Throughout the day, I maintained my act, but with less flirting. I lacked the energy. Instead, I simply spoke like the other ladies and carried myself like them. By dinner, Mr. Hill seemed to be surrendering his claims that it was all an act. He even chose a seat beside Miss Benham after dinner rather than beside me. He did not ask me to sing. He did not wink at me or tease me.

But he did watch me.

He watched me throughout the evening, as if searching for something very important. Perhaps he was waiting for me to make a mistake, to show that I was simply pretending. But I maintained my act the entire day, until I made my way back to my bedchamber, utterly exhausted.

CHAPTER 10

*R*ather than risk finding Mr. Hill in the gardens the next morning, I chose to seek my early morning adventures elsewhere. The hours just before dawn had become my favorite of the day. It was a time when the world was much quieter, when the birds sang the loudest, and the sky seemed to wake from a slumber of its own. With Jessie by my side, we made our way toward the village where I had met Mrs. Roberts and her several children two days before. I held Sophia's reticule securely around my wrist, heavy with coins.

I walked quickly over the path. Perhaps this good deed would help counteract the deceit I had undertaken. I shushed my worries. I had been forced into it, just as I told Mr. Hill. I was not here for Sophia anyway. I was here for Mama. Without our positions at Sedgwick Manor, we would be even more destitute. If there was one thing that gave Papa comfort from his place is prison, it was that his family had a place to live and food to eat. I would do all I could to ensure the Roberts family had the same.

We reached the small house and I knocked softly on the door. The only way to escape Winslow House unnoticed had been to come at this hour, but it was possible that the Robertses would not yet be awake. Just when I thought they wouldn't answer, Mrs. Roberts opened the door.

Her brow creased as she took in my appearance.

"Good morning," I said with a smile. "I'm sorry to be here at such an hour."

She appeared to have already been awake for some time. A low fire burned beyond the door, a weak little flame. The floors seemed to be covered in even more dirt than they had been previously. Mrs. Roberts held her baby on her hip, and beyond the doorway I could hear the quiet whimper of another young child. The little girl I had seen two days before was nowhere in sight.

"Are you stayin' at Winslow 'ouse? Were you here this week?" the woman asked.

"I was." I offered a kind smile. "I had to return to Winslow House to fetch this." I extended the reticule. It was an old one of Sophia's, so I knew she would not care if I gave the entire bag away. She may have minded about the contents, but I could find an excuse for why I had spent it.

Mrs. Roberts stared at the bag, her eyes rounding in surprise. She must have seen the weight of the coins pulling at the fabric.

"Please, take it. You need this money far more than I

do, what with your caring for so many children, even those who are not your own."

When she made no move to accept the bag, I took a step closer. "Where is the young girl in your care?"

"She still be sleepin.' I haven't the heart to wake 'er." Mrs. Roberts scowled down at me from her place on the step above, a deep sadness flooding her expression. "Her father died in the night."

I felt as if I had been struck in the chest, a deep ache spreading out from my heart to the tips of my fingers. I pressed a hand to my chest to stop it. "No." My voice was a whisper.

Mrs. Roberts gave a solemn nod. "Me husband and I'll be takin' care of her now."

I shared a glance with Jessie, whose dark brows were turned downward in distress. How could fate be so cruel? My eyes stung with tears at the thought of losing my own father. In a way, I already had, but to know that he no longer lived and breathed would be too much to bear. To not have hope of ever seeing him again? My heart broke more with each passing second, until I could hardly draw a breath. I couldn't recall ever hurting so much for the pain of another person. If I hadn't already practiced for the last year at keeping my emotions inside, I might have sobbed for the little girl and her family.

"The poor girl. I am so very sorry to hear that." My words were not enough, but I tried to speak my sincerity with my eyes.

"Bless you." She squeezed my hand as she took the reticule, meeting my eyes with unspoken gratitude.

I drew a deep breath, unable to push the image of that little girl with her large brown eyes from my mind. How had I ever dared to complain over my own life? My circumstances could have been so much worse. As Sophia's maid, I was privileged to live in a grand household, to be fed delicious meals, and to be given fresh, clean clothing to wear. I had my mother nearby. In comparison to my previous life, the changes that had occurred in my situation had been drastic, but they had not been entirely bad. I had learned to work, and work hard. I had learned to sacrifice my own desires for someone else. I had learned to appreciate the things I had always taken for granted.

Determination rose in my throat to never again forget just how fortunate I truly was. I might have had a mistress who threatened me for her own gain, but if she hadn't, then I would not have had this opportunity to help the Roberts family in this small way. I would not have had a chance to see Bibury in the spring.

Too many emotions swirled around my heart. Any moment now, I would let them show. Coming to Bibury had already begun to change me. For the first time in months, I felt deeply. My heart seemed to be stirring, unfolding its wings and awakening from dormancy. I felt free to be whoever I wished to be, whoever any situation called for. I could speak when I wished, wear what I wished, smile and laugh and sleep as long as I wanted.

But I was remembering just how similar it had been

being a lady and being a maid. There were expectations to both roles, and consequences for not following them.

I bid Mrs. Roberts farewell before walking out the front door, starting back on the narrow dirt path that led away from the small house. The sun had already traveled much higher in the sky, a faint glow peeking through the clouds. Jessie walked beside me, squinting at something in the distance. "Is that...?"

I followed her gaze, my jaw dropping. Atop his horse, riding up the path toward where we stood, was Mr. Hill. I searched frantically for a place to hide. Had he already seen me? My heart thudded as I pulled Jessie around the side of the Roberts' house, pressing my back against it. As fragile as the architecture seemed, I hoped my weight wouldn't damage it further.

The sound of the horse's breathing and heavy hoofbeats came closer, and I kept my lips pressed together in silence. If Mr. Hill passed without glancing to either side, then he would miss us entirely. But how could I trust that he would stare straight ahead? Tapping Jessie's arm, I motioned behind us, where the ground sloped downward toward a row of trees. She seemed to decipher my meaning, starting down the slope ahead of me. I followed, glancing back just as Mr. Hill and his horse came into view. Distracted as I was, I didn't see the mud.

My foot slipped out from under me and I let out a screech. I caught a handful of grass as I fell, but the force of my fall was too strong to be stopped by a few blades of grass. I slid halfway down the slope before stopping myself on Jessie's ankles. She fell forward to her hands and knees, and I rolled twice before landing in a puddle at the base of the hill. I looked up at Jessie, my face and dress splattered in mud, her clothing only in slightly better condition.

Mr. Hill had likely heard my first screech already, so I clamped my mouth shut. Dragging myself from the ground, I wiped off as many clumps of mud as possible from my skirts before walking forward to help Jessie to her feet. How could I walk back to Winslow House like this? Although, with my hair in disarray and my clothes unpresentable, I felt much more myself—much more like a maid. Miss Downsfield would never be so ungainly as to slide down a muddy slope and land in a puddle. My cheeks burned as I listened for the horse.

Only when I extended my hand to help Jessie up did I notice the way her features twisted in pain. Her breathing was quick as she shifted her weight to one side, pulling up her skirts slightly to examine her right leg. "Tillie," she whispered through gritted teeth. Her brow scrunched as another sharp pain seemed to strike her. "I've hurt my ankle."

CHAPTER 11

"What?" I dropped to my knees, sending another splatter of mud up my skirts. My heart pounded as I followed her gaze to her lower leg.

She bit her lip, nodding fast. "I don't think I can stand. Do you think it be broken?"

My heart pounded with dread. "Oh, Jessie." I touched her arm, helping her sit up straight. "I slipped first. It's my fault."

The hoofbeats grew louder. For Jessie's sake, I couldn't ignore them. Putting aside my pride, I hurried to my feet, climbing up the slope several steps until I could see Mr. Hill on his horse just beyond the path that led to the Roberts' house. My brow furrowed in confusion as he dismounted and started toward the door. Whatever had brought him here would have to wait.

I took a deep breath, replacing my own embarrassment with thoughts of Jessie's suffering. "Mr. Hill." My voice was much softer than I intended. I cleared my throat and tried again. "Mr. Hill!"

He glanced behind his shoulder first before realizing where my voice came from. His eyes met mine from across the path, his expression immediately shifting to one of deep concern. He switched course, moving with long strides toward me, leaving his horse behind. He wore a tan waist-coat and navy jacket, perfectly presentable and handsome. I could only imagine what he must have thought of my appearance. I could feel a drip of muddy water rolling down my cheek, and a strand of hair plastered near it.

"Miss Sedgwick, are you all right?" He stopped in front of me, his blue eyes showing a rare seriousness as he exam-ined my face, then the mud all over the front of my dress. "What are you doing out here alone?"

I shook my head fast. "I am not alone. Jess—er—my maid has been injured." I waved him forward, facing the muddy slope again. I swallowed, eyeing the deep mud that had made me fall the first time. Sophia's old boots had very little left on their soles, and I didn't trust them to keep me upright, even if I was careful.

I took one small step before Mr. Hill stopped me, touching my elbow much like he had the day before. He met my gaze with a shake of his head. "Stay here."

I nodded, wrapping my arms around myself. Some of the mud had already solidified on my arms, cracking and peeling off with the movement. "Do take care, Mr. Hill. It is quite slick."

He acknowledged my words with a nod before walking

down to Jessie with all the ease and grace I had come to expect of him, not even faltering on his feet for one moment. I glanced at his hessians, plastered in mud all the way up to the ankles. I couldn't imagine many gentlemen in London who would risk their prized riding boots with so little hesitation to help a *maid*. Any gentleman might have done so for a lady, but a maid? I could easily envision many men I had met during my Season calling for a physician and waiting for him to come and help the maid out of her plight. My heart skipped with admiration before I gave it a thorough scolding, refocusing on the task at hand.

Mr. Hill scooped Jessie up out of the mud, helping her to her feet. "No, sir, I can't stand. I fear it be broken, sir."

Mr. Hill's dark eyebrows drew together as he glanced at the muddy slope. In a split second, he seemed to make a decision. "I will carry you to my horse."

"You don't have to do that, sir. I can crawl, perhaps?"

He chuckled, glancing up at me. "Was crawling a practice you learned from Miss Sedgwick?"

Embarrassment made me squirm as I was reminded of my crawling across the drawing room floor to clean up the tarts.

"No, sir. I learned in my infancy." Jessie looked up at him with wide eyes, obviously missing his joke. She attempted to turn herself onto her hands and knees.

Mr. Hill shook his head, his face turning serious once again. "I will not allow that. You may injure your leg further."

Jessie cast me a worried glance before nodding her

consent. Mr. Hill bent down, slipping one arm behind her knees and the other around her waist, lifting her up and walking again with unfair ease to the top of the slope. Jessie was quite small, but I still could hardly believe the ease in which he lifted her onto his horse, helping her situate herself on the saddle. She sat awkwardly, her features still twisted in pain. "I'll help her back to Winslow House and have the physician sent promptly," he said, turning toward me. He walked closer, his eyes soft and gentle. "Are you certain you are not hurt?"

My throat felt suddenly dry, words evading me. My dignity was certainly hurt, but nothing more. I pressed my lips together, nodding. "I'm certain." I looked down at my ruined clothes. "I was fortunate to have found you nearby to help us, even if it only further emphasized my propensity of embarrassing myself in your presence." I remembered that I was meant to be acting like Miss Downsfield, but it was too late. In the distress of the moment, I hadn't remembered to keep up my act. I had fallen back into my stumbling, stammering, shy behavior that had first caused Mr. Hill to notice me and tease me the way he had. But today he did not seem inclined to tease me, at least not with his usual frequency. Instead, he stared down at me as if I were a riddle or a poem to be deciphered and studied again and again.

"You should not be embarrassed, Miss Sedgwick. I am simply glad you did not also suffer any injury." A smile tugged his mouth upward. "Aside from the injury to your pride."

"Indeed." I looked down, pressing my lips together. Was it mud I tasted at the corner of my mouth? I grimaced, using the one clean spot on the front of my glove to wipe it off. "I don't believe I have any pride left." I watched the ground, unwilling to meet his sharp blue eyes for a moment longer. It had begun doing strange things to my heart.

"You seemed to have a great deal of it yesterday." He raised one eyebrow.

I opened my mouth to speak, but he began backing away, casting me a questioning glance before approaching Jessie. He took the reins in one hand, guiding his horse back toward the path. "Do you ride, Miss Sedgwick?" he asked over his shoulder.

It had been years since I had mounted a horse, but it was a skill Papa had ensured that I learn. I felt fairly confident, so I nodded. "Well enough, I suppose."

He waved me forward. "If you share the mount with your maid it may be easier to control the horse. I will walk alongside to ensure he behaves." He patted the horse's side.

"Oh, no, perhaps I should walk."

He stopped the horse, stepping toward me. "You have been through a great ordeal."

"I believe you have been through the greater ordeal, helping Jessie out of the mud and lifting her onto the horse." I widened my eyes for emphasis. "It is no great task for me to walk." My head pounded with a returning headache. The walk *was* long, but frankly the thought of

Mr. Hill coming near enough to me to help me onto that horse set my palms perspiring.

"I can see that you are tired," he said. "I must insist that you ride. I wouldn't be a gentleman if I watched you walk all the way home."

I let out a puff of air, suddenly frustrated. I was more frustrated at myself than at Mr. Hill, but my words could not be stopped, nonetheless. "Nor would you be a gentleman if you didn't respect my wish to walk." My voice snapped like a whip. I clamped my mouth closed. I had not meant to be so curt, but my exhaustion had caught up to me. All my efforts from the day before had been for nothing. I had still managed to find myself in this situation with Mr. Hill when I was meant to be avoiding him and driving him away. How could I have let this happen? Each of my failures here reminded me of my failure to keep Papa out of prison. It was *my fault*. I blinked back sudden tears, fighting to keep them from showing.

Mr. Hill's eyebrows shot upward in surprise before lowering in concern. Had he seen the moisture in my eyes? I hadn't looked down quickly enough. His boots moved closer. I watched the mud-covered leather with growing unease. "If you wish to walk, then you may walk. I will offer one last time."

I met his gaze after blinking away my tears, fighting the knot in my throat. I had turned into a watering pot of the most detestable sort. I had resolved myself never to cry in front of anyone, and I would not break that promise to myself. Mama was strong, and so I needed to be too.

Crying would not solve any problem in the world. It would not take me away from Bibury, and it would not bring Papa home. It would not undo the mistakes I had made, nor would it prevent further mistakes. Crying in front of Mr. Hill would be the greatest mistake I could ever make. He would see that I was not as hard and unfeeling as I had pretended to be.

Shame flooded my cheeks over my blunt reply. I couldn't refuse his offer now. "Very well. I will ride. And I thank you for the kind offer, and for being so kind to Jessie." I swallowed. There. I had said it. Even if I was trying to drive him away, there was never any excuse for rudeness. And I had been impertinent too many times toward a man who had done nothing to hurt me.

Mr. Hill still searched my face for a moment before taking a step back toward the horse. I followed, my inhale sharp when he took me by the waist, lifting me easily onto the saddle. After an awkward shift, I managed to steady myself, my wet and muddy skirts creeping too high on my lower legs for comfort. My stockings were also soaked through. I took the reins in hand, leading the horse slowly down the path. Jessie held onto my arms, her hands shaking slightly. She had likely never ridden on horseback, or at least not often enough to not be afraid.

I kept the horse at a slow enough pace to keep Mr. Hill from falling behind, but with his long strides, I did not have to pull too hard on the reins. The horse was very docile and calm, taking well to the change in its riders. Thankfully, the town hadn't come alive completely for the day, still relatively quiet on the streets. The few people who did pass didn't hide their concern and dismay as they observed Jessie and me on the horse, but I ignored their looks, glancing down at Mr. Hill.

Sophia had been correct in describing him as mysterious. I knew so little about who he was. I hadn't learned much from the conversations in the dining room among the guests, as most of the ladies preferred speaking about themselves in order to win over his attention. All I had learned of Mr. Hill was that he had an estate nearby. He was quite rich and respected, and was, according to Mrs. Ollerton's private words to us women, the only gentleman in the town who was eligible enough to deserve any of our hands in marriage. There was the vicar and a few clergymen who were also unmarried, but they were not nearly as eligible a bachelor as Mr. Hill. Or likely as handsome. Or kind. If Mr. Hill had been so kind to Jessie, a maid, then how would he treat me if he knew I was a lady's maid?

I banished my thoughts the moment they came. I couldn't entertain thoughts like that ever again. He wasn't going to discover my true identity, so it didn't matter. He would know me as Miss Sedgwick until the day I departed from Winslow House to never see him again.

"How is your leg?" I asked Jessie, steering my thoughts and eyes away from Mr. Hill. "Am I riding too quickly?" Each bounce of her leg against the horse's side could not have been comfortable.

"No, Till—" her voice trailed off. "Er—No, miss. Carry on." I could hear the grimace in Jessie's voice, but she was trying to be strong. And she was strong. I would likely have melted into tears if I had experienced what she just had.

"How exactly did the injury happen?" Mr. Hill's deep voice was a stark contrast to Jessie's pained squeak. He was addressing me. "What were you doing behind the Roberts property at this hour? I knew you liked arising early," he glanced up at me with a knowing smile, "but I didn't know you enjoyed frolicking in the mud. Does it help you become more amiable by the afternoon, perhaps?" There was an accusation in his voice. I was ashamed enough by my behavior the day before—I did not need to hear the disapproval in his words. He had not been fooled, only confused by my behavior. As much as I needed him to dislike me, it hurt more than I cared to admit. *Your feelings do not matter, Tillie,* I told myself. This was about protecting Sophia and fulfilling what she had sent me here to do.

How could I explain why I was at the Roberts' house? I searched my mind for a response. "I—I was on a walk, and I accidentally moved too quickly over the mud and fell. I collided with my maid and caused her to fall as well." My voice grew quiet at the end. He must have thought so little of me. He had likely never met such an ungainly lady in all his life.

He seemed to be fighting a smile, the dimple on his left cheek flickering in and out. "How did you find yourself *accidentally* in the mud? Would you not have avoided it entirely?"

"I was trying to avoid something else entirely," I grumbled.

"What was that?"

I sighed, turning my attention to the path ahead.

"Were you trying to avoid me?" Mr. Hill's voice stabbed at my chest. His tone was more reserved than usual.

There was no way to avoid his question, and my mind was racing too much to come up with an answer.

A deep chuckle surprised me, and I glanced down to see Mr. Hill's teasing smile. "I will take your hesitation as my answer."

Irritation bit at me, but I pushed it away. Isn't that what I wanted him to think? I had been working to ensure that he knew I was not eager to make his acquaintance, but that hadn't worked. I had been certain my behavior the day before had deterred him, but why then was there an edge of disappointment behind his voice? What on earth could have given him any reason to desire my good opinion?

I sat up straighter on the horse. No good would come from focusing on my own desires. Maids did not think of themselves, but only of their employers and their needs and desires. Sophia had sent me here with one specific objective, and she had been so confident in my success. Even I had been confident. How could a man like Mr. Hill ever look at me with anything but disapproval? How could anyone? My chest tightened with disappointment of my own. Could I not do anything right?

My silence persisted for far too long, and I could feel

Mr. Hill watching me as we moved down a slope on the path, one that was thankfully free of mud and water. There was some explanation he was waiting for, but my thoughts fell silently on my lips. Finally, I managed a few small words. "You are right, Mr. Hill." I swallowed. "I was indeed avoiding you. I didn't wish to be teased about my singing again." I gave a small smile. All the lightness of my words was meant to dispel was the weight in the air, but it only seemed to arouse Mr. Hill's curiosity even further.

"I have begun to notice there are two things you are quite hesitant to give up," he said in a thoughtful voice.

My brow furrowed, and I pressed my lips together. Why was Mr. Hill taking time to *notice* things about me? That went directly against my goals, yet my stomach gave an unwelcome flutter as a slow smile stole over his lips. My curiosity couldn't be helped. "There are a great deal more than two things, but I should like to hear what you think."

He laughed softly. "Well, I do not doubt that. But the two things I have noticed are two things I would most like to see from you. First, the truth, and second, your smiles."

True to form, my face flooded with heat.

"You give up your charming blushes quite easily, though, for which I am grateful." He gave a lopsided smile, and I wanted to bury my face in the horse's mane.

"They are not given voluntarily, I assure you." My voice was nothing but a mutter. "I am simply…not accustomed to men like you."

"And what sort of man do you think I am?" Mr. Hill's blue eyes were soft, but unrelenting.

"You are quite difficult to decipher," I said quietly.

"I cannot possibly be more difficult to decipher than you are."

I sighed, pressing down the smile that threatened my lips. "I suppose that is probably true."

"I should like to hear what you think," Mr. Hill said. "What sort of man am I, according to what you have observed?"

As much as I tried, I couldn't convince myself to be silent. I was supposed to be aloof and distant, but as strange as it was, this conversation was comfortable and easy, even with mud splattered all over me, and with Jessie gripping the backs of my shoulders for balance atop an uncomfortable saddle. "Well, I believe you are quite mysterious, and perhaps you revel in that fact. You enjoy attention from ladies, and you enjoy making them blush and smile and fall in love with you. I suspect it could be a game of sorts, your flirtations. A way to pass the time and entertain yourself." My voice carried an edge of accusation and far more curiosity that it should have. I quickly corrected myself. There were other things I had observed. "And you also seem to be a very kind man, what with your helping my maid today. I have never seen a gentleman behave with such kindness. Well, aside from my father." I cut off my rambling, embarrassed by how much I had revealed. Even a real lady would never venture to say such bold things. I was forgetting my place—forgetting that I was no longer at liberty to speak my mind. These were Sophia's opinions as far as Mr. Hill knew.

What was spoken could not be unspoken. At least the conversation was likely distracting Jessie from the pain in her leg. She had never been a gossip, but she did love overhearing gossip-worthy conversations. My heart pounded as I waited for Mr. Hill's response, not daring to look down at his face. I pretended to be focused on the path ahead and on Winslow House growing closer in the distance.

"Those are very interesting observations," Mr. Hill said. "Though I'm afraid I must defend myself on at least one of your points."

I glanced down, feeling suddenly dizzy from the motion of the horse combined with the lightness in my head.

"I do not flirt without intention or purpose. It is not a game I play. Any attention a lady receives from me is genuine, and not meant to deceive in any way. Any attention I direct toward you is born of sincere interest. Miss Sedgwick, I find you fascinating, and I will not pretend I do not."

I scolded my heart for leaping in my chest. But two words stopped me, leaving my skin cold. *Miss Sedgwick.* He did not find *me* fascinating. He would never have found me fascinating if I had been the maid in the corner, silent and submissive. He never would have looked at me or smiled at me or spoken a word to me. He found Miss Sedgwick fascinating, and if he ever discovered that I was just Tillie, he would be ashamed of his confession. He would never give up a good word toward me again.

"You are wrong, Mr. Hill." I shifted uncomfortably.

"One cannot be wrong in their own opinion." He smiled.

How different would I have felt if the circumstances were different? If it were just a few months before, and Mr. Hill knew me as Miss Matilda Sherbrooke? If he had said these things to me then, I would have clung to every word. I would have allowed myself to be hopeful and flattered, and my heart would not have been so caged. "You are allowed to have your opinion, of course. However, I don't agree with it, and—and I don't think you should have such a high opinion of me."

Mr. Hill studied me for a long moment. "It is the fact that you don't agree with me that makes you fascinating."

Here I was, directly contradicting my behavior from the day before. He hadn't been fooled. My frustration must have shown on my face, because Mr. Hill's expression softened. "You are not like the other women here, despite how much you tried to appear to be so yesterday. May I ask you for the truth?"

"You did just accuse me of delighting in keeping the truth from you." I raised my eyebrows. "I might keep your prize from you a little longer."

"A smile of yours would be a more desirable prize, so if you wish to torment me, you may keep your smiles hidden instead." He glanced at my lips, and my stomach fluttered all over again. "Appease me now with at least a piece of the truth, if you will. Why did you behave the way you did yesterday? And why were you avoiding me today?"

"That is two pieces of the truth, Mr. Hill. I am reluctant even to give you one."

"Perhaps you might give me one for today, and you might tell me the second on a ride with me tomorrow morning?"

I eyed him carefully. How could I decline? I had already reflected terribly on Sophia's name. I didn't really know how far Mr. Hill's influence reached. Who did he know? Who were his relatives? He could very well know someone who knows Sophia, so I had to start treading carefully. I had forgotten all of my manners. "I will agree to the ride, but I may not give up any of my truths."

"That is what I require in exchange."

"In exchange for the pleasure of your company?" I raised one eyebrow. "Perhaps I should enjoy sleeping late in a warm, comfortable bed instead."

He laughed. "There is no question you will already be awake singing in the gardens or sliding down a slope of mud, so a ride with me cannot be an excessively dreadful way to spend a morning."

I shook my head. "My singing is only dreadful to those who hear it, not to my own ears. Though I must confess a ride with you would be slightly less dreadful than sliding down another slope of mud." I hadn't meant to tease him, but the moment the words escaped me I clamped my mouth shut.

"Your performance in the drawing room was one of the most delightful performances I have heard in a long while.

But riding with me will be *far* preferable to mud, not *slightly*."

I smiled before thinking better of it, turning my face away to pretend to study the passing trees. The girlish excitement that burst in my chest was uncalled for, and I pushed it away.

Mr. Hill had never been so easy to talk to, but sitting awkwardly atop a horse, covered in mud, I was somehow more confident than ever before. He had obviously not liked my behavior the day before, so then why was I not trying to maintain it? I was forgetting my purpose. I should have been complimenting him and flirting with him in the way he seemed to despise. I studied him from my elevated seat. He was peculiar. Surely he thought the same about me.

"I'm not certain a ride with you is wise. I'm afraid I have already secured Miss Downsfield's antipathy from the morning walk I took when you happened upon me in the gardens. I—I do not wish to be the cause of any more contention between us."

Mr. Hill had been walking briskly to keep up with the horse, but he still did not appear to be exerting himself. He kept his pace, even speeding up slightly as we came closer to Winslow House. "You are not the cause of any contention." He gave me a reassuring smile. "It is all Mrs. Ollerton's doing. I should never have agreed to this ridiculous plan of hers in the first place."

I frowned. "Why did you agree?"

"You will have to wait until our ride to discover that

answer. Perhaps you'll take that in exchange instead, as a greater value than my company." One eyebrow quirked upward.

Before I could answer, Mr. Hill directed the horse to a place near the front doors, helping me down from the saddle, then Jessie. She let her leg hover in the air, her grimace of pain displaced by her shocked grin as she met my gaze.

She had obviously enjoyed every moment of that conversation.

I had enjoyed it too, far more than I should have. My brow furrowed of its own accord, and my throat was suddenly dry. I had only been at Winslow House for a few short days…how could I survive another few weeks? How many more mistakes would I make? I needed to start mending them, starting with the grave mistake I had made today: letting myself dwell on Mr. Hill's virtues for even a moment.

CHAPTER 12

I wiped the last of the mud off my forehead with the rag that one of Mrs. Ollerton's maids had given me. I had already changed into a clean dress, and I hadn't missed the grimace on the maid's expression when she took away my dirty clothing to be washed. The physician had just taken his leave, declaring that Jessie's injury was thankfully not a broken bone. Her ankle had still begun swelling, so she sat on my bed with it lifted on two pillows, watching me with a look of deep contemplation. It was not difficult to guess at what she was thinking, but I would have rather imagined she was dwelling on her own attraction to Mr. Hill than *my own* far too obvious attraction to him.

Her smile grew. "Are you quite flattered by Mr. Hill's attention today?"

I turned away from the mirror, setting the dirty rag

down on the vanity. "It was quite bold of him to speak so frankly with you listening," I muttered.

"That's one good thing about bein' a maid. You're permitted to be invisible."

"I wish I could be." I let out a long sigh, my pulse still elevated with panic. "Perhaps you should have pretended to be Sophia, and I might have been the maid. You would have done a better job of it than I have."

"Not so," Jessie said amid a chuckle. "I can't talk like a lady, much less walk and eat and behave like one."

"Nor can I, obviously." I groaned, sitting down beside her on the bed. "I am very sorry about your ankle."

"I be grateful for it. Now I shan't lift a finger to work until it heals."

I laughed, grateful for the momentary relief to my worries.

"We must pick a pretty dress for your ride tomorrow."

I shook my head. "I can't go. I will have to send Mr. Hill my regrets."

Jessie gasped, sitting up straight. "You have to go! A true lady wouldn't go back on her word."

Casting her a suspicious look, I crossed my arms. "You are not hoping Mr. Hill will choose me, are you? It is impossible. If I had to reject a proposal from him, Sophia's parents would surely learn of it, and she would be punished. As a result, so would I." I shook my head, the wet hair around my face waving with the motion. "You must see why I cannot go. He is to have no impression that I encourage his affection. I tried to behave like Miss

Downsfield, and I failed. Now all I must do is appear completely genuine in my disregard for him." My stomach twisted. In reality, I regarded him quite highly. He was a good man, and I did not revel in the idea of hurting him. There was still a large part of me that wondered if he really was playing a game. It didn't matter. I would never know.

"I suppose you're right." Jessie pursed her lips. "He's a very good gent, you must confess. And you deserve a good man, Tillie."

My heart warmed at her words, and sudden tears pricked my eyes. I pushed the emotion away, crossing my arms tighter. I had never thought I deserved anything good. "A good man, perhaps, but not a good gentleman." I smoothed out the wrinkles on my clean skirts, picking at a loose thread. "Mr. Hill is far too elevated in society to ever consider me if he knew who I really was. He would lose everything." I looked up, meeting Jessie's eyes. "And I am not worth sacrificing everything for. Even if he does like me for any strange reason, he doesn't love me. I'm not certain even love could encourage a gentleman to marry a lady's maid."

Jessie cast me a thoughtful glance, her eyes turning wistful. "I think love could encourage anything."

I forced a smile to my face for her sake, trying to calm the turmoil in my stomach. "I must accomplish what I came here to do, and that is all. I will send my regrets to Mr. Hill in the morning, but at dinner tonight, I will be polite and reserved."

Jessie seemed to finally see sense, giving a tight-lipped nod. "But what if Mr. Hill tries to speak with you again?"

"I'll direct his attention to Miss Coppins. She is my favorite of all the ladies here, so he might as well take her for a ride in the morning instead."

Jessie sat back on her pillows, interlacing her fingers. "He'll be quite disappointed."

In truth, so would I.

Mrs. Ollerton assigned a new maid to assist me while Jessie recovered, so a young maid named Lydia styled my hair for the evening. She pulled the dark curls into a chignon, leaving loose tendrils hanging about my face. The one evening gown I hadn't worn yet was a pale blue, the sleeves edged in pointed lace and embroidery. I noticed the line of stitches hidden under the arm where I had mended it several months before. Sophia had believed that the stitches were too visible to wear the gown in public, so she had given it to me.

Before I could turn away, the maid pinched my cheeks between her vice-like fingers, bringing a flush of color to them. Sophia had never required that of me, as her face had a natural flush to it. If Mr. Hill had anything to do with it, my face would be flushed enough all evening.

Reserved. Removed. Quiet. Invisible. I let each word course through my mind as I made my way downstairs to the drawing room where everyone was gathered before dinner. Mr. Hill had seen through all my acts. Now I simply needed to act like what I truly was. A maid. If anything could drive him away, it was that. Perhaps I could pretend to be ill after dinner, so my excuses in the morning would be more plausible.

Distracted by my thoughts, I didn't immediately notice the silence of the drawing room when I entered. All the ladies were already gathered, with Mr. Hill at the center of the room. All eyes watched me as I took my first step into the room, then the next, the stares of all the ladies growing more intense with each movement. What had I done now?

"Miss Sedgwick," Mrs. Ollerton said, breaking the heavy silence. "We are so pleased you could make it to dinner after the ordeal you suffered today."

Considering the lack of surprise from the ladies in the room, it seemed Mrs. Ollerton had already told them all what had happened.

"Oh, it was no great ordeal," I said in a quick voice.

"Well, you have Mr. Hill to thank for that. He rescued you in a most gallant manner." Mrs. Ollerton cast him a grateful smile, and he met my eyes, his lips twitching upward, as if tempting me to agree with her.

"I did not require rescuing. It was my maid who was injured, and Mr. Hill helped her to safety." I looked at Miss Downsfield as I spoke, hoping my words would erase the scowl on her brow.

"Well, rescuing a maid is not quite as heroic, but I still believe he deserves praise for it." Mrs. Ollerton gave a sweet smile that contradicted her words, which grated on me. It had been the fact that Mr. Hill dirtied his boots to rescue Jessie that had given me the greatest cause to admire him.

"I must disagree, Mrs. Ollerton," I said, unable to stop my tongue. "I think rescuing a maid is far more heroic than rescuing a lady."

Miss Benham scoffed, sharing a smile with Miss Downsfield. One narrow eyebrow lifted. "How so?"

Mr. Hill's gaze burned on my face, but I avoided his eyes. He was just as curious to hear by explanation as Miss Benham seemed to be. Perhaps more so. Why had I not kept my mouth closed? I wrung my hands together. "Well, I believe the true goodness of a person is determined by what they do when they have nothing to gain. Mr. Hill might rescue a lady in the hopes of winning her affection or her high regard, perhaps to uphold his reputation. But when he rescues a maid, I believe it shows a genuine desire to help her—to see all people safe and taken care of. What could a gentleman have to gain from that?"

Mrs. Ollerton seemed to be pondering my words, a deep furrow in her brow, contrary to Miss Benham's disdainful smirk.

"Very interesting thoughts, Miss Sedgwick." Mrs. Ollerton tapped her chin. "I must agree that Mr. Hill has a very genuine desire for goodness, both in himself, and in his choice of a wife." She smiled at each lady in turn, and Miss Benham's smirk subsided into something far sweeter. I was not the only guest who knew how to put on an act. If Mr. Hill had seen through mine, did he see through hers? Did he see all of us for who we truly were? There was no way of knowing. I caught his gaze by accident, glancing quickly down at my gloves.

A few minutes later, we were all seated in the dining room, and I listened silently while I ate my soup, unwilling to accidentally compliment or defend Mr. Hill again. All the other ladies had already seemed to have selected me as their greatest enemy. Did they think I had orchestrated my fall in town that day?

At one point in the conversation, Miss Coppins took a delicate sip from her glass, careful not to shatter it, as she had often warned me against, and smiled at Mr. Hill. "Do you have any relatives in Kent? I have heard there is much to see there."

He nodded. "Indeed, I do. An uncle."

"Who is your uncle?" Mrs. Ollerton asked. "I do know some families in Kent, including Miss Sedgwick's family."

Mr. Hill glanced in my direction, his gaze hovering on my face for a moment before returning to Mrs. Ollerton. I listened carefully, holding my spoon above my bowl so as not to miss a single one of his words. I had been raised in the same county, so it was quite possible I would know his uncle.

He set down his glass before answering. "Mr. Joseph Baker."

My breath hitched, and I nearly dropped my spoon. Icy fingers seemed to grip the back of my neck. The coldness of my skin spread to every inch as I lowered my spoon with a shaking hand. Had I heard him correctly?

"I have not heard of a Mr. Baker," Mrs. Ollerton's voice

swam groggily through my mind. "Have you, Miss Sedgwick? Perhaps he lives in close proximity to your family?"

After a long moment of silence, I realized she was addressing me. My vision cleared and I took a deep breath, afraid to raise my glass for a drink to moisten my dry throat. My hands were shaking far too much. "His name does sound familiar, yes, but we are not acquainted." To my dismay, my voice betrayed my shock.

Mr. Hill studied me from across the table, and I cast him a small smile, hoping to dispel the concern on his face. Mrs. Ollerton, thankfully, didn't question my odd behavior. Surely she had seen enough of it over the last several days to believe it was a common occurrence.

I stared at my plate. Mr. Joseph Baker was the man who had accused my father.

He was the man who had put him in prison.

The conversation shifted to Miss Coppins and her own uncle, the one who had died on account of his overexerting himself, a subject which I was already familiar with. I continued staring down at my soup, watching a film solidify on the surface as I left it, untouched. My stomach could not tolerate it with what had just been revealed to me.

Mr. Hill was the *nephew* of the man who had put Papa in prison.

I squeezed my eyes closed against a sudden sting in my forehead. How could it be? Did Mr. Hill know what had happened? Had he already heard of my family? What lies had he been told by Mr. Baker?

Papa had been arguing with Mr. Baker for weeks over the expansion of the Baker family's property line, and where it truly ended. It was all for an alcove, a pretty sanctuary in which I was caught by Mr. Baker, reading a book. It had been my favorite place, and Mr. Baker claimed it was on his property, not my father's. Mr. Baker's servant had forced me off of it and threatened to harm me if I was ever found there again. Papa had always been far too protective, and I should never have told him what that man said to me. He confronted Mr. Baker about it, and he was just as unrelenting. Papa's temper got the better of him, and their relationship as neighbors only grew more hostile. One night, Papa sneaked into his great room and stole the prized elephant tusk Mr. Baker had often boasted of from his excursion in India. When it was discovered that Papa was responsible, Mr. Baker had stopped at nothing to have him locked away to await trial. With far greater connections, Mr. Baker had easily achieved his aims. And it was my fault. If I had not told Papa of that day at the alcove, he might not have done what he did. Our house and living might not have been torn away by a distant male relative, leaving us alone in our disgrace. I could only imagine how Mr. Baker reveled in his success.

When the last course was cleared away, I hurried to the drawing room. My heart had finally slowed, but the calmness brought with it a new wave of uncertainty. If Mr. Hill was Mr. Baker's nephew, then how could I continue to avoid him?

This could be my one opportunity to save Papa.

The realization spilled over me like cold rain, unwelcome, yet inescapable. I had promised myself I would do anything to help him. I would be a fool not to use my connection to Mr. Hill to give Papa a chance to be free again, to avoid years behind bars, or worse, an execution. There was nothing I wouldn't risk. Not even my livelihood, not even my heart.

Everything had changed tonight. I could no longer avoid Mr. Hill, nor could I drive him away with false flirtations. I couldn't try to become invisible. It was no longer his antipathy or disregard I was trying to earn, but his trust and friendship. Only then could I ask such a favor as bold as asking him to speak with his uncle about releasing my father, who I would have to pretend was my maid's father. I had already told so many tales for the sake of keeping my identity a secret, so what were a few more? There was no greater cause to lie than seeing my father free and my family complete again.

Still, guilt gnawed at my stomach. Would I really make Mr. Hill into a piece in a game? Isn't that what we all were? It was almost as if Mrs. Ollerton had organized this party for her own entertainment, to watch love unfold as if it could be controlled. Perhaps it could be. By spending time with Mr. Hill—by going on the ride with him the next morning—it did not mean I would fall in love with him. I was the master of my own heart. If I made it clear that I was not interested in marriage, then perhaps Mr. Hill would turn his attention to a different lady who would be much easier to pursue. I could still become friends with him, offering to help him in his pursuit of Miss Coppins, or perhaps Miss Benham.

Then he might help me in return by speaking with his uncle.

My heart pounded with sudden hope, galloping on the back of my fear as if it had suddenly taken the reins.

Mr. Hill did not take long to join us in the drawing room, and when he did, he sat down beside me. It was the second day in a row he had chosen that seat, and each woman in the room sat up straighter as he did. The competition, as they all seemed to view this visit, was becoming much more tense. Even Miss Coppins, who had been the friendliest toward me, seemed to be viewing me as a threat, watching my every move as if to learn from it, as if I were some master in winning the affection of handsome gentlemen.

I would have laughed at the idea, but it was hard to laugh with so many masked glares fixated on me.

"I look forward to our ride in the morning," Mr. Hill said, his voice low as he adjusted his glove. His eyes flicked up to meet mine. "If you have not changed your mind."

There was wisdom in staying away from him, in saying I had indeed changed my mind, but I no longer had a choice. A ride would be the perfect opportunity to question him about his uncle, even if I had to answer some of his questions in exchange.

I took a deep breath. "I look forward to it as well."

He seemed surprised by my response, casting me a suspicious smile before sitting back in his chair.

CHAPTER 13

Mrs. Ollerton appeared equally surprised and amused when she discovered that Mr. Hill had invited me for a ride the next morning and had heartily volunteered to be our chaperone. As much as I would have liked it to, I doubted the ride would stay secret for long. I could easily envision Mrs. Ollerton telling all the other ladies over tea that afternoon, advising them to do all they could to be invited for a ride as well. By the way Mrs. Ollerton spoke, it seemed I was the last lady she would have expected to have been invited on an outing.

We had planned to ride before breakfast, as Mr. Hill had noted that I enjoyed being out in the early mornings. He was even thoughtful enough to note that I would probably prefer the morning so as to not draw attention to myself around the other ladies by leaving for a ride with him in the afternoon. When I stepped outside, the late spring air was cold, and I was grateful once again for the warm lining in Sophia's old spencer jacket.

Mr. Hill was already waiting by his gig, patting the neck of one of the horses and adjusting the reins. As if he had heard my approaching footsteps, he turned around, his chest swelling with a deep breath as his gaze took me in. Beneath the clouded sky, his features were clear and uninhibited by shadows from sunlight or candlelight. The color of his eyes was in its purest form, deep, multi-toned blue, and filled with warmth and questions. "Miss Sedgwick," he bowed before seeming to notice Mrs. Ollerton a few paces behind me. He greeted her as well before stepping forward to offer me his hand.

"I will sit on the back," Mrs. Ollerton said. "I should hate to come between you." Her cheerful smile took on an edge of mischief, as if all her schemes were finally coming to fruition.

I took Mr. Hill's hand, and his fingers tightened around mine as I stepped into the gig. Even through both our gloves, his touch sent a thrill through me. I calmed the leaping of my heart, settling onto the seat and smoothing out my skirts on my lap. After Mrs. Ollerton was seated, Mr. Hill stepped in and sat beside me.

"I must confess, I hardly recognized you in the morning light without mud on your face." His smile tipped to one side, and he studied my features, as if to decipher whether or not I accepted his teasing. I was much more comfortable with his teasing than his seriousness, so I allowed myself a small smile.

"Take care not to offend me, Mr. Hill. You know I can say nothing amiable this early in the day." I glanced at him from the corner of my eye.

He chuckled, looking over his shoulder at Mrs. Ollerton before picking up the reins and leaning closer to me. My breath caught as his whisper met my ears. "You mustn't say anything amiable while our chaperone is listening. She may suspect that you are actually flattered by my attention."

I cast him a scowl from beneath my lashes as the gig moved forward. "Are you suggesting that I *am* flattered?"

"No, but the color of your cheeks is suggesting you are."

Dash it all, why could I not control the way Mr. Hill affected me? Each time he whispered in my ear or smiled that lopsided grin I couldn't help but blush. It was almost as if Mr. Hill's charming smiles were just as involuntary as the darkening of my cheeks.

I sighed, covering the cheek facing him with the palm of my hand. The leather of my glove was smooth and cool against my warm skin. "I would be flattered, Mr. Hill, if I didn't know your true motives behind this ride with me."

He raised his eyebrows. "My true motives?"

I lowered my voice to evade Mrs. Ollerton's attention. From her place behind us, I doubted she could hear much when our words were mingled with the heavy horse foot-falls and the rolling of the gig's wheels over the rocky path. "First, to make Miss Downsfield envious."

He groaned, maintaining his smile.

"And second, to force me to tell you the truth."

"I will not force you to do anything," he said in a firm voice, meeting my gaze. "You have a will of your own." He glanced at the road ahead, then at my face. "A strong one at that."

A will of my own. When was the last time I had felt like that was true? Since becoming Sophia's maid, I had been loyal to her will, to her demands. When had I last considered my own? Even here at Winslow House I had been acting according to how Sophia would have me act. I had known acting above my station would be dangerous—I could already feel the effects of freedom and respect making me long for the life I used to have.

I cleared my throat, unsure of how to respond. "Thank you."

Mr. Hill shifted his grip on the reins. "But—but I would very much *like* to hear the truth on my points of curiosity, if you are willing to give it."

If his questions from the day before had been simpler, then I wouldn't have been nearly as reluctant to answer. He had asked why I had spent a full day behaving like Miss Downsfield. He had also asked why I had been avoiding him. There were so many layers to each potential answer— so many things that I couldn't properly explain.

"I am willing…if you will answer some of my questions honestly as well." I folded my hands together in my lap, watching them with feigned interest.

"That is a steep price, but I will agree to it." The smile in his voice was unmistakable.

"Where are we going?" I asked, surveying the passing trees with their white and pink blossoms. The fragrant scent of flowers wafted through the breeze, and I took it all in, absorbing the scents and sounds and visions of spring like the plush grasses that had absorbed the overnight rain.

"I thought I might show you my childhood home." He met my eyes, his dark lashes casting a shadow over his cheek as the sun peeked out from the clouds. "It is not far from Winslow House, and I thought you might like the gardens."

Mrs. Ollerton's voice made me jump a little. I had forgotten she was there, and Mr. Hill hadn't been whispering that last sentence. "Oh, yes, the gardens at Hill Manor are quite astonishing," she said. "They are even more lovely than the ones at Winslow House."

Mr. Hill pressed his lips together, staring straight ahead.

"Are they really?" I asked him.

He shrugged. "It is a matter of opinion, and I'm sure you shall have your own when you see them. But I must confess I am slightly partial to the gardens at Hill Manor." He smiled as he spoke, and I found myself watching the dimple on his cheek.

I directed my gaze forward, where the path grew more narrow. He guided the horses with ease, and when we followed the curve of the path past a row of trees, a manor came into view, just beyond the next grassy hill.

"There it is!" Mrs. Ollerton craned her neck, nearly rotating completely around in her seat. "Oh, it is such a lovely residence, Mr. Hill. Any lady would be quite fortunate to find herself mistress of such a home."

Her words were as pointed as a sword, stabbing into my back. Mr. Hill's jaw tightened, but he remained silent.

"Do not judge it from this distance, Miss Sedgwick," Mrs. Ollerton said. "It is even more attractive in close proximity."

"I believe you," I said, my voice breathless. It was no wonder why the other ladies were so eager to win Mr. Hill's affection. His handsome face and charm aside, he was to inherit a very handsome property as well. Emotion clawed at my throat as a swing came into view, tucked amid the rose bushes at the side of the house. With the thick ropes upholding the wooden seat, memories of my father flooded through my head, making me weak. Papa had spent hours pushing me on the swing of my childhood home, telling stories and reciting poems, breathing life into my imagination and appreciation for nature. Swinging on that swing, the sky had seemed barely out of reach, the clouds, the moon, even the stars. I would have never guessed that one day Papa would be out of reach too. I wished I had never been taught to consider the sky within my grasp. It had given unrealistic expectations and dreams of what could have been.

"What are you thinking?" Mr. Hill's voice slipped past my memories, soft and gentle.

I couldn't look at his eyes. He would see too much in my own. I tore my gaze away from the swing, focusing instead on the slanted roof and the stone facade covered in flowering vines and ivy. My lungs expelled the breath I had been holding, resulting in something of a contented sigh. "I am thinking of my childhood," I said, trying to pull the joy out of the memories, rather than feeling the pain of what I had lost. "The swing," I said in a whisper. "I had one just like it." As much as I tried, the anguish would not leave my voice—the longing.

"Did you use it often?"

I nodded at my lap rather than looking up at Mr. Hill. "Forgive me for being so wistful." I laughed under my breath.

"I will never judge anyone for being wistful. Do you recall my favorite poem? 'My heart leaps up when I behold a rainbow in the sky. So was it when my life began…'" His voice trailed off. "The moment we stop marveling at things like a rainbow, or a swing…we leave our childhood behind. We leave our innocence and our goodness that was born within us. I will never see a new blossom or a butterfly's wing without pausing to admire it."

I would never have assumed Mr. Hill had such a tender heart and deep mind, but hearing him reflect on that poem, the one that was also so special to Papa, revealed much about his character. And much about my own feelings. The longing in my heart took an alarming turn, and I redirected it as quickly as I could. I was not allowed to feel anything for Mr. Hill but respect and perhaps camaraderie and friendship. He was the only person at Winslow House, aside from perhaps Mrs. Ollerton, who did not want me banished from the property. Even chased away with torches as I was fairly certain Miss Downsfield would encourage, if she could.

Any reply I had hoped to give evaded me, lost in the beauty of Mr. Hill's words and in the beauty of his property. Even above the sound of the gig's wheels, birdsong carried through the sky, the notes cheerful and bright rather than melancholy as they so often were.

"My family is away this week," Mr. Hill said.

"Your family?"

"My parents and brother." He brought the gig to a halt on the drive. There was little endearment in his voice when he mentioned his family, and he didn't seem to care to dwell on them. The gardens were only a short distance from where we stopped. He stepped out the opposite side of the gig before circling around to hand Mrs. Ollerton down, then myself.

For some reason, I had envisioned Mr. Hill living alone. I had never thought of him having a family, and he had never mentioned them. Any questions that had been directed at him by any of the guests concerning his family, he had only responded to with vague answers.

I couldn't imagine what it would be like to rely on something as stable as this house as a guaranteed part of my future, to know that I would always belong somewhere so beautiful. As a woman, even a lady of high breeding, I had been uncertain. My first Season in London had left me even more so. I had been taught to rely on the idea of marriage to a man who could provide for me, but when I had failed to make a match...that idea had become less likely. There was nothing reliable about uncertainty.

"You are quite fortunate," I said in a quiet voice. I did not want to disrupt the peaceful sounds of nature that surrounded us. Even Mrs. Ollerton's humming blended harmoniously with the birdsong. "I have never seen such a beautiful home."

Mr. Hill cast me a sideways glance, his jaw still tight as he turned his gaze back to the house. "Nor have I."

Mrs. Ollerton's voice cut through my pondering, shrill and assertive. "I will be the sort of chaperone all young people desire." She gave a mischievous smile. "I will keep my distance and allow you time to converse alone."

Mr. Hill cast me a smile, one that made my heart jump to my throat. Would I ever grow accustomed to the sensation? My hands began to perspire inside my gloves. A private conversation was precisely what I needed in order to ask him about Mr. Baker, but I was afraid of what he would say. Would he really approach his uncle about such a sensitive subject on behalf of my 'maid'?

"I thank you for your consideration, Mrs. Ollerton." Mr. Hill bowed, making her laugh, before extending his arm to me.

I took his elbow, feeling suddenly shy. No man had ever attempted to court me before, and the exhilaration and guilt that mingled inside me were all too confusing. Before the end of the morning, I needed to make it clear that I had no intention of marrying at all. With luck, I would successfully direct his attention to one of the other ladies.

We began walking toward a small wooden gate that stood between two hedges. The gardens beyond it were nearly completely recovered from winter, plush with leaves and flowers.

"Now that Mrs. Ollerton is far behind us..." Mr. Hill said in a quiet voice. "I shall ask my first question."

"Perhaps I should have asked her to remain closer." I dipped my head, and Mr. Hill laughed.

"Would you like a tour of the house first? Perhaps it will put you at ease." His genuine smile had already begun to melt away my worry.

"I would like that very much," I managed, swallowing against my dry throat.

CHAPTER 14

He started with the gardens, leading me past the rose bushes, then the many fountains and a miniature waterfall in the water gardens. The narrow stone pathway was shaded by trees, and the air was flooded with the sweet scent of flowers and the earthy scent of rain. Even the petals of the roses carried both, where the droplets from the night before mingled with the spiraling petals.

Mr. Hill led me through the back door of the house, into the main rooms, and then to the portrait gallery on the first floor. While grand and spacious, the house was filled with signs of life. Filigree baskets as decoration, framed embroidery, and fresh flowers in vases. The time passed quickly with Mr. Hill telling me the history of each room, and which was the favorite of each member in his family. His voice was animated and filled with fondness, and I could have listened to him all day. From my first impression of him, I would have imagined him living in a dark, spacious home by himself, but now that I had come to know him better, I couldn't picture him anywhere but here. His eyes gleamed with pride over his family and his home; he belonged so perfectly, as if he had been born of the paintings on the wall. Mrs. Ollerton kept her comments infrequent but seemed just as excited to be touring the house as I was.

When we stepped onto the back lawn, Mrs. Ollerton fell back several paces, giving us the privacy she had promised. My heart hammered in my chest. Soon Mr. Hill would ask me his questions, and I would have to answer.

"What was it you would like to ask me?" My voice was quick. It would be better to get the matter over and done with.

Mr. Hill's eyebrows rose. "I had nearly forgotten. I thank you for being courteous enough to remind me."

I narrowed my eyes at him, and he laughed. There was no possible way he had actually forgotten.

"There was the first matter which we didn't have a moment to discuss yesterday as we were helping your maid to safety," he said. "Why were you avoiding me enough to slip down a slope of mud to evade my attention, when just the day before you seemed so eager to receive it? I must admit the contradiction has both puzzled me and frustrated me to no end." Though his voice dripped with his frustration, his mouth was still lifted in a smile.

To my relief, he had combined his two questions into one. There was no better way to get my answers over with than that. I kicked the overgrown grass softly as I walked, letting the tips of Sophia's half boots peek out from beneath the skirts. "Well...I told you before that I was forced to come here."

"Indeed."

"Before I say anything more, I must first apologize for my behavior. I understand how it has left you utterly confused and frustrated. I—well, I have never found myself in this position before."

His eyebrows lifted again, and he tipped his head to one side as he studied me. "You have never found yourself in a competition of sorts with four other ladies for the attention of one gentleman? How surprising."

My cheeks grew warm as I formulated my words in my mind. "Yes...and I have never found myself in receipt of attention from *any* gentleman, not as you have given me." I swallowed. "I must have you know, Mr. Hill, that I did not come here with any intention of seeking your attention at all. I came here by obligation, and I think it would be wise for you to pursue the other ladies, all of whom are much more eager to marry and will make much better wives that I ever would." I stammered to correct my mistake. "I am not suggesting that you intended to—er—to make any such offer to me, but I thought it prudent that you know from this moment onward that I would never be inclined to accept an offer of marriage from *any* gentleman. Any gentleman at all."

My face grew warmer as I tried to dig myself out of the mess I had made with my explanation. How had I forgotten how to speak clearly and eloquently? Had I spent too much time with Jessie? "That is the reason I was avoiding you, Mr. Hill. I did not want you to think I had followed you to town, or—or that I was eager to have you notice what I was up to." I bit my lip. Why could I not hold my tongue?

I dared a glance at his face, surprised to find it calm and contemplative, even a bit amused. "Would it ease you to know that I came here with no intention of marrying either?"

My eyes widened. "Truly?"

He smiled, clearly amused by my surprise. "My parents were determined that I would be much happier and fulfilled should I marry. They have been pestering me about it for years, and when Mrs. Ollerton successfully hosted a matchmaking party such as this for my friend, she discovered that I was the last eligible bachelor in Bibury, and that I ought to have the same fate. So she gathered up a new collection of young misses. To appease my parents, if not prove to them that I was determined not to marry, I agreed to it. My parents have promised that they will no longer pester me to find a wife if Mrs. Ollerton finds herself unsuccessful in finding me a match." He leaned closer to my ear. "I must confess, the idea of humbling Mrs. Ollerton in her matchmaking abilities was also too enticing to resist."

The relief that flooded through my limbs left me weak, and a smile slipped past my defenses. I dipped my chin in an attempt to hide it.

"Was that a smile?"

I shook my head, attempting to correct the expression. The effort was futile the moment I saw the look of pure victory on Mr. Hill's face. My smile spread, pulling on my cheeks. It felt as wide as the expansive lawn of Hill Manor, and I couldn't stop it. His gaze swept over my face, his eyes growing softer somehow, more careful as he watched my newfound expression. "I never thought I would convince you to give up an honest answer and a smile all in one day. What else might you be reluctant to give up? I should like to test my good luck."

I shook my head. "That is all for one day, Mr. Hill."

"I suppose this new joy on your face is born from your belief that I don't have hopes of marrying you?"

My heart leaped, not at his words, but at the look of intense curiosity in his eyes. "No. It was born from the fact that Mrs. Ollerton is bound to be quite humbled."

He tipped his head back with a laugh. I savored the sound, trying to memorize it before it disappeared. I had heard his flirtatious chuckles, but never a laugh as hearty and full as this one. It was contagious, and I had to bite my cheek to keep my own laughter at bay. Had I been trying so hard to avoid him for nothing? If he had no intention of actually selecting a wife from the guests at Winslow House, then I had been making a fool of myself, mistakenly thinking he had intentions toward me other than friendship. He had likely only gravitated toward me because I did not fawn over him like the other ladies. The realization caused every muscle in my body to relax, and I could finally enjoy his company without worry and fear. It felt as if a weight had been lifted from my shoulders, and I could finally breathe.

When Mr. Hill's laughter subsided, he threw me a look of curiosity. "Now I must ask what you were up to that you didn't wish for me to discover yesterday morning."

"It was nothing."

He raised both eyebrows, unrelenting. "What mischief were you about?"

I let out a sigh. "No mischief."

"Will you really refuse to tell me?"

"Oh, very well, if you must know, I was visiting a family with whom I was recently acquainted." I looked down at the grass as we passed a large tree, watching the bright spots of sunlight succumb to the shade. "I felt the need to help them in any way I could. I learned that they were looking after the daughter of a family in much greater need, and that her father had recently died."

"The Roberts family?"

I gave a slow nod. "Do you know them?"

"I had heard of the death of Mr. Shaw as well, and I was on my way to visit them when I saw you." Mr. Hill's brow furrowed. "What were you able to offer them?"

"Nothing I offered could comfort the family like I wished it could." My throat tightened at the memory of the little girl and her sad eyes. "But I gave them the money I had and my condolences. I wish there was more that could be done."

Mr. Hill stopped under the tree, turning to face me. "Why would you wish to hide such a kind deed?" The flash of admiration that now burned in his eyes was the reason I had hidden it from him.

I shrugged one shoulder. "I believe kindness done in secret is worth far more. Kindness is not meant for anyone but the recipient of it. What I did was a small deed, and it was not meant to elevate anyone's opinion of me, nor was it meant to elevate my pride, or anyone's pride in me."

Mr. Hill stared at me for a long moment, as if searching for something deep within my eyes. His gaze seemed to scrape at my soul, and I felt completely exposed by it. "Is that why you didn't make a basket, that day when we all walked into town? All the other ladies made one but you."

I dipped my chin. I hadn't known he had noticed. "I didn't wish for you to think I was generous in any way."

He scoffed, rubbing one side of his face. "Would it surprise you to hear that I admired you for it? I knew precisely why the other ladies were assembling their baskets. They did not care for the people to whom they were giving the baskets. They only cared that they were seen carrying them."

"That might not be entirely true..." my voice trailed off, not even convincing myself. "The women at Winslow House are good women. I believe you would find happiness with any of the four of them."

He glanced down at me with a skeptical frown. "You have never told a greater lie than that."

Little did he know, I certainly had. Guilt drove its blade deeper into my skin. If there wasn't so much depending on my silence, I would have told him right then who I really was. He didn't deserve to be tricked like this. My conscience was relieved slightly by the fact that he didn't actually intend to marry me, or anyone else at Winslow House, so his heart at least would not be affected by my departure at the end of the month. My heart, on the other hand, I was not so sure would remain untouched.

My stomach flipped when his lips curled into a smile, and the teasing glint entered his eyes again. "Are you still worried that I will propose to you? Is that why you are advising me to see the good in the other ladies?"

"No." My voice was too quick. "And even if you did, you know what my answer would be. Remember? I do not care to marry either."

"Why is that?"

I had told him before that I wouldn't marry any *gentleman*. I couldn't explain the reason without telling him of my lowered position in society. No gentleman would ever marry a maid. So I simply shrugged. "The idea has never appealed to me."

"Ah, so you haven't been in love."

I frowned.

He took a step closer. "If you were in love, the idea would appeal to you much more, I suspect."

There had been a time when I had dreamed of falling in love, long before my life had changed. "How can you be so certain?" I raised one eyebrow.

His expression faltered slightly, and so did his smile. My heart picked up speed at the look he was giving me, the intensity of his gaze in the shade of the tree. "It doesn't matter." His voice was heavy with uncertainty, and it made my breath stall.

Who had he fallen in love with? I was afraid to ask, so I kept my mouth closed, searching for a way to break through the silence between us. To my relief, Mr. Hill's smile returned, and he lowered his voice to the mischievous tone that had become familiar. "We mustn't allow Mrs. Ollerton to hear us discussing such improper things as love and marriage. She will assume an engagement has taken place between us."

I followed his gaze behind me, where our chaperone was standing in the shade of a nearby tree, her neck craned as if she were trying to hear anything she possibly could over the breeze. I shared his mischievous smile for a brief moment, the elation in my chest disconcerting. When had I come to enjoy Mr. Hill's company so much? "That would be disastrous, indeed."

He offered his arm to me again, and we walked beyond the tree toward the one side of the house he hadn't yet shown me. My legs were surprisingly tired from all the walking, but I didn't mind at all. "There is another matter I wished to discuss with you," I said, before I could lose my courage. "When you mentioned that you are a relative of Mr. Baker…the name sounded quite familiar."

"Oh? Do you know my uncle?"

"I know of him, yes, from one of my maids." I took a deep breath to calm the turmoil that had resumed inside my stomach. This was for Papa. After all he had sacrificed for me, I could sacrifice for him. "My maid, Matilda Sherbrooke." Speaking my own name to Mr. Hill set my heart pounding. "Her father—a gentleman—was well acquainted with Mr. Baker, and they were friends and neighbors, until a certain enmity developed between them. Matilda's father was at fault when he stole from Mr. Baker's property. He returned the item shortly after, but Mr. Baker, using his connections to his advantage, had Mr. Sherbrooke placed in Canterbury Gaol, where he is currently awaiting trial." I swallowed, tugging on the side of my skirts. "My maid is quite troubled by this, as you may imagine, and I hate to see her in such distress."

I could feel the intensity of Mr. Hill's gaze as he listened to me, but I couldn't begin to imagine what he was thinking. My words spilled out fast. "I wondered if you might speak to your uncle on her behalf. On my behalf." I glanced up, meeting his gaze quickly before looking down again. "You might ask that he retract his accusations and see him released from prison. He is a good man. I can vouch for his character as much as any other person of his acquaintance. He does not deserve the sentence he might receive."

Several seconds passed before Mr. Hill spoke, and I held my breath. "If this man is indeed a thief...should he be allowed to avoid the consequences?"

"Surely his months in prison have been enough. He apologized. He returned the stolen item. He was defending his family and took his actions too far. A man who steals once with regret is not a thief. Only one who makes a habit of it and feels no guilt."

Mr. Hill gave a slow nod, observing me for a long moment. "I will write to him today and investigate the matter." He gave me a reassuring smile. "It is very kind of you to be so concerned for your maid. I know you despise having me see your kindness, but it is impossible to miss. You have a heart unlike any lady I have met."

The sincerity in his voice matched that of his eyes, and I had to look away again. What would he think if he knew I was the maid from that story? How betrayed would he feel? I tried to focus on the relief and the hope that gripped me, but I was robbed of any celebration by my guilt. If Mr. Hill had been less wonderful, I might have been happy at this moment. Instead, I felt rather empty.

As we walked around the side of the house, I caught sight of the swing that had set my emotions spinning. The breeze tossed the ropes, causing it to sway side to side. If I closed my eyes, I was certain I would feel Papa's strong hands on my back, lifting me high into the sky and letting me go; I would feel the breeze against my cheeks and my teeth as I smiled and laughed.

"Would you like to try the swing before we leave?" Mr. Hill asked.

I opened my mouth to refuse, but he was already walking toward it, gesturing at the seat. "I assure you, it's secure." He sat down on the wooden plank, clutching the ropes with both hands before pushing off the ground with his feet. The branch above rustled slightly but held his weight. With the broad smile on his cheeks as he swung, he appeared more youthful than he ever had. I could easily picture him as a boy, with his golden-brown hair slightly lighter, perhaps freckles on his cheeks and those deep dimples ever-present.

He stood, taking hold of the rope to stop the motion of the swing. "Come," he said with a cajoling smile.

My legs shook as I walked forward, and I tried to hide the concern on my face as I approached. It had been years since I had been on a swing, or even thought of the swing from my childhood. With a deep breath, I sat down, clutching the ropes so tightly my fingers ached. This swing seemed to have been built much taller than the one I was accustomed to. My toes barely brushed the ground as I tried to push away from it.

Mr. Hill's deep chuckle came from behind me, and then I felt one strong hand press against the center of my back. A sound escaped me, half-laugh, half-shriek, as he pushed me high into the air. The pressure of his hand deserted me, and all I felt was the wind against my back as I swung backward, then skyward once again. Mr. Hill's laughter carried up through the air toward me, and I was choked by laughter of my own. This was what freedom felt like. It was pure joy, relief, and weightlessness. It was like the freedom I now had a chance to give to Papa, with Mr. Hill's help. Papa, my family complete again, it was no longer out of reach. But the sky still was.

I opened my eyes, looking up as I swung back and forth, higher and higher. The clouds: out of reach.

Mr. Hill: out of reach.

Love: out of reach.

CHAPTER 15

*I*f the stares from the other ladies at Winslow House had been cold before, then I didn't know how to describe the iciness that enthroned me now, as I sat in the drawing room that afternoon.

Mrs. Ollerton had not been secretive at all about my morning ride with Mr. Hill, and there was no doubt that I was the sole object of envy in the room. It was a position I was not accustomed to being in, so I shifted my weight from one side to the other as I drank my tea. If only I could tell them all that Mr. Hill had no intention of marrying any of them. How disappointed Miss Downsfield would be. The thought brought a slight smile to my face—one that was likely mistaken for gloating. There was no success to gloat about…only that Mr. Hill had agreed to contact his uncle about Papa. I told myself that that was the only explanation for my jovial mood, but the images of Mr. Hill and his kind smile that coursed through my mind begged me to reconsider.

Stop, Tillie.

I gulped too much of my tea at once, swallowing hard before coughing to dispel the liquid that had made its way into my lungs. My coughing was the only sound that had filled the room for a long moment, drowning out the faint ticking of the clock in the far corner.

"Please excuse me," Mrs. Ollerton said with a pained smile. "I will return shortly." She stood, seemingly just as uncomfortable with the tension in the room as I was. It only took a few seconds after she closed the door for Miss Downsfield's teacup to clatter against her saucer. She composed herself slightly with a deep breath, but the rage behind her eyes was as clear and blue as the afternoon sky.

"How did you manage it?" Her voice was shrill as she addressed me. The other three ladies sat up straighter, just as eager to hear my response, no doubt.

I set my teacup down, folding my hands in my lap. "I'm not certain to what you are referring."

"How did you manage to be the first lady invited for a ride with Mr. Hill? Did Mrs. Ollerton arrange it?" Her eyes had narrowed slightly, but her mouth held a smile, as if she were still trying to be polite, even against her frustration.

I had never been so tempted to boast in my life, but no good would come from it. Keeping my expression indifferent, I shrugged. "There was no significance to our ride, I assure you. I believe Mr. Hill took pity on me because of the ordeal with my maid being injured yesterday."

"An ordeal which was surely orchestrated by you and your designs on him." Miss Benham piped in, her eyebrows lifting with accusation as she stared down her nose at me. "Do you truly expect us to believe that you happened upon him a *second* time in the morning without any conniving on your part? We have contemplated the matter together," she gestured at the other ladies, "and we have concluded that you are attempting to ensnare him."

I glanced at Miss Coppins, who avoided my eyes. Did she believe this ridiculous idea too? I shook my head, refraining from releasing the exasperated sigh that hovered in my lungs. "You are entirely mistaken. It was coincidence that placed Mr. Hill in my path yesterday, and I am most grateful that it did. If he had not been there, my maid would not have been cared for so quickly."

Miss Downsfield exchanged a frown with Miss Taplow, then the other two ladies, before fixing me with her intense stare again. "I suppose there is no other explanation for how this all came about. Mr. Hill cannot possibly favor you." She touched her fingertips to her collarbone, raising her chin as she studied me from head to toe. "After your disgraceful behavior with the tea upon your first day here, and your lack of charity toward the beggars in town, as well as your ridiculously flirtatious display during archery...Mr. Hill is sure to take pity on you for your utter lack of manners and ladylike conduct. There is nothing remarkable about your appearance that might tempt him to overlook your shameful behavior, and your accomplishments are... questionable. I have never heard a lady sing who sounded so much like a scullery maid scrubbing dishes in the kitchen." She touched her glove to the bottom of her nose as she laughed, and the other ladies joined her.

My heart pounded fast, and a knot formed in my stomach. I had known just how ridiculous my behavior had been, and just how pathetic my attempts at being a lady were. But to hear it in such a snide, cruel manner made my face heat with shame. There was nothing I could do to stop it. As much as I wanted to be strong, to defend myself, the words were choked from me by Miss Downsfield's sneer.

As a child, I had once seen two young boys in the woods near my home with a squirrel in a trap, approaching the frightened animal with expressions similar to Miss Downsfield's. Victory. Spite. Superiority. The poor creature had nowhere to run; it was cornered. I had shouted at the boys to let the squirrel go. Whether they had been intimidated by my crazed screams or the fact that they were trespassing on my family's property, I didn't know, but they listened to me. They released the animal unharmed.

Where had my confidence gone? When it came to defending myself, it was nonexistent. There had been a time when I would not have taken spiteful words to heart, but they struck hard, piercing my heart like only the truth could. My frustration rose as I sat in silence, my face growing hotter. A lady might have defended herself, but I was not a lady. I had been taught a new way of living. I was to be submissive and quiet. But why? Right now, I was not a maid. Would Sophia have listened to such cruel words without refuting them?

Before I could sort out my emotions, the drawing room door swung open. The footman would have opened the door gently, so as to not disturb the guests too greatly. But the door made contact with the opposite wall with a thud, and I glanced up to see Mr. Hill in the doorway, hardly recognizable with the scowl on his brow, and a hint of anger burning in his eyes. Had he heard all the things Miss Downsfield had said about me? My shame would swallow me up at any moment.

"Oh, Mr. Hill." Miss Downsfield corrected her posture, fiddling with her necklace. Her smile faltered as she seemed to notice his expression. "I did not know you intended to join us. What brings you here?"

Several seconds passed, and I stared at the rug at my feet rather than meeting Mr. Hill's gaze. When his voice finally came again, it was deep and determined.

"I have come to seek a private audience with Miss Sedgwick."

For the first time since my arrival at Winslow House, Miss Downsfield seemed to be at a loss for words. Her cheeks even darkened a shade, and she cleared her throat with a small, squeaking sound. The rest of the room was silent, but even if it hadn't been, the sound of my pulse would have drowned out any noise.

"I see," Miss Downsfield said. "Well…"

I would not have expected to see her confidence or elegance falter for even a moment, but Mr. Hill's request had ruptured her facade.

And mine.

I could hardly breathe as the ladies traipsed out of the room. Their whispers of disbelief could only be heard once they were in the wide hallway where every sound echoed. The clicking of their feet against the floors grew more distant, and I wished Mr. Hill were just as distant. Instead, he was standing only a few feet away from me in a quiet drawing room, with nothing but the red sofas and Mrs. Ollerton's little brown dog, always sleeping beneath the pianoforte, as a chaperone.

I squared my shoulders and forced myself to look up. Now was not the time to be timid and submissive, despite the confusion that threatened to consume me. Mr. Hill's brow was still furrowed, his arms tight at his sides. When he finally spoke, his voice sent a tremor through me. "You were wrong to say those ladies were good." His eyes met mine, heavy and filled with disgust. "I commend your ability to endure their cruel words with such grace." He shook his head, walking closer.

So he *had* overheard Miss Downsfield's words.

I shrugged one shoulder. "They spoke the truth, which is often most cutting."

The furrows in his brow deepened, and he tipped his head down to look at me. "You are wrong again. Miss Downsfield's words could not have been further from the truth. Anything you might be lacking in accomplishments is exceeded in far more important things. If any lady should hope to be accomplished in anything, it should be kindness. Honesty. Goodness and generosity, and you are the most accomplished lady here in all of those aspects. Do not listen to Miss Downsfield. Promise me you will not listen? That you will not change to suit what she thinks you should be? What society thinks? I am tired of it." Half his mouth lifted in a smile, but the sincerity in his eyes still begged for my assent.

The raw sweetness of his words sent a surge of warmth to envelop my heart. I drew a deep breath through my nostrils, filling my lungs to their capacity as relief flooded over me. The fleeting fear that Mr. Hill had requested this meeting in order to propose had been ridiculous. He had made his feelings on marriage clear, and so had I. "I will not give any heed to anything Miss Downsfield says."

Mr. Hill's smile grew to one of relief. "Unless she speaks of my virtues?"

I smiled. "That is when I will ignore her the most."

He laughed, and the sound filled the room.

I tried to draw a breath, but it was suddenly difficult with him standing so close and his smiling eyes looking down into mine.

"As you should," he said softly. "I would prefer that you come to know me yourself, rather than rely on the opinions of anyone else."

"How am I to do that?" I meant it as a sincere question, but by the quirk of Mr. Hill's eyebrow, I feared he had taken it as a flirtatious remark.

"You may begin by joining me for a horseback ride tomorrow morning...if the speed of our riding allows for conversation. You have already proven yourself comfortable atop a horse."

I fiddled with the sides of my skirts, unsure of how to answer. "I was not comfortable, actually, sharing the saddle with my maid in a wet, muddy dress." I gave a weak smile.

"How is your maid faring? Jessie, was it?"

"She is well. She quite enjoys the extra rest." I smiled, thinking of how Jessie had been earlier that afternoon when I had visited her, reclined on her bed with an expression of complete content.

"I have already written to my uncle concerning your other maid's father," Mr. Hill said. "I informed him of my connection with you and Matilda Sherbrooke. We shall hope he offers mercy on her father's behalf, but he is a stubborn man."

My heart sank. Mr. Baker was just as stubborn as my father, but far more powerful. "Thank you," I said in a quiet voice. "I'm certain she will be most grateful for your interference, even if nothing comes of it." My throat tightened as the ever-present image of Papa behind bars entered my mind. It was shaken away by the softness of Mr. Hill's gaze.

"I will do all in my power to ensure something does come of it. A man should not be exiled or executed for such a small thing, especially if it was unlike his character to do so."

I nodded my agreement, fighting back the tears of hope and gratitude that welled behind my eyes. Papa had paid enough for his mistake. Mama and I had paid for it too. I was still paying for it, charading as Sophia and coming to regard a man very highly whom I could never marry. "That is very kind of you," I managed through my tight throat.

He smiled, looking down at his shoes. The modesty on his face was unfamiliar and endearing, and I found it strange how much my opinion of him had changed. He was not the pompous rake who I first thought him to be. He was far more than that.

"You never did give me your answer." He glanced up to meet my eyes. "Will you come riding with me in the morning?"

A surge of uncertainty gripped my chest. "For what purpose?"

He chuckled softly, clasping his hands behind his back. "Do you still fear I will propose to you?"

I searched his eyes. "A little."

His laughter grew, and I couldn't help but join him. If he thought it was ridiculous enough to laugh at, then I was safe. At least I hoped so.

"You have made your opinions clear enough." His lips curved upward at the corners, but the smile didn't reach his eyes. "So you may be sure to avoid such an unpleasant conversation."

I raised my eyebrows. "Then why do you wish to take me riding? Do you realize how angry that will make Miss Downsfield?"

He frowned. "You said you would not pay any heed to her."

I sighed. "Yes. Sorry."

"But you have discovered one benefit to coming riding with me."

"To make her envious? To torture her?"

"Perhaps a little. You may call it revenge for her spiteful words toward you today. You may also call it proof that you are my favorite." His smile tipped more to one side, and my stomach gave its familiar flutter.

"Your favorite subject for teasing, perhaps?"

He laughed. "That is certainly true, but there is far more to my regard for you than that."

I swallowed, my smile fading as his words sank into my chest. I almost let them reach my heart, but I stopped them before they could get too comfortable in a place where they didn't belong. I had done enough of that already.

"Have you considered that this private conversation has likely already given Miss Downsfield a great deal of distress? She likely assumes you are proposing to me at this very moment." I wrung my hands together.

Mr. Hill's eyes widened. "Are you truly worried over Miss Downsfield's feelings after her treatment of you just now?"

I shrugged one shoulder. "Miss Coppins has warned me on many occasions that distress can cause one's heart to burst. I should hate to be the cause of an unfortunate event like that."

Mr. Hill tipped his head back with a laugh and I joined him, watching the way his shoulders shook and his eyes sparked with amusement. His laughter subsided with a sigh, and he tipped his head to one side, shaking it slightly.

"You are exceedingly thoughtful. And loving. I daresay you could love anything or anyone."

I studied his expression for too long—causing it to turn inquisitive. I looked down at the toes of my boots. By the way his gaze burned on my face, I could tell he was guessing at my thoughts. He would never guess that I had been wondering if he was the same...if he too could love anything or anyone—even a lady's maid.

"That is not true." I searched for anything I could plausibly claim to despise. "I do not like spiders. Or snakes," I added after a pause.

Mr. Hill chuckled. "Well, Miss Downsfield's behavior today was rather snakelike; would you agree?"

After a moment of hesitation, I nodded, biting my lower lip guiltily. "Yes."

Mr. Hill paced over to the pianoforte, running his fingers over the keys casually before looking up with a grin. "She may even hiss when she discovers our plans for a ride."

A laugh escaped me before I coached my expression back to normal. "She might *not* discover that if I don't agree to accompany you."

He crossed his arms. "Would you really deny yourself the opportunity to witness Miss Downsfield hissing?"

The image of Miss Downsfield with her teeth bared letting out such a sound made another giggle escape me. "No."

Mr. Hill's smile grew. "Then we shall meet at the stables at eight o'clock."

I opened my mouth to refute him, but his grin left no

room for argument. I snapped my mouth closed, pressing my lips together. Drat it all, Mr. Hill had managed to charm his way to what he wanted yet again. Why he wanted me to ride with him was still a mystery. If he truly didn't wish to marry, then why bother with me at all? My heart hammered, but I ignored it. He had explained his reasoning well enough, but for some reason, I still didn't believe him.

I cast him a suspicious glance, but he didn't seem to notice. His expression was all triumph, and it melted the stone walls around my heart before I put them up again, stronger, more resilient to a certain set of blue eyes and undeniable charm. No, I would not fall in love with Mr. Hill. Not now, not tomorrow, never. We were friends. He was the only person here besides Jessie who did not intend to hurt me in some way or another.

Yet, no matter his intentions, I still feared he would.

CHAPTER 16

*I*n the drawing room before dinner, I felt very much like a piece of taxidermy on display. I was not dead...yet. But if Miss Downsfield had her way, I might be. By the way she held one of her wrists encircled tightly in her other hand, it seemed she was practicing for how it might feel to squeeze my neck in a similar manner.

I swallowed, pressing my lips together to keep my laughter at bay. Mr. Hill had intentionally chosen a seat on the opposite side of the room from me in an attempt to further confuse the group. The question of why Mr. Hill had requested a private meeting with me hovered in the air, unspoken, and leaving it so was proving quite amusing.

Perhaps Miss Downsfield would burst from her curiosity.

Miss Coppins sat at her right, casting her gaze at me periodically with a look of concern, as if she blamed me for Miss Downsfield's current state.

It was cruel, really, that Mr. Hill had come here at all with his determination not to marry any of the ladies. By the desperation on their faces, it struck me just how unfair he had been—how unfair he *still* was being not to make his intentions clear. Whether he had meant to or not, he had stolen many hearts he didn't intend to keep.

When we stood to head to the dining room, Miss Benham looped her arm through mine so abruptly I jumped at her touch.

"How do you do, Miss Sedgwick?" Her large brown eyes blinked up at me. "It has been far too long since we have spoken."

I sensed the ulterior motives immediately that she must have had in now attempting to befriend me. Surely she suspected Mr. Hill would find her kindness endearing, as she hadn't spoken to me since Mr. Hill had chosen to sit beside me in the drawing room my second day here.

"I am well." I smiled as we made our way out the door.

"You look quite refreshed from your ride this morning."

"Ah, yes." She certainly did not take long to find her way to her desired subject. "I thank you for noticing." I wouldn't be the one to tell her that I had a second ride planned for the next morning.

Fortunately, the walk to the dining room was short, and I was able to separate myself from Miss Benham. The first course was served in relative peace and generic conversation, then the second was placed on the table. The restlessness in the air was becoming more evident by the minute.

My fork scraped across my plate a little too loudly, and I glanced up to meet Mr. Hill's gaze. He smiled, just a slight upturn of his lips before turning his attention back to his roasted goose and potatoes. Mrs. Ollerton had been cheerfully relaying her plans for the next day for at least ten minutes while the rest of us ate in silence. With Mr. Hill as my ally, the envious, dark looks from the other ladies were much more tolerable. It was still difficult to rein in my laughter when I thought about their expressions when Mr. Hill and I had exited the drawing room earlier that day without an engagement to announce. The ladies had been equal parts relief and confusion, and Mr. Hill had yet to explain himself to them.

Silence fell with renewed heaviness, and I didn't dare move as I listened to the repeated clearing of Mrs. Ollerton's throat, a sign that her upcoming choice of words would not be pleasant.

"Mr. Hill," she said around a stiff smile. "I have heard a rumor which I think ought to be clarified."

I stared at my goblet, watching the shadows of the nearby candles flicker off the glass.

From the corner of my eye, I saw Mr. Hill's posture straighten. "In my experience, rumors are never to be believed." How could he manage to sound so calm? So charismatic? I was gripping my fork like a trident, pressing it into the meat on my plate as if I meant to kill it.

I dared a look at Mrs. Ollerton as her lips pursed into a forgiving smile. "Yes, I believe that does apply to most rumors…but I'm afraid the rumor I speak of came from a reliable source." Her eyes flicked to Miss Downsfield before settling on Mr. Hill once again.

I would have never considered Miss Downsfield to be a reliable source for information, unless it was skewed toward achieving her own designs. "I see." Mr. Hill smiled. "What is this rumor? Does it concern me?"

The room was so silent I didn't dare move my fork from its place, spearing the meat unforgivingly. It seemed I would soon be just as trapped.

"Well, yes." Mrs. Ollerton shifted uncomfortably. "It is rumored that you spoke privately with Miss Sedgwick this afternoon." Her eyelids fluttered, as if to beg him to refute her words. "I thought it would be prudent that you deny or confirm this rumor, for the sake of my other guests. You might also explain what the purpose was in such an endeavor, taking Miss Sedgwick aside from all the ladies here." There was a distinct arch to one of her pale eyebrows.

I sat up straighter, lowering my fork as I watched all the other ladies do the same. My heart thudded against my chest, but Mr. Hill, ever collected, simply smiled. "It is true, I did speak with Miss Sedgwick." He paused to take a sip from his goblet, and a collective force seemed to pull every woman forward in her seat, leaning just enough to ensure not a single one of his next words were missed. He met my eyes, and I shot him a questioning look.

Mrs. Ollerton's brow twinged with annoyance when he

failed to explain further. It seemed even *she* lacked the impropriety to force the answer out of him. It had been a private conversation for a reason, after all, but I feared that if he didn't explain, it might reflect badly on my—or rather —Sophia's reputation.

Mr. Hill met my gaze as he took another drink from his cup.

I held back my smile. My amusement with the entire situation was uncalled for, especially considering the risks his plan posed. But for tonight, I tried my best to relax. Roasted goose and potatoes were my favorite, after all.

"Ah, so you did." Mrs. Ollerton's voice raised at the end, making the phrase sound more like a question.

Mr. Hill smiled. "I am glad to have appeased your curiosity."

Her nostrils flared slightly as she returned his smile, and the ladies around the table sat back in nearly perfect unison, the disappointment clear in the slip of their postures.

The conversation shifted to other, less intriguing things before it was time for the ladies to retire to the drawing room. Mr. Hill remained behind for port, as was customary, and I had the distinct impression that I was on my way to something of a war zone. Without Mr. Hill present, the drawing room would be just as it had been that afternoon. At least Mrs. Ollerton would be there to prevent any impoliteness from occurring. I squared my shoulders, willing myself to feel confident.

I glanced back at Mr. Hill as I left the room, catching the concern on his brow. I cast him a reassuring smile. Was he still worried that I couldn't endure the company of the other ladies without being hurt? How fragile did he suppose me to be? Straightening my arms at my sides, I flexed my hands. I was not fragile. I was not weak. In something of a chant, I let the words echo in my mind as I exited the dining room and sat down on one of the red sofas.

Mrs. Ollerton took the seat on the cushion beside me, her rouge-covered lips stretching into another of her stiff smiles. "Miss Taplow, will you favor us with a song on the pianoforte?"

"I would be most honored, Mrs. Ollerton." She beamed as she stood and found her seat at the bench, obviously quite pleased with the opportunity to showcase her talents.

The moment she began playing, Mrs. Ollerton leaned toward me to whisper in my ear, her moist breath uncomfortably close. "As your hostess, I must insist that you tell me the matter you and Mr. Hill discussed today in the drawing room. It is my responsibility to ensure your reputation remains…unscathed, if you will."

I kept my gaze fixed on Miss Taplow at the pianoforte, too afraid to turn and see just how close Mrs. Ollerton's face was to mine. "It was nothing of importance."

"I do not mean to suggest that Mr. Hill is a dishonorable man, as I am certain he is not, but if he has developed an attachment, then you mustn't deny me the reassurance that he did not succumb to any passion he may have in regard to you or compromise your reputation in any manner." She inhaled deeply when she finished, the entirety of her warm, moist breath having been expended at my ear.

I shuddered. My face grew hot at her implications. "No, he did not. I assure you. At any rate, Mr. Hill does not have any passion for me."

Mrs. Ollerton chuckled. "How I wish that were true. I would have preferred he choose Miss Downsfield, as they would make the handsomest couple in the entire county."

I leaned away to look at her eyes, insistent that not a single one of my words be missed. "He has not chosen me."

"So he did not propose today in the drawing room? I am glad to have eliminated that possibility." Her voice could barely be heard above the pianoforte, but the song was almost finished. "Tell me, child. What did he say to you?"

"He—er—he wished to invite me horseback riding in the morning."

Mrs. Ollerton's eyes flashed with victory at having been told what she had been fishing for, yet her disappointment was just as obvious. "Oh, dear. I was not mistaken in his passion."

I really wished she would stop using the word *passion*. A passion for teasing me, perhaps. My heart pounded at the thought of Mr. Hill having any real attraction to me. He had made it clear that he esteemed me highly, and he had become something of a trusted friend. We shared a passion for poetry and nature. But romance? Love? That was likely the farthest thing from his mind when he looked at me. He enjoyed making me blush with his flirtations, and that was all.

But the fact that Mrs. Ollerton believed his attachment was genuine was dangerous.

"Mrs. Ollerton, please understand, I am quite certain he does not—"

Miss Taplow's song ended just seconds before the drawing room door opened. Mr. Hill had never left the dining room so quickly. Mrs. Ollerton moved to a far more comfortable distance, but Mr. Hill seemed to have noticed her quick movement. He likely noticed the blush on my cheeks and discomfort in my expression as well. I quickly put on a pleasant smile, willing my face to cool.

He sat on the chair beside my end of the sofa, joining in the applause that was being offered for Miss Taplow.

"Are you all right?" he said in a quiet voice, just soft enough to evade Mrs. Ollerton's ears.

I nodded, knowing full well any word I spoke to him would be carefully observed by the rest of the party. They would all be reading my lips.

"What did they say to you?" He lowered his voice further.

Miss Taplow began a second number without invitation, seemingly unwilling to lose her place at the instrument now that Mr. Hill was present.

"I cannot explain here," I breathed, careful not to draw attention to myself. Mrs. Ollerton was already watching from the corner of her eye, the blue irises shifting in my direction.

"Tomorrow?"

"Yes."

I met his gaze, suddenly far more comfortable than I had been moments before. Ironically, the way he put me at ease instantly was rather unsettling.

One corner of his mouth curled upward. "Now, shall we tell a certain snakelike guest of our morning plans?"

"We must wait until the song is over," I said in a hushed tone. "Or we shall not hear the resulting hiss."

He made a choked sound, dipping his chin as if to lodge his laughter in his throat before it could escape. The corners of his mouth still twitched, and I found my own smile particularly strong in its fight against me.

"But there will be no need to tell her," I said. "I daresay I have vexed everyone enough already." I adjusted my left glove, enabling me to turn my face far enough away from Mrs. Ollerton to avoid being overheard. "And our hostess already knows."

"Is she pleased?"

"Not in the slightest."

Mr. Hill laughed under his breath, and we both sat back, our whispering becoming far too obvious. Miss Taplow's immaculate performance was not even enough to distract me from the ripple of excitement in my chest.

With the downward spiral of each trill she played, I was reminded of the risks I was taking.

For Papa, I told myself.

But the longer I sat against the red sofa resisting the urge to glance at Mr. Hill and his broad smile, the more I realized that my time spent with Mr. Hill was not *just* for Papa.

CHAPTER 17

"My horse is much faster than yours, I'd wager," Mr. Hill said as we rode over the first hill beyond Winslow House. The landscape was more rugged here, less manicured. Dandelions sprouted all around us, trampled underfoot by our horses.

"This is not my horse, so I will not take any offense to that, though I sense *he* is offended greatly." I patted the tan mane of my mount before tossing Mr. Hill a smile.

His eyes widened in a look of mock dismay. "He did glare at me just now. It was almost as cutting as one of yours."

"I have not glared at you in a long while."

"I do miss it."

I raised one eyebrow. "Please do not give me a reason to glare at you simply because you enjoy making me angry."

"It is not your anger I enjoy, but rather the creases in your forehead when you scowl." His eyes swept over my face, half his mouth lifting in a smile. "And the way your nose scrunches as if you have just smelled the inside of a horse's stall."

I exhaled sharply, and almost glared at him before thinking better of it. "You are very observant."

"Not always." He smiled, keeping his gaze fixed ahead, as though he didn't want to risk me discerning more from his gaze.

When we had promised Mrs. Ollerton we would stay within view of the estate, she had agreed to simply observe our ride from the back window rather than venture outside on horseback to follow us. She would never leave us unchaperoned, even if she was uncharacteristically relaxed in her duties today.

"Do you have a horse? In Kent?" Mr. Hill asked.

Not anymore. She had been one of the first things to be sold. "My father had a mare he taught me to ride," I said in a quiet voice. My heart protested the memories, but they floated to the surface anyway. The sensation was much like an experience I'd had as a child, when I had eaten too many sugar cubes when Mama wasn't watching. My stomach had protested almost immediately, but they had tasted too sweet for me to leave behind.

"Did she have a name?"

"Cinnamon." I smiled. "My father allowed me to name her whatever I wished."

"Perhaps he will regret giving you that privilege when he learns that you attempted to deflect every opportunity to become engaged on your visit to Bibury." Oh, yes. I was to be speaking of Sophia's parents, not my own.

"Surely your parents will revoke some of your privileges if they learn that you have done the same," I said.

Mr. Hill laughed. "It vexes them to no end that I have such a firm wish to deny them their intentions for me."

"Why do you have that wish?" He had never fully explained it to me before.

His expression turned more serious, and he looked down at the reins he held. "Because they have denied me mine."

What did he mean by that? I scowled in confusion.

"There it is," he said, a slight smile reappearing on his face. By the teasing in his voice, I could guess he meant my scowl. It had been meant to prompt him to explain further, but he seemed content to drop the subject. We passed a shallow stream, and I inhaled the earthy scent of the water as it trickled over the rocks. The sun had begun rising, and I let the warmth of it soak through the fabric of Sophia's old riding habit.

After a long moment of comfortable silence, Mr. Hill spoke again. "Considering that we are both trapped here at Winslow House against our wills, and we are both quite tired of the company of our fellow guests...I wondered if you might consider indulging one request I have of you."

"What is it?"

He seemed uncharacteristically shy, rubbing one side of his face before pressing his lips together, as if uncertain of whether he would make his request or not. "We have three weeks remaining of our stay, and three weeks is all I ask of you."

"Three weeks of what?"

"Courting me."

I raised my eyebrows as the color drained from my face. Had he misunderstood what I had said on our first ride? I had no intention of courting or marrying any gentleman, and Mr. Hill was certainly a gentleman. A very eligible one at that.

He must have noticed my shock. "*Pretending* to court me," he corrected.

I recovered from my shock for long enough to answer. "Considering that this is our second ride in two days, it seems you already have been doing just that."

"Time in your company is never something I will regret, and I assure you, I have not been seeking it in order to instigate any false courtship without your permission. The idea only struck me this morning." He checked my expression before continuing. I kept my dread from showing. "Mrs. Ollerton will have a taste of her much desired success, the other women will be sufficiently humbled, and I might depart here in three weeks claiming to my family that you have broken my heart and I might plausibly renew my determination to remain a bachelor for all of my days. There will be no risk to your reputation. I will ensure discretion. You might even claim to your family that it was I who broke your heart, and you failed by no fault of your own."

The panic in my chest reminded me of the moment

Sophia had suggested her 'clever idea' to me. Seeing how disastrous that plan was turning out to be made me even more wary to agree to Mr. Hill's idea. Pretending to court the very man I was supposed to be avoiding could only result in disaster. Pretending to court a man whom I was in great danger of falling in love with was even worse. A man I could never, ever consider marrying, and who would never, ever consider me.

There was far too much that could go wrong.

The claim that Mr. Hill was the one to break my heart could become much more factual than I would have liked it to be.

Mr. Hill awaited my response, his blue eyes boring into mine.

"I question the wisdom of…a fabricated courtship," I said in a quiet voice. "Mrs. Ollerton will likely boast of her success to all of her friends. She may even write home to my family and tell them. They will be very displeased when I return home unattached."

To *Sophia's* family. Mrs. Sedgwick *would* be quite angry with Sophia if she returned unattached after receiving such a promising letter from Mrs. Ollerton.

Mr. Hill seemed to consider my worries, eyes narrowing as he surveyed the field ahead. "You might tell her that you wish to tell your family yourself? That you wish to have them be happily surprised when you return to them at the end of the month."

I let out a puff of air, looking down at my hands. I did want to help Mr. Hill, but he had agreed to come here of his own will. He hadn't actually been forced like I had. Had he expected *not* to have ladies fawning over him and fighting for his attention? If he were truly a rake, he would have delighted in it, but I was discovering that he was much more noble than that. "Perhaps not a *courtship*," I said. "Perhaps you might just pretend to favor me?"

Mr. Hill's lopsided grin appeared again, and my stomach fluttered. Yes. This would be far too dangerous.

"There would be no pretending involved in that," he said. "And it seems the other guests already believe that I favor you, and it has caused them to behave in a way that is much to your expense. I refuse to allow them to speak so cruelly to you again. There needs to be absolutely no question that I have chosen you."

A pang of longing struck my chest, and I pushed it away as fast as possible, unsettled by the emotion accompanying it. Mr. Hill hadn't *actually* chosen me. He couldn't. The dangers of this game were already presenting themselves, and Mr. Hill's persuasive words were becoming difficult to resist. He was right. I should not be forced to endure any cruel, unkind words from the women here. I had Sophia for that, and in three weeks my life would be back to the way it was.

Could I not enjoy these three weeks?

It was the last chance I would have to be a lady, to be respected. And there was the matter of staying in Mr. Hill's good graces. I needed him to be willing to keep contact with Mr. Baker on my behalf. That was the most important issue, and if I refused to help him with this request, how could I expect him to help me with mine?

Summoning all my courage, I nodded. "Very well. I will pretend to court you." It was a faint whisper, my courage already fading. "But only if it is presented as your fault when we part ways."

His gaze hovered on me for a long moment before returning to the field ahead. "Very well."

We had reached the edge of Winslow House's property. Mrs. Ollerton would be fit to be tied if she could no longer keep us in view. She would be fit to be tied, nonetheless.

A laugh bubbled out of my chest at the utter ridiculousness of my current situation. Perhaps Mr. Hill was right. No harm could come from this. He never had to know I was not Miss Sophia Sedgwick. At the end of the next three weeks, we would depart as coconspirators, and even friends, and never speak again. I would go back to being Sophia's maid, and Papa might have his chance at freedom.

Mr. Hill's laugher joined in mine. Laughing with him like this was not wise. He was far too endearing when he laughed.

"A third outing ought to confirm any suspicions the guests have regarding my choice." He smiled, glancing upward in apparent thought. "Perhaps a bit more archery tomorrow afternoon? You are in desperate need of practice."

"I did not shoot as terribly as you think."

"I meant your flirting."

I scoffed. "I was attempting to turn your attention away."

"Yet I enjoyed every moment of it." His smile turned mischievous. "If we are to convince everyone that you love me, then you must do all you can to improve your acting skills."

I would have laughed, but my stomach felt as if it had formed one large knot.

It would not require as much acting as he seemed to believe.

CHAPTER 18

"*O*h, my."

Little did Mrs. Ollerton know, I was listening to her conversation with Mr. Hill from the other side of the banister, hidden behind a statue.

"If you are certain." Her voice was skeptical. "Would you not consider taking Miss Downsfield on a walk through the gardens? I suspect you might find much to admire in her."

"That would be counterproductive, Mrs. Ollerton." Mr. Hill spoke with confidence, and I could envision him with crossed arms and a lifted chin. "I consider it unfair to give any other woman than Miss Sedgwick the idea that I intend to court them. You might advise them all to simply enjoy the rest of their stay as fellow guests rather than competitors."

"Do you intend to...offer for Miss Sedgwick?"

"That is the purpose of a courtship, is it not? To determine the answer to that very question." The smile in his voice was charming—there was no way Mrs. Ollerton wouldn't be convinced by it.

Her inhale was slightly labored. "I suppose so."

"*If* I were to select a wife from among your guests, it would undeniably be Miss Sedgwick. But of course, I will not be making such a decision yet. We have just begun to come to know one another."

I pressed my palm against the cool stone of the statue, keeping myself steady and quiet. "Well, thank you for informing me, Mr. Hill." I caught the last few echoes as Mrs. Ollerton's feet clicked across the floor and away from the staircase before peeking out from behind the statue.

Mr. Hill appeared behind me, and I stepped out from my hiding place. His smile was contagious. "Considering that you will be absent from tea this afternoon, I suspect our courtship will be the topic of conversation," he said.

I interlocked my fingers in front of me. "Let there be no doubt."

He chuckled. "Perhaps it would be wise for me to arm you with a bow as soon as possible. And teach you how to use it so you may have a means of defending yourself."

I laughed. "You may be right."

He extended his arm to me as we walked outside, where two targets had already been set up. After proving to Mr. Hill that my archery did indeed require just as much practice as my flirting, he walked me back to the house. My cheeks ached from smiling as I made my way to my room to change before finding Jessie in her room. She had hardly left since injuring her leg, and I decided I had been neglecting her nearly as much as she had been happily neglecting her responsibilities.

"Tillie!" She sat up straighter in her bed when I entered, licking a bit of jam off her finger. A half-eaten slice of bread sat on a tray on her lap. She had been treated far kinder here than I would have been had I been injured working at Sedgwick Manor. Here, she was more of a guest, and Mrs. Ollerton had been generous enough to ensure she was comfortable while her ankle recovered.

"How is your leg?" I asked.

"The swellin' has gone down a bit," she said with a smile. "The doctor said I'll be up and about soon enough. 'Twasn't as severe an injury as we thought."

"I'm relieved to hear it." I eyed her crutches where they rested against her small bed.

"Would you like to take a walk outside? The ladies are still gathered in the drawing room with their embroidery and I would rather not guess at what uncharitable thoughts they have for me." I bit my lip.

"Are they still fit to be tied over your ride with Mr. Hill?"

"There is a matter I must discuss with you." I gulped. "And yes. Very much. I suspect they have all named the handkerchiefs on which they embroider after me, so they may happily puncture the fabric again and again. Well, all the ladies except Miss Coppins. She does not enjoy embroidery because she fears she will puncture her finger with the needle."

Jessie's eyes widened. "Oh, dear." A grin overtook her face so suddenly I took a step back. "What have you done now?"

"Let us walk outside," I said, helping her to her feet and handing her the crutches. "You are surely in need of fresh air, and the story I have to tell will be most invigorating."

Jessie seemed to have gained a great deal of energy, following me out the door and up the stairs with little assistance. Despite the reputation servants had for gossip, I trusted Jessie entirely, and I needed someone to share the anxiety that had been unfolded upon me. I told her everything that had transpired—including the details of Mr. Hill's connection to Mr. Baker and the false courtship we had concocted. Jessie's limp had nearly disappeared by the time I finished, her eyes reflecting her shock.

"Sophia will not be pleased," she said amid a chuckle of disbelief. "How will she explain to her parents?"

"I don't know." I put my forehead in my hands.

"Do you trust him?" Jessie asked.

"I do. Should I not? He seems very trustworthy."

Jessie studied me for a long moment. "One may *seem* trustworthy. I suspect he thinks you are to be trusted. But little does he know, your name is not Sophia Sedgwick."

My stomach dropped and guilt flooded through my chest.

"It's not your fault, o'course." Jessie touched my arm. "You're not at liberty to tell him your real identity, and I wouldn't trust him to keep a secret like that, at any rate. You could have the constable at your door if he wished it."

"That is why he will never know," I affirmed. *And that is why he can never actually care for me, or I for him.* With those words, I jostled the locks around my heart, just to ensure they were still secure.

"I wonder how Mistress Sophia is enjoying Hampden Park," Jessie said in a distant voice. "If she'd seen Mr. Hill, I suppose she wouldn't have ever sent you here in her place."

"If she wanted him, she would have secured him too. Sophia is not one to accept defeat. She always gets what she wants. Her idea was foolish from the beginning to have me try to pretend to be her."

"Mr. Hill's idea to have you court him is foolish too." Jessie chuckled. "All that pretending to be in love is bound to turn into the real thing sooner or later."

My face flushed.

Jessie grinned. "*Sooner*, I'd wager."

I shot her a scowl, shaking my head, though it spun at the truth behind her words. Before I could respond, we turned the corner beneath the archway where Mr. Hill had discovered me singing my first morning here. On the bench just beyond it, Miss Coppins sat, her ankles crossed, a book on her lap. She must have heard our approach, because the book was closed, and she was staring straight at us.

My stomach pinched with dread. Jessie did not have a talent for speaking quietly. Had she overheard our conversation? All she could have heard from her place on the bench were Jessie's last words. *Sooner, I'd wager.*

"Miss Sedgwick." Miss Coppins smiled. "Have you come to keep me company? It does get quite lonely out here when all the other ladies are embroidering. I have no desire to lose a finger."

"I was just taking a walk with my maid." I smiled.

"May I join you?"

There was no way to refuse in a kind way, so I simply stayed silent as she stood and hooked her arm through mine, not waiting for an invitation. I considered reminding her of the dangers of extensive walking, but thought better of it.

Jessie fell silent, bobbing a curtsy before stepping back to trail behind us. Not only did I hope that Miss Coppins hadn't heard our conversation, but also how casually my 'maid' had been conversing with me.

"Why did you not join the other ladies in the drawing room this afternoon?" Miss Coppins asked.

"I—er—Mr. Hill was instructing me on my archery."

"Oh, I was not aware." Miss Coppin's voice seemed to grow higher in pitch. "How fortunate you are to be the center of his attention."

I bit my lower lip, unsure of how to respond. "Mrs. Ollerton has surely explained my absence to her other guests in the drawing room, and that is why you were not informed."

"Mrs. Ollerton is on a call this afternoon," Miss Coppins said, her voice clipped.

"Oh, I see."

We walked in prolonged silence for several seconds before she spoke again, her voice abrupt. "I must go now. It was quite diverting to walk with you, Miss Sedgwick, but as you know, I prefer not to exert myself for longer than necessary."

What had been necessary about that walk? My brow furrowed as she smiled and retreated back to where we had found her.

"I've never met such a strange woman." Jessie hobbled up beside me, frowning in Miss Coppins's direction as she disappeared within the shaded gardens once again.

"I have come to expect such from any conversation with Miss Coppins." I sighed. "But you are right. That was particularly strange."

Jessie and I finished our walk, and my thoughts wandered back to other things. Mr. Hill was among the most prevalent. But arching over it all was a heavy blanket of fear that I couldn't seem to displace, no matter how hard I tried to remain calm and positive. Mr. Hill did not seem entirely confident in his success with persuading his uncle to be lenient toward Papa, and I was not confident in my success with continuing our false courtship undiscovered.

When the next three weeks ended, how much will have changed? How much further will I have strayed from my purpose?

My worry refused to leave all afternoon, and when Mrs. Ollerton stood abruptly in the drawing room after dinner, it only increased. Her expression sprung into a look of panic. It wouldn't have been so out of the ordinary if it had been directed at me.

Instead, she was staring at the table in the far corner of the room.

"Where is my mother's pendant?" Her face took on a grey hue, and she rushed toward the bust, touching the sculpture with dismay. She whirled to face the room, taking a deep breath as she touched a hand to her collarbone.

It took me a moment to recall the image of the necklace she spoke of, with the ruby center that sparkled in the sunlight each afternoon. There had yet to be a day Mrs. Ollerton hadn't commented on its beauty. But, as she said, it was gone. Miss Downsfield gasped, putting one gloved hand against her cheek. The other ladies made similar sounds of dismay, walking forward to examine the statue that had been left bare.

"I should never have gone out this afternoon," Mrs. Ollerton said under her breath.

Miss Taplow frowned. "Surely you don't suppose it was one of your guests who stole it. Perhaps a maid took it to clean and forgot to replace it? Did it fall on the floor?"

Mrs. Ollerton shook her head, the color still missing from her cheeks. "I have strictly forbidden any of the servants from touching it. If it needs cleaning, I have made it clear I will perform the task myself." She turned back toward the table, her shoulders slumping.

I glanced at each of the ladies surrounding her, catching a ghost of a smile curl one side of Miss Downsfield's lips.

Her expression quickly transformed back to dismay when Mrs. Ollerton turned once again.

My eyes narrowed.

"I will not allow this misfortune to ruin our evening." Mrs. Ollerton exhaled through pursed lips. "First thing in the morning I will have every room searched as a precaution. I do doubt there is a thief among us, but one can never be too certain of anything." Her smile was weak as she surveyed each guest in turn.

If the evening wasn't ruined by the missing pendant, it had already been ruined by Mrs. Ollerton's recent announcement. Mr. Hill had yet to rejoin us in the drawing room when she had detailed her conversation with him that morning concerning our courtship, and consoled the other ladies with the hope that he might soon *change his mind*. I pretended not to be offended by the hopeful tone in her voice and the complete disregard she showed for my presence in the room.

"There is no need to worry, really," Miss Downsfield said. "Surely Mr. Hill will come to his senses."

For a moment, I felt as if I were sinking into my chair. But then my hands tightened around my skirts, and my spine straightened. "Mr. Hill is a very sensible man," I blurted, willing my voice to sound confident. "He has already come to his senses, and he has chosen me. He is quite firm in all his convictions, and does not change his mind easily." I wished I could tell them that one of those convictions was never to marry *at all*, but I held my tongue.

"You must be so very proud," Miss Downsfield said between gritted teeth. It may as well have been a hiss. I would have laughed, but the spite in her eyes struck me silent. Her body was angled just far enough away from Mrs. Ollerton to hide her expression, and her voice somehow managed to sound polite.

I took a deep breath. The pride that coursed through my veins had nothing to do with Mr. Hill, but the fact that I had not sunk into the chair. My hands shook in my lap as I found my voice again. "In truth, I am not *proud*," I said, shaking my head. "And perhaps that is why Mr. Hill chose me over you."

Miss Downsfield's jaw unhinged slightly.

I stood, offering a curtsy. "Excuse me."

I made it to the door and out into the dim hallway without stopping to catch my breath. The moment the door closed behind me, a smile stole over my cheeks. I covered my mouth to hide it, as if the portraits on the wall would scold me for it. Before Mrs. Ollerton or any of the other ladies could have a chance to come after me, I hurried toward my room, not stopping until I was safely behind the door.

My smile faded as I pressed my back against the wall. Where were my manners? What had I been thinking? I couldn't risk displeasing Mrs. Ollerton too much, or she would simply send me back to Kent. My heart pounded with a warning, and my cheeks burned with shame despite the victory I had just recently felt. My words were not my own, they were Sophia's.

I had forgotten that.

There were too many important things I had forgotten of late, the most important being that I was not a lady. I was not at liberty to say and do what I wished, not really. I was still a lady's maid in disguise, no matter how unsavory that reality tasted now that I had tasted something sweeter.

I rubbed my right temple with my fingertips as I paced toward the chair by the mirror. Breathing was suddenly difficult—perhaps due to the maid who had laced my stays too tight. As I sat down, something small caught my eye in my reflection, tucked beneath the brush that rested on the vanity. Something red and shiny.

I moved the brush, and the chain of a necklace fell in a tangle onto the vanity.

The ruby glared up at me. It was Mrs. Ollerton's missing pendant.

CHAPTER 19

I stared at the necklace for a long moment.

With the chain tangled up near my brush, I could only assume it had been hastily placed there.

My heart thudded as betrayal crept over the edges of my mind, rimming my vision in darkness. Of course Miss Downsfield had placed it here. She hoped to have me sent home, or even punished further. My thoughts flashed to Papa. All it had taken was a stolen tusk to put him in the Canterbury Gaol. How much worse would a punishment be for stealing an expensive heirloom like Mrs. Ollerton's pendant?

Considering the fact that I was likely not currently in Mrs. Ollerton's good graces, I didn't dare take it back down to the drawing room, claiming innocence. Papa had tried to return the tusk and had still been sent away. Pressing a hand to my chest, I tried to calm my breathing, a sudden panic overtaking my lungs. I collected myself, meeting my own eyes in the mirror.

You are innocent, Tillie.

That single thought sent a wave of calm over my shoulders. I had already known the ladies were combating against me. I just hadn't expected to be framed for thievery. Even Miss Downsfield seemed too refined to do something like that. And there was no reason Mrs. Ollerton wouldn't take my word if I told her I didn't take the necklace. Was there? I could tell her I found it on the floor in the hall.

With shaking fingers, I scooped up the necklace, planning to take it to her that very instant.

But as I made my way to the door, I stopped in my tracks.

Mrs. Ollerton might take a lady's word, but she would never take a maid's. If it were ever discovered that I was not Sophia, then Mrs. Ollerton would hold this against me.

There was only one safe option. I had to put it back before morning.

Before I could lose my nerve, I slid the necklace inside my glove on the underside of my hand. The ruby left a large bump beneath the fabric on my wrist, but I bunched the fabric around it to make it less noticeable. The ladies would likely still be in the drawing room for a few more hours, especially after Mr. Hill joined them.

My stomach clenched. The cold metal of the necklace dug into my skin, reminding me just how much more suspicious I would appear for having fled the room. What if Miss Downsfield was, at that very moment, convincing

Mrs. Ollerton to search for her pendant tonight rather than in the morning? My worries continued their course through my head as I sat on the edge of my bed.

If I were to venture back to the drawing room, it would be unwise to leave the necklace anywhere near my room, on the chance Mrs. Ollerton did send servants in search of it. But approaching Mrs. Ollerton about where I had found it was not a safe option, nor was trying to sneak it back onto the bust in the drawing room while everyone else was gathered there. I would have to wait until late in the evening, after everyone else had gone to sleep. For now, I would do all I could to evade any suspicion. Keeping it under my glove felt like the safest choice at the moment. It was undetectable, and I would ensure it didn't get lost.

With my mind made up, I stood and made my way quietly down the stairs. A lively melody streamed through the house from the drawing room, where one of the ladies must have been playing the pianoforte. I stopped several feet away from the door in the dimness, fisting my hand to keep the necklace from sliding around inside my glove. How would I explain my abrupt departure? I didn't regret what I had said to Miss Downsfield—especially now that I knew that she had attempted to frame me.

"What have you done now?"

I jumped at the sound of Mr. Hill's voice. He walked toward me from the direction of the dining room, brow quirking upward in curiosity. I put a finger to my lips, backing away from the door. He followed, and I eyed the nearby footman suspiciously.

"This way," I said, waving Mr. Hill toward me as I walked with quick steps toward the library.

He didn't question it, but followed me as I slipped behind the heavy library doors. They closed with a thud behind us, and the large windows let in just enough light from the sunset to show the curiosity on his face. "If you wished to be alone with me, you could have simply asked." A slow smile spread over his lips.

Drat. I hadn't thought of how it would appear if we were seen alone in the dim library. The necklace inside my glove, however, was a reminder that my sneaking that evening had only just begun.

He seemed to notice the worry on my brow. His expression softened, and he took a step closer. "What is the matter?"

"The missing pendant," I said, swallowing. "It was in my room. I think one of the other ladies put it there in the hopes that it would be discovered and I would be blamed."

Mr. Hill's jaw tightened. "You cannot be serious."

"I don't know how else it could have gotten there."

He rubbed the back of his neck, the spark of anger in his eyes growing hotter. "Do you know who did it? I can speak with Mrs. Ollerton and have her held responsible."

"I don't know for certain." I wrung my hands together. "And there is no need for that."

He eyed me carefully, the anger instantly fading from his gaze. "How can they be so cruel to someone so kind? I don't understand."

I looked down at my shoes, a sudden surge of emotion

gripping my throat. How was it he could make me so vulnerable, all with one look and a few sweet words? My emotions would have never been allowed so close to the surface before, but he somehow managed to untether all my defenses.

"I am not entirely kind," I said, still staring at the floor. "In fact, what I said to Miss Downsfield before leaving the drawing room this evening was not kind at all." My voice turned into a mutter.

Mr. Hill nudged my chin up with one knuckle, his smiling eyes boring into mine with inquiry. A string of shivers spread down my neck at his touch. "What did you say?"

My mind was suddenly quite blank, and I grasped for the memory like grasping at smoke in the air.

Mr. Hill had never touched my face before.

If he had, I would have certainly remembered it. Perhaps not now, however, as every thought seemed to have fled my mind. I could already feel the cursed heat spreading in my cheeks, and I willed it to stop, but it refused to obey. I prayed the room was dark enough to hide the color. But the warmth could not be hidden. Mr. Hill's fingers grazed my cheek as he tucked a limp curl behind my ear. There was a certain reluctance in his movements, and his smile faltered slightly as he lowered his hand to his side.

I breathed as steadily as I could, taking a minuscule step backward. The extra distance served to clear my mind for a brief moment. "You will tease me for it."

"Surely what you said was deserved," Mr. Hill said

before clearing his throat, taking a step backward as well. Perhaps he had also noticed how improper our proximity was, especially being alone in a dim room.

"In essence, I called her proud."

His eyebrows rose and a fresh smile tugged on his mouth. "That is not unkind at all. That is entirely truthful."

"The truth can be unkind at times." And cruel, and bitter, and unfair. A pang of guilt struck me again at the reminder that I had not been truthful with Mr. Hill. I *could not* be. The fate of my family rested on my lies, and I couldn't escape it.

"Indeed." Mr. Hill's eyes searched my face. "And that must be why you are often reluctant to give it. You cannot stand being unkind."

I smiled at the ground, unsettled by the warmth in his gaze.

"There are times when I think the world does not deserve you. Surely I do not, and that is why our courtship is false." There was a hint of teasing in his voice, but it seemed half-hearted.

My breath caught in my lungs like fabric snagging on a dull needle. How could he think he didn't deserve me? He, the kind, generous, wealthy, handsome Mr. Hill—the man every woman wanted to marry. He could have anyone he wanted. So why did I feel as if it was me he wanted most? His words told one story, but his eyes told another, and I didn't know which to believe. All I knew was that there was some truth hidden inside his voice and eyes and smile, and I would prefer the lies.

My voice shook as much as my hands. "Our courtship is false because you wished it to be. It is not a matter of whether or not you...deserve me. It is a matter of our own goals and convictions." I bit my lip. "And I am fairly certain you have the matter backwards, Mr. Hill. It is I who is undeserving of you. Of-of your friendship. You have already helped me many times."

He studied me for a long moment, his expression serious and contemplative. After several seconds, he smiled, but it was the same weak motion as before. "Well, it is a good thing we have our goals and convictions then. Otherwise we might have fallen madly in love by now."

My heart leaped before I recognized the teasing glint in his eyes. My shoulders relaxed, but only a little. I took another step away from him, licking my lips and glancing at the floor. "I—I think we have strayed from the matter at hand." I lifted my glove. "What to do with the necklace."

Mr. Hill nodded, correcting his expression to one of solemnity. "We must put it back."

"How?" I glanced at the closed doors of the library behind us. The ladies would be wondering where Mr. Hill was soon, and I couldn't risk them finding us here.

He rubbed one finger under his chin in thought. "Meet me here again this evening. At midnight. Everyone will have gone to bed by then."

My brow furrowed and I opened my mouth to speak, but he stopped me.

"We will sneak into the drawing room and replace it. In

the morning, Mrs. Ollerton will assume she imagined it being missing at all."

I gave a slow nod, though my stomach twisted. How wise was it to sneak around the house alone with Mr. Hill? A thrill of excitement cut through my misgiving. It would be an adventure of sorts, and seeing the surprise on Miss Downsfield's face the next morning when she discovered her scheme was ruined would be well worth the risk. I took a deep breath. "Very well."

"We shall plan on it," he said.

"And if we're seen?" I raised my eyebrows. "What then?"

"Your reputation could be in danger." He turned toward the door before glancing behind his shoulder with a wink. "I suppose you would have to marry me."

My eyes rounded in shock and he turned toward the door again with a deep chuckle. "We won't be seen," he said in a reassuring voice, peeking out the crack between the double doors before opening them slowly.

He slipped into the hall before facing me. "I will join the guests in the drawing room first."

"And I will come in a few minutes."

He nodded, casting me a smile before fading into the dark hallway.

CHAPTER 20

paced nervously in front of the flickering candle by my bedside, stopping to unpin my hair and arrange it in a loose braid over my shoulder. The pain in my head subsided with my hair lower on my scalp. I still wore my gown from that evening, and I hadn't dared remove my gloves. The pendant still rested against my hand, the metal having long lost its coolness after the hours it had spent against my palm.

Mrs. Ollerton hadn't bothered to hide her displeasure with me after I had returned from leaving the room in a rush. I could only imagine how much more displeased she would have been had she known what was hiding in my glove the entire evening.

My heart thudded as I checked the time. There were two minutes until midnight.

Picking up the candle, I sneaked out of my room, careful not to make a sound as I walked downstairs to the library. The house was silent, evidence that the rest of the guests had gone to sleep. Or at least to bed. My feet moved noiselessly along the ground floor, and I searched the hall for any sign of Mr. Hill. I touched the door handle at the library, dreading the slight creak I knew the doors to make. Thankfully, I didn't have to open them.

"Miss Sedgwick, you look quite clandestine this evening." Even in a whisper, Mr. Hill's amusement came through unmistakably.

I turned to face him, unable to control my smile at the sight of his mischievous grin. "As do you."

He held a candle of his own, the small flame flickering and casting shadows over his face. I hadn't thought it possible for him to look more handsome, but the candle-light did him all sorts of favors. My gaze caught on his open collar, where his cravat was regrettably missing. That combined with his mischievous grin and slightly unkempt hair, not only did he look handsome, but he looked *devilishly* handsome.

My stomach fluttered with nervousness as I glanced around the hall, half-expecting to find Mrs. Ollerton in her nightdress, watching us with shock and disapproval. "We ought to hurry," I whispered, starting in the direction of the drawing room.

Mr. Hill followed in silence, his footsteps nearly as quiet as my own as we made our way down the dark hall.

"Did you hear that?" Mr. Hill whispered, a hint of panic in his voice.

I stopped, my heart thudding. I strained my ears, but

all I could hear was my own pulse and the rush of air exiting my lungs. "No." I whirled to face him, eyes wide. "What is it?"

His lips twitched, betraying an amused smile. "Nothing."

My jaw dropped. The *incorrigible* tease. He had no mercy for my anxiety over this entire situation—replacing the missing pendant, being here at Winslow house at all, and especially being alone with him in an empty hallway after midnight.

He chuckled, his eyes dancing in the candlelight.

I scowled. "You know, I could set fire to your shirt right now, Mr. Hill." I held up my candle, letting it hover dangerously close to his blasted collar. "If you dare test my nerves again." I was only half-jesting, but he seemed to take it as a full jest.

"If you did, I would have to remove it, and I daresay our situation would be far more improper than it already is." He raised one eyebrow, as if to reprimand me for suggesting such a thing.

I managed to control my blush for once, trying not to dwell on the image he had just placed in my mind. "Why must you take such pleasure in my discomfort?"

"It seems it is *you* who takes pleasure in *my* discomfort, wishing my shirt to be set on fire." He laughed under his breath. "That would not be comfortable in the slightest."

My smile escaped its confines before I could stop it, and I shook my head. "You are ridiculous. Do you not recognize the danger in what we are doing?"

He leaned closer, both eyebrows raised. "It was not dangerous until you threatened me."

There was a different sort of danger that he seemed unaware of. The danger that was the flame that flickered in my chest, urging my heart to feel things it certainly was not allowed to feel. It was a different kind of fire—the sort that could not be stamped out or smothered or drowned. It was forbidden and disobedient, spreading and catching in my chest with each playful smile Mr. Hill cast in my direction.

"It has been dangerous all along."

His eyes met mine with a question, but I refused to answer, pressing my lips together. What exactly had I meant by that? The words had slipped out, unbidden. In truth, I had been in danger since the moment I walked into Winslow House. But my heart had been more in danger than anything of late. I banished my thoughts. Acknowledging it did not make the matter any better.

"Did you hear that?" I asked, craning my neck toward the staircase. What had sounded like footfalls had been clear just a moment before. My heart thudded too loudly to hear it again.

Mr. Hill chuckled, adding to the excess noise.

Another sound came from down the hall, then another, each growing louder and more frequent, as if someone were walking toward us.

But Mr. Hill didn't seem to hear any of it. "If you are going to start teasing me, be unique at the very least."

Panic seized my limbs, and I reached for his arm, tugging him toward the drawing room door. My own strength surprised me, and he stumbled, his feet making a loud thud against the marble floor.

I pulled the door open and thankfully didn't have to grab him again. He followed me inside, and I reached around him to close the door.

"What the devil—"

"Hush!" I held a finger to my lips, taking a step back when I realized how closely I stood to him. He finally obeyed, his eyes rounding slightly as he heard what I had— the footfalls coming even closer from outside the door.

"Drat," I whispered under my breath. "Drat, drat, drat." I searched the room for a place to hide, my mind racing. Whoever it was in the hallway seemed to be heading in our direction. Dread sank through my stomach, and my legs shook.

Mr. Hill sprung into action, taking me by the wrist and pulling me toward the red sofa, hardly recognizable in the darkness. He blew out his candle first, then mine, squatting down in the space between the window and the back of the sofa. I followed suit, the drapes brushing against my back as I settled on the ground beside Mr. Hill. He reached around me, taking hold of the drapes to stop the swaying I had caused. I pulled at my skirts, making sure they were not showing on the other side of the sofa, and to my dismay, he looped his arm around my waist, tucking me in closer against him.

I ignored the effect his touch had on me, directing my focus back to the anxiety I felt. I waited, holding my breath as the footsteps grew closer and the door unlatched. The hinges gave a slight creak, and I ducked, even though I knew my head wasn't showing above the sofa. Mr. Hill did the same, his eyes just inches from my own. Was he smiling? I checked the curve of his lips, my suspicions confirmed. What on earth was he smiling about? His exhale rustled my hair, and I pretended not to notice the thrill it sent over my skin. There were far more pressing matters at hand, like the two quiet voices that carried through the room.

"I cannot sleep knowing it is still missing." It was Mrs. Ollerton, the distressed tone less masked than it had been that evening. Her skirts rustled as she walked, the sound growing closer. "Look. It has been gone since I returned home this afternoon. Who do you suppose might have taken it?"

"I assure you, the entire household staff is most trustworthy." I recognized the nasally voice of the housekeeper. I could envision her dark hair with the streaks of silver and her high cheekbones, made more gaunt and hollow by the candlelight that now filled the room. Mr. Hill's arm tightened around me, a warning in his eyes. I glanced to my other side, my heart leaping when I saw the hem of Mrs. Ollerton's dress. When had she moved so close? I didn't dare move a muscle, tipping my head down and squeezing my eyes shut. Mr. Hill inched toward the other end of the sofa, keeping his arm around my waist. With careful movements, I followed, any rustling drowned out by Mrs. Ollerton's voice. I released the breath I had been holding, careful not to make a sound.

"I do trust them all. You are right." Mrs. Ollerton's voice came from above. If she took another step, she would see us for certain. A distressed sigh escaped her. "And I should hate to accuse any of my guests."

"Miss Sedgwick's maid…the one she brought along with her….she's been giving herself airs of late." The housekeeper's voice was quiet, heavy with accusation. "She thinks she can do whatever she likes since she injured her leg."

"Are you suggesting it was Miss Sedgwick's maid who took the necklace?"

A surge of anger rose in my chest, and I nearly stood to defend Jessie. My heart pounded against my ribs as if trying to escape, and I had to force myself to remain still and silent.

"I think her innocence should be questioned, yes. I will not directly accuse her, but she should not be brushed aside without scrutiny."

"Nor should Miss Sedgwick, herself, I daresay." Mrs. Ollerton's voice was distant, and my stomach sank. Had Miss Downsfield planted that idea in her mind? My blood boiled, and dread continued its course throughout my veins. I felt Mr. Hill grow tense beside me.

Though I was closer to the other side of the sofa, I still didn't feel safe. All it would take would be one sound, one extra step from Mrs. Ollerton and we would be caught. Mr. Hill's words burned in my mind. *I suppose you would have to marry me.*

He was just the sort of honorable man who *would* marry me if my reputation was at stake, or at least if I were *actually* Miss Sedgwick. There was no telling how far his honor went. Would he do the same if he knew who I really was? If he knew I had been lying about it and befriending him with the hope he could free my father? I took each breath silently, careful not to focus on the feeling of his hand around my waist, and the way his body pressed against my side and his breath rustled my hair against my forehead. I glanced up to meet his gaze. His eyes burned with anger, and for a moment I thought he would stand and defend *me*, just as I had been tempted to do for Jessie.

"There is simply something odd about Miss Sedgwick," Mrs. Ollerton continued. "She is not nearly as elegant and pretty as her mother's letters suggested."

"A mother is likely to exaggerate her daughter's virtues."

"I suppose." Mrs. Ollerton paused. "But I still do find her strange. And stranger yet, Mr. Hill's decision to court her."

The familiar sinking sensation started in my chest, reminding me just how far I was from truly being like Sophia. She had been a fool to think I could have ever portrayed her accurately.

Mr. Hill leaned impossibly close, making my shoulders tense. His voice was so soft—quieter than Mrs. Ollerton's footfalls as she paced away from our hiding place—barely more than a breath. "And stranger yet, the fact that the two subjects of her conversation are listening to every word she is speaking." His lips grazed my ear, and heat flooded my cheeks. I could hear the smile in his whisper, and I would have smiled too if I were able. Instead, I scolded my heart for leaping.

He replaced the distance between us—if just a few inches could be called *distance*—leaning his head against the back of the sofa once more. My smile finally came, but it was weak, and his eyes were too warm and mischievous as he studied my face, as if awaiting my reply. If he thought I would whisper in his ear in the same manner, he was mistaken.

I clamped my lips shut, relieved to hear Mrs. Ollerton's voice growing more distant as she crossed the room.

"We shall search Miss Sedgwick's room tomorrow," the housekeeper said. "Simply to rule out the possibility."

"And her maid?"

"Her room will be searched as well."

The latch clicked on the door, and their conversation faded into the hallway, as well as the light from their candles. The room filled with darkness once again, our place by the window drenched in silvery moonlight. The moment they were gone, the hammering of my heart became more evident, and I willed myself to relax. The relief that flooded my chest caused a quiet laugh to escape me, and soon Mr. Hill was chuckling too. I felt the vibration of his laugh against me. He was still holding me close, his smiling eyes still staring into mine, just inches away. I had never been so loath to leave the floor.

"You're lucky you had the foresight to return the necklace tonight," Mr. Hill said, his voice hoarse and quiet from lack of use. He did not seem any more inclined that I was to leave our place between the window and the sofa. Laughter still punctuated his words, and I couldn't help but join in.

Another giggle burst from my lips, and I put a hand to my forehead. "Do I have an air of suspicion about me? Why is it Mrs. Ollerton would think me a thief?"

"You *did* manage to steal me."

I laughed. "Ah, yes, the most treasured prize of all."

"It was far past time you realized that." A wink accompanied the words, his smile growing wider and even more infectious.

I scoffed, shaking my head, though my laughter betrayed my amusement. "One cannot steal something that is willingly given, or rather…forced upon them." I raised one eyebrow. "I made no effort. You came to me willingly, as I was the only one *not* attempting to steal you."

He laughed, his gaze softening as he searched my face. My own laughter faded at that look, a deep, penetrating flutter starting in my chest and spreading through my stomach. I knew his eyes were blue, but in the dim light, they appeared grey. For a moment, I had forgotten that it was past midnight and we were sitting most improperly on the floor, hidden and risking my reputation as well as Sophia's. I had forgotten about the pendant digging into my palm. I had forgotten our courtship was false.

I had forgotten that I wasn't supposed to feel anything for him.

I recognized the flutter in my chest as longing, and it seemed to be encouraged by my acknowledgement. The flutter surged, sparking a flame in my chest as I glanced at Mr. Hill's smiling lips.

"Since we have now established you are not indeed a thief," he began, "we are forced to face the truth that I am one."

I met his eyes, my heart leaping when his gaze flickered down to my mouth and back again. "Are you?" I choked. "Was it you who stole the pendant in order to frame me?" I spoke in an effort to tame that wild thing in my chest, but it pounded harder than before.

"No, but I would have, had I known it would lead to this." His voice carried an edge of mischief, but I lacked the strength to scold him for it. What did he mean by *this*? Was it our hiding place? His arm around me? Each time he glanced at my lips my breathing stalled.

I maintained a confused expression. "Surely the other ladies didn't intend for it to lead to this," I said in a hoarse whisper. I tried to cast him a look of reprimand, but his smile distracted me.

He leaned his head closer, all traces of his laughter gone. My heart still pounded, no matter how much I told it to slow down. "May I steal something from you, Miss Sedgwick?" he asked in a murmur. He seemed just as unaware of our improper situation as I was becoming. Or perhaps he simply didn't care anymore.

"That will depend on what it is." I swallowed, careful not to glance at his grinning lips. He may have been teasing me, but I had never felt more serious in my life. More trapped or vulnerable or safe. I looked up at his eyes, and

Mrs. Ollerton's choice of words flashed through my mind. *Passion.*

My head swam.

"A kiss."

I closed my eyes for a moment, trying to calm the rate of my pulse and the shaking in my hands.

"If it is willingly given, I shouldn't have to steal it at all," he said. The note of teasing still carried in his voice, but it was different now, more uncertain. His eyes found mine in the dark, as if asking for permission.

If he kissed me now, it would be willingly given—far too willingly to ever earn him the title of thief. His lips were just a breath away. If I shifted on my hip, I would be close enough to kiss him. I fought against the pull in my chest, the desire that still burned there. He didn't realize what he was asking for. He didn't recognize the consequences. It might have been a game to him, but it was far more than that to me.

"I do not give up kisses easily," I said in a quick voice, turning my face away.

He was silent for a long moment. "Nor truth, nor smiles," he finally said, letting out a deep sigh that rustled unjustly against my hair again. His arm slipped away from my waist, and he stood, offering his hand as I followed. My legs prickled from being in the cramped space. He smiled down at me. "Although I did manage to earn both in due time."

Did he think he would eventually convince me to kiss him? Annoyance and frustration surged. "You wouldn't actually kiss me." I said, my voice less confident than I intended. "You simply enjoy teasing me." Surely he had only meant to taunt me with his suggestion, to catch sight of the blush on my cheeks which he found so entertaining. Our courtship was false. Our feelings were *false*. The more I told myself, however, the less I believed it.

He chuckled under his breath, tipping his head to one side. "I do enjoy teasing you. But I daresay I would enjoy kissing you more."

He was unbelievable. *Incorrigible.* "Well, you will never know which you prefer, because you shall never experience the latter." I rushed past him, feeling once again how I had when I had first arrived at Winslow House, unsure of his intentions and afraid that they didn't match my own. I hurried toward the bust, eager to replace the necklace and return to my bedchamber in solitude.

I sensed Mr. Hill behind me, and I took a deep breath before turning around. "Let us replace the necklace before Mrs. Ollerton comes back."

He nodded his agreement before moving a step closer. While his expression had been filled with teasing before, it was now serious as I slid my glove down and pulled the necklace out. Concentration marked his brow as he took the necklace from my outstretched hand, his fingers brushing mine. He replaced the pendant on the bust, centering it just as it had been before.

"We shall call this a successful mission." His gaze found mine, and my heart gave another wayward leap.

"We haven't made it back safely yet."

"We will." He smiled, and my shoulders relaxed. "We have made it this far. It would be unfair to be caught now."

Unfair. The word stuck in my mind as we sneaked back into the hallway. Our paths parted where the hall divided between the direction to his bedchamber and mine.

"Goodnight, Miss Sedgwick." He backed away with a smile, and my heart told me what I already knew. Despite all I had done to avoid it, I had fallen in love with him.

"Goodnight." My voice was just a choked whisper, one I wasn't even certain he heard before I turned and walked away. I felt his gaze on my back as I went, but I refused to look behind me until a door separated us.

When I was finally safe, I leaned against the wall in my room, pressing a hand against my chest. I had been a fool to come so close to Mr. Hill. My original tactic had been the best, no matter how difficult it had been to avoid him. I could no longer continue spending time with him if I hoped to keep my secret. For his sake, I would allow the guests to believe he still favored me, but I would force myself to believe that I did not feel anything for him. Nothing real. He had already written to his uncle, and I knew him well enough to know he wouldn't abandon the effort to free Papa if I asked him to try. He was too honorable and kind.

My heart ached as I renewed my determination to put a bit of distance between us. As difficult as it would be, the next three weeks would be much harder if I didn't.

And leaving Winslow House at the end would be the hardest thing of all.

CHAPTER 21

My efforts to avoid Mr. Hill were less obvious than my past efforts to flirt with him and imitate Miss Downsfield. I was subtle, careful, and sneaky. Although he invited me for a ride each morning, I made sure to speak less and ride faster, so as to avoid any flirting and teasing which might have occurred. I invited a chaperone each time as well, as there was nothing that hindered flirtation like Mrs. Ollerton on our heels. We couldn't speak of private matters, and we couldn't be improper in the slightest.

Mr. Hill was not a fool—he recognized the change in me—but I never gave him the opportunity to question it. Thankfully, Mrs. Ollerton had several activities planned for the last fortnight of our stay, and I made sure to engage one of the ladies in conversation on each group outing, and Mr. Hill's arm was always eagerly claimed by someone else.

I had written out the days on a sheet of foolscap in my

room, penciling an X through each day that passed, bringing me closer to the end of my charade. I had thought my distance from Mr. Hill would make me care for him less, but the effect was the opposite of what I had intended. I missed him. And I hadn't laughed since the night we sneaked the necklace back to the drawing room. Mrs. Ollerton had been shocked the next morning to find it returned to its proper place, and had attributed the entire ordeal to a miracle.

Mrs. Ollerton, much like all the other ladies, seemed to have noticed the distance I was putting between myself and Mr. Hill. It made them all much more civil toward me. Even as hard as I tried not to feel it, guilt pooled in my stomach at the confusion on Mr. Hill's face each time I turned away from him or avoided his gaze. During the more idle times of each day, I moved from place to place within the house, making my way secretly down to Jessie's room where he could not find me.

All of my efforts would have to be stopped eventually though, when I gathered the courage to ask about his uncle and my father. But by then I would be closer to my departure and I would never have to see him again. The pain would lessen, this entire month would become a memory, and I would return to Sedgwick Manor without having failed completely. And with luck, Papa might be free. There was no cost too great for that. Not even my heart. Not even Mr. Hill's.

Tears burned behind my eyes as I walked up the stairs from Jessie's room. I blinked them away, listening to the quiet prattle drifting through the air from the sitting room. In the last week, I had formed the habit of tucking myself away in the farthest corner of the library most afternoons. From the doorway, I couldn't be seen in my hiding place.

The tricky part was getting there without being caught, but I was well-practiced.

With quick steps, I hurried past the partially open door of the sitting room, holding my skirts up to avoid excess rustling against the floor. When I was out of sight, I slowed my steps, trying to envision the shelves and which book I would select from among the many I had already finished.

When I opened the library door, I stopped, my legs rigid.

"Oh, forgive me, Mr. Hill," I stammered when he glanced up at me from the table at the center of the room. Afternoon light filled the library, and my favorite place to read was tucked in a ray of sun near the window, tucked behind the farthest shelf. I couldn't simply go to it now. A second ray of sunlight fell upon Mr. Hill's broad shoulders, bringing out lighter tones in his hair and eyes.

"So this is where you have been disappearing every afternoon, is it?" He set down the book he had been holding, coming to his feet.

"Most afternoons." I shifted awkwardly, pressing my lips together. We had hardly spoken since the night we sneaked through the house, and it showed in the hurt that shone behind his eyes. Didn't he see it was for the best? His convictions about marriage might have been just that: convictions. He could change them if he wished, but I couldn't do anything about the fact that I was a maid in disguise. He would never want to be near me again once he knew. The feelings that swirled around my heart reminded me just how wise I had been in avoiding him during the past week. And how *unwise* it was to be with him now.

"I will leave you to it, Mr. Hill." I offered a curtsy, backing away two steps before turning around.

I heard the scrape of his chair across the floor. "Stop. Please." His exhale sounded like an exasperated sigh. "Where are you going?"

I paused, turning toward him slowly. In truth, I didn't know where I had been going, simply that it was away from him. Words refused to come, so I stood there like a child who had been caught sneaking dough from the kitchen.

"Come, sit down." He motioned at the chair across the table, his voice something of a grumble. I hadn't known just how upset my absence would make him. "Perhaps you might explain why you have a sudden fascination with the library." He raised one eyebrow. It wasn't as playful as usual, as if he were attempting but failing to tease me through the true frustration he was feeling.

I swallowed. Why had I thought he wouldn't notice? He always did. I crossed the room and sat in the chair he had selected for me. "I have always been fascinated by the library," I said.

He eyed me with deep curiosity. "You are keeping the truth from me again. There is a reason you have been avoiding me, is there not?"

With his blue eyes boring into mine, I could hardly

think up a lie that he might believe, and I certainly couldn't deliver it in a plausible way. After several seconds of silence, the tension in my shoulders relaxed. I couldn't tell him the entire truth, but I could tell him part of it. My stomach twisted, but I managed to nod my head. "Yes."

He sat back in his chair, crossing his arms in front of him. I couldn't look away from the hurt in his eyes. It shouldn't have captivated me, but it did. Had he missed me as much as I had missed him?

"Why?"

There. The dreaded question. I searched my brain for a way to explain myself, but could think of nothing that wouldn't reveal my true feelings or my secret. "I—er—I was worried."

His eyebrows lifted. "Worried?"

"Concerned."

"That is essentially what worried means."

"You asked for clarification," I said, my voice too defensive.

A smile flickered on his lips. "On your reasoning, not on the definition of the word."

I sighed, resuming my search for a good explanation. There would be no way to avoid embarrassing myself. Heat was already creeping up my neck. "I was worried that..." That our courtship was becoming real? That he might have truly cared for me? There was no way to phrase it correctly.

"That I would try to kiss you again?"

My heart leaped, and my cheeks burned hotter. "Well, yes, I suppose." That was certainly part of it, but not all of it. I tried to read his expression, but was afraid of what I might find. Had he felt the things I had that night in the drawing room? Did he feel what I felt now? What had become far too real to me might have still been entirely pretend to him. A kiss to him surely meant much less than it would to me. It might be pleasurable, diverting, sensational, even, but it would not leave his heart in complete disrepair like it would leave mine.

"Agreeing to not kiss you…" He gave a half smile, "that is a price I am willing to pay in exchange for your company." He looked down at the table. "I have missed it."

A thread of warmth pulled through my heart, and I tried to focus on the puncture of the needle instead: the pain, not the joy. "I-I think it may be best if we interact only when necessary." My heart ached with the words, but they had to be said. "You should not desire my company," I said in a quiet voice.

He met my eyes. "You may deny me anything I want, Miss Sedgwick, and I will concede. But that cannot stop me from wanting it."

I felt tied to my chair, to his gaze, to the implications in his words. If I hadn't turned him away, would he have kissed me that night? If I hadn't told him how I never wished to marry, would he have abandoned his own convictions and proposed? I shushed my thoughts, willing my heart to slow. It didn't matter. Even if it were true, it didn't change the fact that I had to keep denying him what he wanted. Even if what he wanted was me.

My stomach tugged at the idea; a surge of longing filled

my heart. I searched for a distraction, my thoughts traveling back to one of our previous conversations.

"You said your parents denied you your dearest wish," I said in a careful voice. "And that is why you defy their wishes to see you married. What was it they denied you?" I had lacked the confidence to ask him before, but now I needed to know. I held my breath as he studied my face.

"Are *you* demanding the truth from *me* now?" he asked.

Relief bounded through my chest at the light tone in his voice. I was much more comfortable with this. "We may call it an exchange."

He drew a deep breath before exhaling, long and slow. "It is not a pleasant story. And you might think badly of me when you hear it."

"Everybody has such stories to tell." I wrung my hands together. I had my fair share.

He shifted in his chair, the discomfort obvious in his features. "It will help you understand more fully why I cannot offer my hand to any of the ladies here, and why I never intended to raise their hopes." He paused, as if collecting his thoughts. His eyes met mine. "I am not inheriting Hill Manor."

Shock collided with my chest. "You were disinherited?"

He shook his head. "It is far more complicated than that."

I waited, watching the signs of unrest in his expression with growing dismay.

"I have an older brother, one who only recently returned home from Spain. My parents haven't yet announced his return, and have been keeping the secret since just weeks before my invitation came from Winslow House." He glanced up at my face, tracing his finger over the table as he spoke. "All my life I was raised to believe I would not inherit my childhood home. It was the reality I was resigned to, and I tried not to envy my brother his prize. He never loved the home like I did. He never even wanted it. He lived in a manner that disappointed my parents greatly. He was frivolous and daft, choosing to leave it all behind for a life in another country, as far away from his family and their upbringing as he could manage to live. His abandonment was a devastation and a disgrace, and so my father was able to disinherit him and leave the house to me. My belief, and the belief of everyone in town for the last five years has been that I would inherit Hill Manor." He followed the lines his fingers had drawn on the table, silent for a long moment.

"What happened?"

"My brother returned, penniless and rueful, begging for all that he had left behind. Trust, love, respect...and Hill Manor. His wishes were granted without hesitation, and after all I had done to maintain my parents' trust and respect, learning to manage the household and the farms, I was left without it."

My jaw fell open, and I touched a hand to my chest. "You were left with nothing?"

"A small property in Sussex as consolation. It has not been occupied for years, and for good reason." He gave a small smile. "And so, when I leave Winslow House, I will travel there to make my best attempt at reviving it." He met my gaze. "I am not the prize Mrs. Ollerton believes me to be. In fact, there is little to prize in my character as well. My ambitions of vexing my parents by remaining a bachelor for all of my days, of disappointing them as they did me..." He shook his head, his smile resurfacing. "It sounds worse when I say it aloud. There is no reward, is there? It will not bring me Hill Manor. All it will bring is loneliness and regret."

My heart pounded at his words, at the way he looked at me when he spoke them—as if he intended to have no regrets at all, especially when it pertained to me.

"And you, Miss Sedgwick?" His eyes searched my face. "Have you reconsidered the worth of your defiance toward your own parents?" Although his voice was light, he spoke with genuine curiosity.

If the story I had told him before had been true—that I was simply defying my parents wishes to have me married —then I would have abandoned it in an instant. But instead, my livelihood and my family depended on a different answer.

"No," I said in a whisper. I cleared my throat, looking down at the table. "I am still quite determined."

I counted to five in my mind before looking up. My intention was to hold my head with confidence, but the moment I saw Mr. Hill's expression, all my confidence fled. He looked...disappointed.

"That is a shame." He gave me a soft smile before standing, taking his book with him as he moved toward the door. I stared straight ahead, listening to his retreating footfalls and watching his empty chair.

My heart lurched, begging me to tell him my secret—to explain that my circumstances were the only thing denying my wishes. And just because I could not have him didn't mean I didn't want him.

Instead, I made my way to my hidden place by the window.

CHAPTER 22

*M*y habit of arising before the sun had persisted through my entire stay at Winslow House, so when Mrs. Ollerton planned a bit of bird watching for the next morning, it wasn't out of the ordinary for me to be awake at such an hour. The other ladies, after offering a few complaints, had agreed to join us. Nervousness twisted in my stomach, but I pushed it away. I couldn't be afraid to face Mr. Hill. I still had a week remaining at Winslow House.

When I reached the drawing room, he was already there, trapped between Miss Taplow and Miss Downsfield, who seemed to be taking advantage of my absence as they likely had been all week. It seemed they still hoped he would choose one of them instead. Would they have been so eager to be near him if they knew what I knew? The story he had told me of his brother had refused to leave my mind. He had been hiding something too. Would he understand if I told him what I had been hiding? Would he keep my secret?

I looked down at my hands, realizing that I had forgotten my gloves. Drat. My mind had been quite scattered of late. The room was filled with candlelight, and I was reminded once again of the night Mr. Hill and I had hidden behind the sofa. My gaze took in his blue waistcoat and dark top hat, the polite way he smiled down at the ladies. If he truly had reconsidered his choice not to marry, perhaps he would choose one of the other ladies by the end of the week. I ignored the rush of envy to my heart, focusing instead on the other four guests. If I were to choose just one of them to marry him, it would have to be Miss Coppins. She would entertain him far more than even I did, and overall, she still seemed to have the kindest disposition.

Lost in my thoughts, I hadn't noticed Mrs. Ollerton enter the room. She wore a headdress covered in feathers for the occasion, a gleam of excitement in her eyes.

When the group was all gathered, we headed outside into the crisp morning air. I stayed close by Mrs. Ollerton's side, who led the group across the property. Just enough light seeped through the sky to illuminate our path, though it was still too dim to see far into the distance.

"This excursion was inspired by a song I heard from my window just yesterday," Mrs. Ollerton called over her shoulder. "I do not usually arise so early, but I was having difficulty sleeping that day." She continued on describing the events of that morning for several minutes as we walked through the gardens toward the trees, where most of the birdsong came from. I had learned that birds liked sitting high in the trees when they sang, as if they knew their voices would reach the farthest from there.

"So," Mrs. Ollerton continued, "Our objective today is to find the bird, or species of bird, whose song I heard. I should dearly like to hear it again. Stay close, but we may all spread out throughout the trees in search of it."

"Shall we make it a competition?" Miss Benham asked.

Mrs. Ollerton raised one eyebrow. "Of what sort?"

Miss Benham's smile grew, her eyes slightly less vibrant than usual, as if she were still half asleep. She yawned, covering her mouth with one gloved hand. "Perhaps the first lady to discover your favorite bird…will win an outing with Mr. Hill." She smiled coyly, glancing his way. "Would you agree to that plan, Mr. Hill?"

He seemed to have still been trying to maintain his partiality to me, but I had not been helping him convince the group. It appeared Miss Benham still assumed she had a chance to compete. I glanced at his face, and he met my eyes before looking away.

Mr. Hill would have likely refused her idea, but before he could, Mrs. Ollerton gasped with delight. "That is a wonderful idea, Miss Benham. I don't believe Mr. Hill would object to a bit of diversion this morning, nor would he object to an outing with any of you lovely young ladies, would you Mr. Hill?"

It seemed Miss Benham wasn't the only one he would have to convince of his partiality to me. Mrs. Ollerton still seemed to be holding out hope that he would form an attachment to one of her other guests, perhaps one prettier or more accomplished than I was. She had only a week to ensure it happened.

I glanced up at Mr. Hill, who looked vastly uncomfortable. "I could never object, Mrs. Ollerton." He gave a smile, but I could tell it was forced.

"Oh, how exciting." She clasped her hands together, surveying the area with her nose in the air, her fluffy, pale curls spilling out of her hat. "Now, we must make haste. As soon as the sun fully rises, the cacophony of beautiful birdsong begins to diminish."

"What bird are we in search of?" Miss Taplow asked, suddenly far more eager about the activity than she had been before.

Now there was a prize.

Mrs. Ollerton continued scanning the skies, closing her eyes for a long moment. "He was small, with dark wings, and his song sounded something like this." She cupped her hands around her mouth, letting out a loud noise that sounded much like the words, *lurkey, lurkey.*

I pressed my lips together to contain my smile when Mr. Hill's eyes met mine with a look of dismay. I scolded myself. I was not supposed to be smiling at him.

"As soon as you hear a similar sound, call for me and I will see if it is my bird." Mrs. Ollerton grinned. "Are there any questions?"

I shook my head, and Mrs. Ollerton glanced my way before looking up at Mr. Hill. "Should our bachelor find the bird before any of you do, then he will have his choice of who he would like to take on an outing."

All eyes fell on me in unison, and I shifted uncomfortably. I had never been the one everyone sought to outperform—the one whose every move was watched for a sign of weakness that could be exploited. I had always been the one in the far corner of the room, unnoticed, disregarded as someone who could easily be defeated if given the chance. The change of role was unsettling.

On the count of three, Mrs. Ollerton sent all of us toward the trees. She followed at a slow pace, clapping her hands together in an attempt to hurry us along. I moved ahead of Mr. Hill, following in Miss Coppins's trail, stopping only once I came behind a broad tree trunk. Under the cover of the leaves, the world felt even more still, despite the hurried footfalls of all the ladies over the twigs and leaves on the ground. I listened closely. There were at least three different birds singing above me, all with different melodies and articulations. I tried to turn the sounds into human speech as Mrs. Ollerton had done, and I caught one call that sounded like *teacher, teacher.* And another that could not be assimilated to words, but that was deeper than all the others, a trill that made me imagine a larger bird. And the wren—I recognized his tune. He was the smallest bird, but had the biggest voice.

Of course, I wasn't actually trying to win. I was trying to get as far from Mr. Hill as possible.

I walked farther into the trees, away from the places I knew the other ladies to be standing still, listening. A set of heavy boots became louder on the ground, and I glanced back to see Mr. Hill watching me.

"I didn't think you were a competitive sort." One eyebrow quirked upward, almost indiscernible in the dimness. "Especially when it comes to spending time with me."

A pang of guilt struck me, and by his knowing smile, I could see he had intended it.

"You should be listening too." I glanced up as the leaves rustled. It was the wren again. "If you don't find the bird first, then one of the others will, and you heard the consequences of that. It would ruin your plan to not give any of them false hope."

"I already know which bird Mrs. Ollerton speaks of," he said with a nonchalant flick of his hand. "The blackbird is the only one I have known to say the words, *lurkey, lurkey*. I heard it outside my window this morning."

I stared at him with disbelief. "When do you plan to tell her?"

"As soon as I am finished thoroughly enjoying this peaceful morning with you. Next time we are together we are sure to have Mrs. Ollerton following closely behind."

"Well, she is still somewhere nearby." I glanced behind me, surprised to find the area empty. I hadn't realized how far into the woods we had walked.

"Not near enough, I suspect," he said with a chuckle.

Near enough for what? My heart hammered, and I shushed it. He leaned one shoulder against a nearby tree before pushing away, crossing the ground that separated us.

He stopped when he reached my side, following my gaze to the tree above us. "I have often wondered what madness caused Mrs. Ollerton to concoct an idea like this match-making party." His voice had taken on a serious tone, one that was more inquisitive than flirtatious. I let my shoulders relax, though my heart still pounded.

"To a dishonorable man, this situation would be very dangerous," Mr. Hill continued. "To have five ladies fighting for a moment with him, which he would be ever-willing to give."

"But you are not a dishonorable man," I said, surprised by the steadiness of my voice. Glancing up at his face made me realize just how close he was standing. In the quiet of the morning, the cacophony of the birdsong seemed to disappear, and all I could hear were Mr. Hill's steady inhales and exhales, and the beat of my own pulse as it passed my ears. He met my gaze, and the dim morning light left his features soft and blurred, not as easy to distinguish. His eyes appeared more grey, and his lips smiled softly.

"What would you consider a dishonorable man to be?" he asked. "What do you suppose a dishonorable man might do at this very moment?" The teasing in his voice was unmistakable, but there also a hint of genuine curiosity.

I took a step back, then another, until my back made contact with that large tree trunk I had passed. Mr. Hill did not allow me the space I had created, walking with two large strides until he stood in front of me, even closer than before. "I, well—I suppose a dishonorable man would likely lie to Mrs. Ollerton about finding her bird. He might continue speaking too loud so that the lady in his company cannot have her chance at finding it herself." I gave him a pointed look. I kept my voice even and calm, though my heart raced. I wasn't afraid of Mr. Hill—but only afraid of the things he made me feel. No man had ever had this much of an effect on me, and it was unfamiliar and breathtaking. *Breathtaking.*

I remembered to breathe, taking two handfuls of the fabric of my skirts to steady myself.

Mr. Hill's smile grew, and he glanced upward at the trees. The air grew still for a short moment, but all I could hear was the wren and the other bird, the one that did not sound anything like the blackbird.

"It doesn't matter how loudly I speak," Mr. Hill's voice cut in. "I already told you which bird Mrs. Ollerton is searching for." His voice seemed to be intentionally loud.

I scowled at him, pressing a finger to my lips as I gazed up at the trees. "Hush! I want to hear it."

When I met his eyes again, my heart gave an alarming leap. His smile had grown again, but it was more uncertain. And in the moment I had been looking away, his gaze had lowered to my lips.

"A dishonorable man might take this as the opportunity he had been waiting for." His gaze danced between my eyes and my lips, lingering just a moment longer on the latter. The birds had stopped singing. The wind had stopped. The leaves no longer rustled. The entire world held its breath as Mr. Hill leaned closer with his smiling lips. My breath refused to come too, stranded somewhere between my throat and my lungs. I swallowed, letting a breath of air fill my chest, but it only seemed to draw him closer. He pressed his hand against the tree behind me, just above my shoulder. This opportunity he spoke of…it could only involve kissing. He could tease me all he wanted, but I didn't know how to spar with him when what he was suggesting was so…unfair. He knew I wanted to kiss him. It showed in his devilish smile.

I found my voice. With the way he was standing, trapping me between himself and the tree…my guess could not be too unreasonable. "An opportunity to…abduct me?"

Mr. Hill laughed under his breath, leaning back slightly. I relaxed, but it was brief. "Guess again."

I glanced at his lips; I couldn't help it. I looked away as fast as I could, focusing on his eyes, but the effect of his gaze on mine was not any better. It was as if he could see my secrets—all of them, swimming far too close to the surface. If I wasn't careful, I would tell him everything. And I would probably kiss him first.

I pressed my hands against the tree trunk behind me, focusing on the feeling of the mottled bark against my palms rather than the turmoil inside my chest.

Guess again. If Mr. Hill thought I was a simpleton, he was mistaken. I knew what he implied, but I didn't want to say the words out loud.

He kicked a twig near his boot. "I have been thinking

about our conversation yesterday, and I found I had an unanswered question."

I froze, trying to appear nonchalant.

"If your feelings for me are not real...what then would be the purpose of avoiding me?" His smile had faded. "If what you feel for me is nothing more than friendship, then there would be no risk in spending time with me."

The rough bark scratched between my shoulder blades. I had no where to go. I should have known he would read me so easily. When would I learn to hide my feelings from my face? He had likely known all along how much I cared for him. I struggled to breathe, and my voice came out weak. "Do you really think I would be so stubborn?"

"Yes, and it drives me mad."

"You are just as stubborn." I scowled. "You will not even give the other ladies a chance to impress you because you wish to remain a bachelor for all of your days."

"They would have never impressed me." He shook his head, his voice growing softer. "Not with you here."

He leaned closer. I recognized the look in his eyes as clearly as it burned inside me. Longing. Real, raw, and unguarded emotion.

"You wouldn't dare kiss me," I blurted.

"Wouldn't I?" He seemed to take my words as a challenge, so I hurried to correct them.

"I might mistaken your intentions. An honorable man wouldn't steal kisses from a woman he doesn't intend to marry."

Mr. Hill's expression shifted, his eyes becoming more

serious, searching mine with a new intensity. "Perhaps I do hope to marry you."

"You don't."

"I do." His hand moved from the tree trunk to the back of my neck, his fingers curving into my hair. He tipped his head down, and his other hand touched my face. I couldn't breathe. "And I would ask you, if I didn't already know your answer. I suspect you have been avoiding me because you feel your determination never to marry is at risk. If I asked you...you might hesitate to refuse me."

What was my answer? I could think of nothing but the way he cradled my face between his hands. I could feel nothing but longing, fierce, deep longing, far more than a desire to kiss him. I *did* want to marry him. I wanted to laugh with him and see his charming smile for the rest of my life. I wanted him to tell me over and over that I was good enough. That Tillie Sherbrooke was good enough.

"Tell me you have changed your mind," he said. "Tell me if you ever will. I have changed mine." His thumb traced over my cheekbone, and the intensity of his gaze softened. "*You* have changed mine. I asked three weeks of you, but now I am asking for much longer than that. I know I cannot offer you Hill Manor, and I know how much you loved it there, but I offer you my heart and my love and a comfortable future that I will work hard to provide. I understand if that is not enough, but I offer it nonetheless."

Before I could stop myself I shook my head. It was more than enough. It was more than I had ever dared to dream of. Tears stung my eyes. When had my heart taken control of the reins? What had been my first mistake? I couldn't trace it back to a specific moment, but a slow weakening of my resolve—little by little. Mr. Hill had taken my heart piece by piece, and there it was now, reflecting back at me from his eyes. How had I missed it? Why hadn't I been more careful? It was just like the day I had chosen to read my book in the alcove. I should have known Papa's temper, that he would have confronted Mr. Baker about his unkindness to me then. Those little mistakes had led to me losing Papa, just like my little mistakes with Mr. Hill had led to me losing my heart.

"You do not want to marry me," I whispered again, shaking my head against his hands.

"Yes, I do." His voice was firmer now, more determined. "You cannot tell me what I want and what I don't. I want you. I have never been more certain of anything. This courtship has never been false to me. Not really. The moment it began I regretted ever starting. You made me too blasted happy to ever consider sending you back home." He took my chin between his thumb and forefinger when I looked away, bringing my gaze back to his. "I will admit how very wrong I was, thinking I couldn't fall in love, or that I didn't want to. I stand here with no pride, and with nothing to prove besides how much I am willing to try to change your mind."

My stomach flipped at his words, and emotion gripped my throat. It wasn't my mind that needed to be changed. It was my station. My identity. My life. I could not stand here and let Mr. Hill confess his love to a lady's maid. If only he knew how little *I* truly had to offer. I would drag him down in society farther than his loss of inheritance ever could. His heart would be broken either way—if I told him the truth, or if I lied and told him that I didn't love him.

I closed my eyes for a short moment, letting the moisture disappear behind my eyelids. I didn't have the strength to break him, to speak the words that I knew would. But I couldn't lie either. "If you are no longer opposed to marriage, please consider Miss Downsfield," I said. "Her affection for you seems to run deeper than your inheritance, so I suspect she would accept your offer even without Hill Manor. She is much more inclined to the idea of marriage than I am. I have also considered that Miss Coppins might suit you best—"

Mr. Hill groaned, cutting my words short with his lips. They pressed against mine like an iron against silk—gently, as if he were afraid I would burn if he kissed me with any less care. My head spun. His kiss was like one might approach a bird, slow, restrained, so as to not risk the creature flying away. I wasn't going anywhere. The roots of the tree might as well have encircled my feet, and Mr. Hill's lips might as well have been two anchors. So long as he was kissing me, I couldn't move. I couldn't breathe.

His boots crunched over the twigs. I flattened against the tree. The chain holding my heart at bay snapped just like the twigs beneath Mr. Hill's boots, and I touched his neck, near the corner of his jaw, the skin warm and thrumming with his pulse. My fingers slid into his hair, and my toes lifted me higher.

I might have scolded myself, but I kissed him instead, weakened by the feeling of his gentle fingertips in my hair and his mouth moving slowly with my own. His kiss deepened at my encouragement, forbidden as it was.

Two female voices met my ears from the distance, growing closer with each second that passed. It sounded like Miss Downsfield and Miss Benham, but I didn't trust the accuracy of my judgement at the moment. Mr. Hill pulled back just enough to glance over his shoulder. I caught my breath, eyelids heavy, heart racing. My lips tingled.

"We mustn't be seen," I whispered, panic rising in my throat. I pushed against his chest, but it was a weak effort, my fingers curling into limp fists instead.

His eyes found mine, and he took my hand, pulling me past the large tree in the clearing and into the thicket, where the shadows were much heavier, despite the slow rise of the sun. I had to run to keep up with his long strides, but my legs shook, and I almost laughed.

Almost.

Our kiss had been interrupted, and Mr. Hill was nothing if not determined. He led me several paces into the trees before stopping and turning toward me. "We can't go back until I've changed your mind," he muttered, his eyes serious and unwavering. His dark lashes swept downward, and he cupped my face in his hands. His thumb traced over my lower lip, and my eyes closed. "Or until you tell me to stop trying."

My eyes fluttered open. Morning light filtered through the leaves, taking advantage of tiny pockets between the foliage. The sunlight left spots on Mr. Hill's hair and jacket, but lacked the strength to fill our entire space between the trees. My mind ordered me to tell him to stop, but I was even weaker than the morning sunlight. I hesitated for too long.

His lips lowered to mine again, and his hands gripped my waist. My heart hammered, and he must have felt the same knocking against his chest. His kisses were more confident now, more fervent, as if he realized I was not as fragile as he thought—as if he no longer worried I would push him away. I couldn't, even if I wanted to. Not when he was kissing me the way he was—as if he really did want me. Not just for now. Forever.

With each touch of his lips, I believed him more. Reckless abandon swelled inside me, and I let myself forget all the reasons why he shouldn't want me. A lady's maid may not have gotten what she wanted, but here in the trees with the sun rising around us, I could. I could be who I wanted. I could kiss Mr. Hill for as long as he would let me. I did not have to give him to Miss Downsfield or Miss Taplow or Miss Benham or Miss Coppins because they wanted him first. I did not have to curtsy and step away from him if they demanded it. The only thing I was capable of listening to at the moment were the demands of my heart, and it demanded *more*.

Reason was gone. Logic abandoned. Responsibility lost in the feeling of Mr. Hill's lips against my own. If not for the blackbird, our kiss might have never ended. I might have never realized my mistake.

Lurkey, lurkey, lurkey.

Our kiss broke abruptly. My cheeks burned with the realization that I had not been the aloof bystander I should have been. I had kissed him just as thoroughly as he had kissed me, and my heart had been completely exposed by it. My hands still clung to his jacket. His eyes followed mine to the sky, and I held my breath, schooling it back to a normal rhythm.

"The blackbird," he whispered. "Just as I said." He smiled with a hint of mischief. But his eyes were still heavy, filled with the same awe and emotion that flooded my chest.

"This cannot continue," I whispered. "I cannot marry you."

My heart stung at the way his smile fell. "You cannot or you will not?"

I shook my head, turning away.

"Please, Sophia." He took hold of my arm, stopping me.

My senses came back to me in one harsh blow, striking my chest and pounding that one dreadful word against my skull.

Sophia.

A tear slipped out the corner of my eye, and I wiped it away before he could see it. "I'm not Sophia." It took me a moment to realize I had said it aloud, and I clamped my mouth closed, my heart thudding. Before he could question me, I pulled my arm away from his grasp, hurrying out of the thicket and back to the place where we had almost been seen.

To my relief, Mrs. Ollerton stood nearby with Miss Benham, both staring up at the trees. I glanced back just as Mr. Hill joined us. I tried to correct my expression, but Mrs. Ollerton seemed to notice my distress.

"What is the matter, Miss Sedgwick?" She raised her pale eyebrows in alarm.

"Nothing is amiss." I forced a smile to my face. My heart still thudded in my ears, drowning out all the birdsong. Had Mr. Hill heard me say I wasn't Sophia? I didn't dare look at his face and find out.

She seemed satisfied enough with that response, turning her attention to Mr. Hill. "Oh, I am most pleased to tell you that Miss Benham has identified my bird. I suppose you will have to take her on a ride this afternoon."

Miss Benham smiled proudly, her large brown eyes enhanced by her red bonnet.

Mr. Hill's footsteps crunched behind me, and I kept my gaze fixed on the ground. Surely he had questions to ask me, but I couldn't give him that chance. My tongue had slipped, and I would pay for revealing that secret, one way or another.

"I look forward to it, Miss Benham." Mr. Hill's voice was hoarse and quiet. It tugged at my heart.

After the group had gathered together again, we made

our way back to the house. The sun had fully risen by the time we stepped through the doors, but all I wanted was to go back to sleep. After debating over what to do with the rest of the day, I decided to pay a visit to Jessie. It was the one place I knew Mr. Hill would not come looking for me, and she was the only one who understood why I couldn't marry him. With luck, he would have an enjoyable time with Miss Benham that afternoon.

With luck, he would forget all about me and that forbidden kiss.

CHAPTER 23

*I*t seemed Mr. Hill was not the forgetful sort.

When I sneaked back to my room that afternoon, a letter rested against my door. I took it inside before sitting on my bed and unfolding it. The note itself was short, and another pang of despair struck my heart when I saw who it was written to.

Sophia,

I could hardly read the rest, my eyes blurring with tears. Perhaps he hadn't heard me deny that name as my own. Or he hadn't realized what I meant—that I wasn't really Miss Sophia Sedgwick.

. . .

Meet me by the stables at four o'clock. This is simply a request, but one that will be enlightening, and will allow you to convey your feelings without the need to speak to me again. If you do not come, I will know that what you said this morning is true. If you do come, I hope you will, at the very least, provide me with the answers I seek.

I threw the note onto my bed, falling back against the covers. He must have left it at my door before his ride with Miss Benham. It was nearly four o'clock already.

It would be better if I didn't go. Or rather, better for *me*, but not for him. I owed him an explanation. There were risks in telling him the truth, but he deserved to know it. And I trusted him enough to know that he wouldn't tell anyone here at Winslow House, and would ensure I made it back home safely in my disguise. He might think badly of me, but at least he would know why I had so heartlessly refused him.

I reminded myself that he had treated Jessie with kindness, and she was a maid, so there was a chance he would still be kind to me. He had even written to his uncle in an effort to save who he thought was my maid's father. My heart ached at the reminder that that was also another piece of the truth I would have to reveal if I met him at the stables. Mr. Hill would likely think I had only befriended him as a way to achieve my own designs. What he didn't know was that I had always wanted to be near him, and helping Papa had been my best excuse to allow it, even though it had been dangerous. If both our hearts broke because of my choice, at least Papa had a better chance at the rest of his life than he had before. That thought was the consolation I needed as I stood, taking a deep breath before the mirror.

I would be honest and forthright. I wouldn't allow any of my emotions to show. As I made my way down the stairs, I replaced the barriers on my heart, willing them to be strong enough to withstand the storm that was coming.

A shrill laugh made me stop at the base of the stairs. I walked closer to the sound, my heart pounding. I had become quite familiar with the voices of each guest at Winslow House, but this voice was even more familiar.

"She will not be punished for it. I only wished to give her the opportunity to experience what it is like to be a lady. But I have come now to enjoy the last week of your house party in her place. I did not know Mr. Hill had such a beautiful property, or I might have come sooner."

Dread sank deeper in my stomach as I approached the drawing room door.

"My dear friend Anne likes it even more than her own family's Hampden Park, and so I couldn't resist coming for my chance to be mistress of it."

I closed my eyes against the sting in my head.

This could not be real.

Sophia couldn't really be here.

"I believe you are underestimating the extent of your deception, Miss Sedgwick." Mrs. Ollerton's voice was quiet and somewhat nervous. "You have led me, as well as all of my guests, to believe that your maid was eligible to marry Mr. Hill, and that she bore your name and station."

"Did you all really believe it? Oh, my. She must have behaved better than I expected." She giggled again.

I leaned closer to the door, emotion gripping my throat.

A voice from behind me made me jump. "Oh, there you are Sherbrooke."

I turned to see Miss Coppins, a smug smile on her lips. My mind raced, and it took a long moment to recognize the name she had just called me.

Sherbrooke.

She drifted past me, placing one hand on the door. "It seems you have now been made aware of our new guest."

My brow furrowed, pain stabbing at my chest.

"I heard you speaking to that maid with the injured leg in the gardens about your little ruse." Miss Coppins grinned, as if she were proud of her discovery. "I thought it prudent to write to your mistress to inform her of your deception. I was quite surprised to learn she was already aware of it. After receiving my letter, she simply had to come take her chance on him herself. I would have told Mrs. Ollerton directly, but the anxiety such a betrayal to you, a dear friend, would cause would be a great strain on my health." She drew a deep breath. "I did try to have you removed from the house before your secret could be revealed, but that effort did not succeed."

My heart pounded. "What effort?"

"As soon as I discovered your secret, I took the pendant

from the drawing room." A slow smile spread on her lips. "It would have been for your own good, you know, if it had been found in your room. You might have gone home before the entire household learned that you are a lady's maid." She glanced upward with a sigh before pushing lightly on the drawing room door. "It seems we are now too late for that."

I didn't have time to recover from the shock of what she had just revealed to me, nor the time to process the strange logic behind it all. How could she have possibly thought she was being helpful? Sophia arriving here was infinitely worse than my secret being revealed in some other way, and having me sent home for thievery would have been even worse.

Beyond the open doorway, Sophia sat beside Mrs. Ollerton on the sofa, appearing graceful and comfortable enough to have been a guest here for weeks. Her golden curls were piled atop her head, blue eyes rounding with surprise when she saw me. "Oh, Sherbrooke, you must be quite surprised to see me here."

Surprise did not begin to explain all the things I felt. My head spun, my breathing shallow.

"Come, come." She waved her hand for me to enter the room, a pleasant smile on her face. Miss Downsfield, Miss Benham, and Miss Taplow were all seated on the other sofa, watching me with a mixture of victory and shock.

In an instant, I was no longer a lady. I was no longer their equal. I was now a maid who was expected to obey a demand from her mistress.

I walked into the room, stopping by Sophia's side. She looked up at me with a doting smile, reminding me of how Mrs. Ollerton looked at her dog. I knew Sophia was not nearly as caring as she pretended to be for her spectators. "I have missed your attention to detail these weeks, Sherbrooke. The maid Anne let me use at Hampden park did not have your talent."

Sophia turned her attention to the other guests. "I truly have the most talented maid. It will be quite advantageous for me to have her here to help me look presentable during this final week. You all have had weeks to make an impression on Mr. Hill, and I have only one week to do that." She laughed.

The awkwardness in the room was nearly too much to bear. Mrs. Ollerton looked vastly uncomfortable, shifting in her chair and touching her curls repeatedly. "It may be unwise for Miss—er—your maid to remain here at Winslow House."

"Why should it be unwise?" Sophia glanced at me, then at Mrs. Ollerton, her blue eyes wide with curiosity.

For the first time in my life, I felt keen to faint. I touched my fingertips to my temples, drawing a shaking breath into my lungs. Mr. Hill was waiting for me at the stables. I could already see what would happen next. When he realized I was never coming, he would return to the house and find the real Sophia, and me, the imposter. I couldn't explain the truth to him now. He would see it all for himself instead. I was no longer in a place to do or say as I wanted. Sophia was here, and I was a slave to her every wish, or my employment would be taken away.

I begged Mrs. Ollerton with my eyes not to say what I feared she would.

She didn't listen. "I believe it would be best to sever Mr. Hill's attachment by sending your maid home at once."

Sophia blinked.

My eyes squeezed shut.

"Attachment?" Sophia scoffed, a laugh escaping her. "Do you mean to say that Mr. Hill has fallen in love with...Sherbrooke?"

Mrs. Ollerton was silent for a long moment. I had never seen her so uncollected. Her chest rose and fell rapidly, and she began fanning herself. "Oh, dear. This is not good."

Sophia turned to me, one eyebrow arching. "Is it true?"

I swallowed, searching for a way to placate the situation. "It is speculation, that is all. We are friends. He hasn't expressed a wish to marry me." The lie burned on my tongue.

Her gaze traveled to the other ladies in the room with scrutiny, as if she were searching for any reason why Mr. Hill might have favored me over them. She wouldn't find the reason. Even I did not fully understand it.

"Well, then. I see no reason why she cannot stay." Sophia met Mrs. Ollerton's gaze. "Now that he knows her true identity, any thought he may have had toward marrying her will be extinguished. A man of his station would never consider a maid as a wife."

"No, of course not." Mrs. Ollerton's lips pinched together. "However, if we wish to avoid a scandal of any sort, I think it is best to take precautions. I am certain your parents would agree. I will have my own carriage convey Miss Sherbrooke and the other maid from your household back to Kent first thing tomorrow."

Sophia's brow furrowed, as if she hadn't considered the fact that her parents would be informed of her late arrival. If Jessie and I went back now without Sophia, they would have to be given an explanation, and then there would be no one to accompany Sophia back home in a week.

"That will not do," Sophia said, shaking her head. "I think so long as Sherbrooke remains below stairs for the rest of the week, not even Mr. Hill should know that she is still here. Then she may still be present to accompany me back home when the time comes." She smiled. "Unless, of course, it is expected that I stay to court Mr. Hill."

It was refreshing not to be the recipient of all the envious glares. It seemed the other ladies were thinking the real Miss Sedgwick was far more of a threat to their success than I was. Little did they know that he *had* proposed to me, and I had refused. My heart ached as I thought of him, standing by the stables as he waited for me. Had he given up hope yet? I glanced at the long case clock in the corner of the room. It was fifteen minutes past four.

"I suppose that will suffice," Mrs. Ollerton said, glancing at me briefly before turning her attention back to Sophia. "She will share a bedchamber with your other maid, and you may tell Mr. Hill she was sent home."

"Wonderful." Sophia clasped her hands together, as if the matter were settled and completely behind her. "Where is Mr. Hill? I should very much like to meet him."

"I believe he is still at the stables," Miss Benham said. "He and I went riding this afternoon." She gave Sophia a pointed look.

Mrs. Ollerton stood, smoothing her hands over her skirts with a huffed breath. "I suspect he will return at any moment." She turned toward me. "Please make haste. I will have your things sent down to your new room."

My mind still raced, but I obeyed, walking toward the door. The moment I was alone, tears sprung to my eyes. I wiped angrily at them, ridding my face of the tiny droplets as I made my way toward Jessie's room. My chance to explain myself to Mr. Hill was gone. I would never see him again.

In a matter of minutes, I had been harshly reminded of who I really was. My freedom was gone, and so was the new strength and identity I had found. Sophia had taken away that which she had given me, and now she planned to take away Mr. Hill too.

I stopped myself. He was never in my future. I couldn't be robbed of him if he was never meant to be mine at all. It was simply a foolish hope, a dream, a wish, that could never be. The entire time I had been at Winslow House was a dream, and now I was finally awakening. My place was not on the arm of the handsome gentleman who I loved. It was below stairs. Invisible, quiet, alone, and forgotten.

CHAPTER 24

J hadn't expected Jessie to become such a dear friend, and I certainly hadn't expected her to become my eyes and ears. During the week I was trapped below stairs, she seized the opportunity to act as Sophia's lady's maid. Each night, Jessie would relay to me all the gossip she had heard, and everything she had observed among the guests.

"Sophia claims that Mr. Hill's taken an interest in her, but I've seen nothin' to support that idea," Jessie had said one night, her lips pursed. "His heart's loyal to you, Tillie. Feelings don't simply disappear."

I wished they would. My heart had felt sickened all week as I wondered what he must have thought of me. How foolish he must have felt for caring for me like he did.

On the last night before our departure, Jessie had been particularly attentive, watching for any sign that Mr. Hill had decided to marry one of the ladies after all. I had hardly been able to sit still all day in terrified anticipation, and when Jessie burst through the door, her expression was difficult to read.

"Mistress Sophia's not pleased," Jessie said, her eyes wide. After a brief moment, her expression melted into a smile. "Not pleased in the slightest."

"What happened?" My heart pounded hard against my ribs.

"Mr. Hill made an announcement at dinner, she told me." Jessie's eyes lit up. "He told the entire party how privileged he felt to meet them all, but that the woman he wished to marry wasn't among them. He then explained that he was no longer to inherit his family's home." Jessie sat down beside me on the bed. "Can you believe it? All this time he's known, but didn't care to publicize it until now. And when he said the woman he wished to marry wasn't among them...surely he spoke of you."

I swallowed against my dry throat, bunching fabric from my dress into my fists. "That cannot be what he meant." I cast her a berating look, softening it with a faint smile. "Please do not hint at that again. I cannot afford to hope." My heart stung as I looked down at my hands. Hope was what caused me so much pain now. As much as I had tried to keep it at bay, hope had escaped its confines for long enough to dream of a future with Mr. Hill. And that was where I had gone wrong. I couldn't control the feelings in my heart, but I should have controlled my dreams.

"If he loves you as much as I think he does, he won't simply forget you." Jessie's gaze was firm. "The first thing he'll do when he leaves Winslow House is go find you, I'm sure of it."

"No, he will not." I gave her the best smile I could muster. "And I am content with that fact. Even if he did wish to marry me still, I couldn't lower him to such a state. Society would frown upon him forever. Surely he is already enduring enough scrutiny for the change in his inheritance."

"You're not content, Tillie." Jessie shook her head, clasping my hand in hers. "You don't have to pretend you are in front of me."

At her words, tears pricked the back of my eyes, and a lump formed in my throat. I had been holding back the emotion that throbbed in my heart, painful and unjust, for the last week. I never would have thought something as soft as Jessie's words would break the dam. I breathed deeply, failing to keep my tears from falling down my cheeks. I tipped my head back, as if that would aid the situation. "And I'm glad," I said, sniffing. "I have done enough pretending already." I rubbed my nose, laughing despite the pain.

"You need never pretend to be Sophia again. Tillie is much better, I think." Jessie wrapped her arms around me, and I leaned my head on her shoulder.

"Do not tell Sophia that, or we shall both lose our wages," I muttered.

"Aye. But since she banished you below stairs for a week, she deserves our ill words."

I laughed, wiping my cheeks with the back of my hand.

Though the future was uncertain, there were still many good things in my life that hadn't been taken away. Soon, I would return home and see Mama. I still had sunrises and birdsong and friends like Jessie. I had memories of Papa, sweet, beautiful things to reflect on when I was worried or sad. And now, I had memories of Mr. Hill.

"I wish I could have an opportunity to explain." The words spilled out as I sat up, drying my eyes. "Sophia could have told him any number of lies about me. I cannot imagine what he must think of me. I do not want to imagine it."

Jessie's eyes rounded. "You *can* explain! Write him a letter, and I will deliver it."

I bit my lip, my heart picking up speed. "Truly?"

"Yes!"

"I don't have any writing supplies."

Jessie grinned. "Leave that to me."

Jessie left my letter at Mr. Hill's door late the night before our departure. We were leaving early enough that it was unlikely he would see it until after I was already gone. He wouldn't have time to wonder how it had gotten there, or wonder if I had still been at the house all along.

He wouldn't have time to come looking for me.

The birds sang as Jessie and I waited outside the carriage for Sophia. The footmen had finished loading the coach with our belongings, and were beginning to find a place for Sophia's as she walked out the front doors. She didn't appear as disappointed as I had expected, but rather relieved to be leaving Winslow House behind. Perhaps the other ladies were too, now that they knew Mr. Hill was not as rich as they had hoped. Handsome, yes. Kind, yes. And so many other things worth more than money. I shushed my thoughts, trying not to wonder if he was awake or asleep—if he had found my letter or not.

The note hadn't been an outpouring of my feelings, but rather a simple explanation for why I had been unable to tell him the truth, and that I had still planned to tell him that day at the stables. I apologized, and I thanked him, and wished him all the happiness he deserved. Although we had never been entirely proper, a maid couldn't write a love letter to a gentleman. I didn't know if he would keep my letter or throw it aside, but at least I knew he would read it. That eased something inside me.

When all the bags and trunks were secured, we entered the carriage. I stretched my legs, preparing for the long journey ahead. There was much to occupy my mind, so it wasn't boredom I feared. Sophia would likely have plenty of prattle to pass the time.

As the carriage doors were closed behind us, the front doors of the house opened.

Mr. Hill walked down the steps.

My heart seized, and I flattened against the back cushion of my seat so I wouldn't be seen through the window. Mrs. Ollerton followed closely behind him, reaching for the back of his jacket as if she might actually grasp onto it and stop him.

How had I forgotten? Mr. Hill always arose early.

"Hide yourself!" Sophia said, swatting her hand through the air above my head.

I ducked lower in my seat when the carriage began to move. Sophia waved out her window, and I remained unseen. He didn't know that I had been there all week, and it would be better if he never found out. I closed my eyes against the pain in my chest, only sitting up once I knew we were too far for him to see through the window. I could still see his outline, standing beside Mrs. Ollerton on the drive at Winslow House. Even from the carriage, I could see the slump to his shoulders and the folded piece of foolscap in his hand. My letter. What else could it have been?

I watched him as we drove away, careful to keep my face hidden. My heart ached. My head throbbed. Everything hurt as Winslow House disappeared behind the hills, taking Mr. Hill with it.

"I never should have left Hampden Park to come here." Sophia let out a sigh, adjusting the curls beneath her bonnet. "I see why Anne finds Mr. Hill attractive, but without his property he is not the prized bachelor Mrs. Ollerton supposed him to be. It shocks me that he would create such a ruse and only tell the party at the end of his stay." She shook her head. "I suspect the woman he hopes to marry will reject him now that he does not have Hill Manor to offer. What a disappointment. I daresay my arrival at Winslow House was the most diverting thing the guests experienced their entire trip." Her blue eyes met mine. "I will not have you punished, of course, and Mrs. Ollerton intends to keep the situation confidential as well, since she would hate to have any scandalous impersonation tied to her." She eyed me with suspicion. "However, I do wonder what you did to encourage Mr. Hill's attention."

"I did nothing. I acted as you advised me to."

She laughed under her breath. "I suspect he was quite embarrassed by his regard for you once I told him you were my maid."

I looked out the window. I felt as if the heaviness in my heart would never go away. It crushed down on me, as if I might sink to the bottom of the carriage.

If only I could ask her what his expression had shown when he learned the truth. Was he embarrassed? Betrayed? Hurt? To think that I had caused him to feel any of those things brought the heavy stone of ache to sink lower in my stomach.

The rest of the journey passed slowly, and by the time we reached Sedgwick Manor the next day, I could hardly wait to return to what was normal and safe.

Mr. and Mrs. Sedgwick stood outside, awaiting the carriage, and the moment it stopped and Sophia stepped out, her mother burst into tears, throwing her arms around her. After Sophia told her that Mr. Hill did not propose, Mrs. Sedgwick appeared to be offering her daughter words of consolation that she certainly didn't need, asking for every detail of her trip and declaring every shortcoming Mr. Hill *surely must have had* to have not chosen Sophia.

I walked closer, spotting Mama behind the Sedgwicks. Although she didn't know the ordeal I had been through, her eyes were filled with the same softness and kindness as Jessie's, and my emotions overflowed again. What had felt like a failure didn't feel quite so much like one anymore. I was still allowed to work at Sedgwick Manor with Mama, and that was something to be grateful for.

"My dear Tillie." She smiled as I approached, pulling me into her arms. Two tears soaked into her sleeve, and I wiped my cheeks before stepping back. Why was it so much harder to be strong when surrounded by so much love? Perhaps that's exactly what love was: weakness. But if loving Mr. Hill had made me weak, then I was content with that. One day I could be strong again, but for now, I was allowed to hurt.

Mama seemed to notice the heaviness in my expression, but she didn't say a word, pulling me back into her arms and squeezing me tighter.

CHAPTER 25

NE MONTH LATER

As content as I was to be home, I feared I would always have another hole in my heart, one right beside the one Papa had left behind. I had hoped Mr. Hill would be easy to forget, but I had never been more wrong.

Despite the painful things that still lingered in my heart, I had never felt more free.

My circumstances had not changed, but my heart had. My confidence had. Being a maid was not my identity, but my opportunity to help Sophia every day, and to learn new things. My knowledge on hair arrangements and current fashions had never been so extensive before, and I was taking pride in my work for the first time. Jessie hadn't been pleased to go back to her duties, but we still enjoyed our happy conversations each day, and I even began arising a few minutes earlier, singing in the mornings alongside the birds. Each time I heard the blackbird's song, I remembered Mr. Hill, and our kiss, and the many times we had laughed. The memories grew lighter each day, and I tried not to allow them to be weighed down by reality.

Jessie had been wrong.

He didn't want me anymore.

If he wanted me, he would have come, just as she had said. But I couldn't blame him for staying away.

Mama had been unable to afford any more trips to Canterbury, but we had enough to send new letters to Papa each week. He didn't write back, but we allowed ourselves to hope that he was well. As dangerous as hope was, I had also learned that life was bleak without it.

Summer had come, and the warm air was a balm to my soul. Today, I walked alongside the stream behind Sedgwick Manor, listening to the buzzing insects and thick sloshing of my boots on the wet grass. Sophia was spending the day with Anne in town, who had come to visit, so my duties were few.

I followed the stream to the edge of the property before sitting down on a patch of dry grass, leaning back on my hands. The sun warmed my cheeks, making my eyelids heavy, and I nearly fell asleep sitting up.

"Tillie!"

I jumped at the sound of Mama's voice, blinking the orange and yellow sunlight spots from my vision. She came slowly into focus: Her gray dress, white apron, dark hair, and tear streaked cheeks.

I scrambled to my feet, fear knocking against my chest. "What is the matter?"

She covered her mouth with one hand, and when she pulled it away, she was smiling. Relief crashed over my shoulders, but it was quickly replaced by curiosity. "Mama, what is it?" I walked closer, taking her by the shoulders.

"I received a letter from Mr. Baker." She wiped her cheeks, her eyes flooding with a new bout of tears. "He has repealed his accusations against your father. He was released last week and is expected to return home any day now."

I gasped, throwing my arms around Mama. The joy and relief that flooded my entire body was indescribable, and I could hardly catch my breath as tears filled my own eyes. "How?"

Mama shook her head, her hair sticking to my wet cheek. "Mr. Baker's explanation was brief, but he did apologize for the state he left our family in. He claims he was humbled by a relative who ultimately convinced him to have a change of heart."

I pulled back, blinking rapidly to clear my vision. "A relative? Did he mention a name?"

"No." She glanced heavenward. "But he is an angel, whoever he is."

My heart hammered against my chest. Had Mr. Hill's efforts truly succeeded? The last time we had spoken he had not sounded very hopeful that his uncle could be persuaded. What else had he done? Had he realized that *I* was the maid I had spoken of, not Jessie? If he knew my name, he would surely recognize my connection to my father. Tears filled my eyes again, my emotions too scattered to be contained. "But where will Papa go now? How will he find work? Disgrace will follow him wherever he goes."

"We will find our way as we always have." Mama squeezed my hand. "What matters is that he is free and alive."

I nodded. I hardly noticed how wet my feet were inside my boots and how soaked the hem of my dress had become, standing so close to the stream beside Mama. My heart and head swirled with too many emotions and questions to dwell on anything else.

Papa was coming home.

"I've another letter for you," Mama said, digging into her apron pocket. She sniffed, wiping her nose as she extended the letter to me. "I do not recognize the name of the gentleman."

My heart gave a leap before I even took the letter from her hand. There was only one gentleman who would ever write to a maid. My hand shook as I took the letter, and I struggled to tear the seal. The moment it unfolded, a long blue silk ribbon fluttered to the ground. I picked it up before it could become soaked, rubbing the soft fabric between my fingertips. My heart pounded so hard it hurt, and hope gripped me so hard I was sure I couldn't move even if I wished to. My eyes took in the writing on the page, and I held the ribbon against my chest.

. . .

Dearest Tillie,

I do not know what you are thinking, but I can make my best attempt at guessing your thoughts. I have become quite skilled in trying to understand all the things you will not say aloud. At this moment, you are likely thinking how strange it is that I remembered the very ribbon you admired at the modiste's, but you should not be surprised. You and everything you do and say are unforgettable to me. I could not forget you even if it was my dearest wish, and I assure you, there have been days over the last month that I have wished to forget you and all the pain that comes with not having you, but I cannot. My heart is yours and always will be.

It took a great deal of effort, but I finally managed to discover your real name from Miss Sedgwick. In the case of Miss Sedgwick, as rare as it is, I find that I like the imitation much better than the reality. It doesn't matter that your name is actually Tillie Sherbrooke. It suits you much better than Sophia ever did. I do not care about your station, nor the consequences to my own if I were to tie myself to you. I have come to realize that happiness is not found in respect from others, but in respecting oneself. I have put aside my pride, my dear Tillie, and I never wish for it back. I only wish for you, and I must respect that wish, no matter who in my family or in society does not. You are my happiness. You are my heart. I love you.

I would have come to you sooner, but there was a matter of business which I had to attend to. It is my privilege to tell you that your father is now free, and will be returning to you at Sedgwick Manor at the same moment I do. Your father is a good man, just as you said. Of course, a large part of my regard for him comes with the fact that he granted my request to marry you, should you agree.

Others may say that the matter of your station means you do not deserve to marry a man of my station, but the truth is quite to the contrary. I cannot give you all that you deserve, but I have tried. In the month we have been apart, I have worked tirelessly on my new property, and if it suits you, I think we could be quite happy there. The land is expansive, and I have offered the Roberts family a place as one of my tenants, where I believe they will be far more prosperous.

Tears spilled down my cheeks as I thought of the little girl who had lost her father, and the family who had taken her in. Mr. Hill had not forgotten them either. I wiped my eyes so I could see the rest of the letter.

My path did not lead me where I thought it would, and I have been foolish far more times to count, but all the disappointment that led me to where I am today was worth every moment. I might have never found you, and that is a thought I don't care to dwell on.

If my estimation is correct, this letter will have reached you just a day or two before I do. If by the time I arrive you haven't received it, I will repeat all the things I have said here. I will say it again and again if it means you will finally grow tired of my persistence and agree to be my wife.

With all my love,
  Mr. Frederick Hill

When I finished reading, I nearly forgot Mama was still standing in front of me, her face heavy with concern. A smile overtook my face, and I read the letter again, unable to believe that Mr. Hill had really written those sweet words for me. My tears dripped off the tip of my nose, and I dried them with my sleeve. I felt as if I were floating, all the heaviness that had been weighing on my heart for the last month turned to feathers, wings that lifted me higher than the trees. I looped my arm through Mama's, keeping the letter and ribbon tucked safely in my apron.

I had never explained to Mama the reason for my tears the day I returned from Winslow House, and she had never asked, patiently waiting for me to tell her when I felt ready. So on our walk back to the house, I told her everything, including what Mr. Hill had written in his letter.

"I esteem him highly already." Her smile could not have been wider than my own. "It seems both our hearts will be returning to us tomorrow."

A flutter coursed through my stomach, and I tried to

imagine what it would be like to see Mr. Hill's face again, to feel his arms around me, to kiss his lips. To hear him tell me that he meant every word in his letter. It didn't seem real. How could I wait an entire day, or more, to see him? And to see Papa! My heart couldn't contain all the excitement even now when the news was so fresh. I could only imagine how rampant my emotions would be after being left to flourish all day and night.

When we reached the house, we were stopped in the hallway by Mrs. Sedgwick's voice. "Sherbrooke!"

Mama and I both turned at the sound. She walked with purpose in our direction, her blue skirts swaying with the motion. As she came closer, I noticed the glaze over her eyes and the pallor on her cheeks. "You will never believe who is in our drawing room."

My heart leaped, and I exchanged a glance with Mama.

"Is it my husband?" Mama asked, her voice barely above a whisper. "Already?"

Mrs. Sedgwick nodded, shock reflecting in her eyes. "How did you know?"

"I just received word this morning." Mama squeezed my arm, as if to steady herself. The nearby bannister would have provided much better stability than I currently could. My lungs felt like two large rocks, heavy and unable to expand amid the wild pounding of my heart.

Mrs. Sedgwick's throat bobbed with a swallow. "And Mr. Hill has come with him." She eyed me carefully. "He has asked for *you*."

I felt suddenly frozen, torn between running to him

and hiding in my room again. What if he came to regret his decision? What if he begrudged me one day for lowering him in society? I shushed my fears. They had ruled me for long enough. At any rate, Mr. Hill's mind was not easily changed.

"Why is he asking for you?" Mrs. Sedgwick continued to stare at me, likely noting the emotion that I had never been skilled at hiding from my features. "How are you acquainted?"

"I'm afraid that's a question you must ask your daughter," Mama said.

Mrs. Sedgwick appeared even more confused, but Mama seemed unable to stand still for a moment longer. She pulled me toward the open door of the drawing room, and Mrs. Sedgwick followed closely behind.

I saw Papa first, sitting on a chair near the window. His hair was much longer than the last time I had seen him, dark and coarse, just like the beard he had grown. His blue eyes filled with tears the moment they took in Mama, then me, and he stood, rushing forward to pull his wife into his arms. She cried into his shoulder, and he kissed the top of her head. She turned, waving me forward, and Papa hugged me at the same time, holding us both as if he never wished to let go. "I'm sorry," he whispered, his voice more gruff than I remembered. His eyes found mine, wrinkled at the corners, just as I had always known them. "My dear Tillie. Only a man like Mr. Hill could ever deserve to marry you. You both have saved me." At the mention of Mr. Hill, my heart jumped. Amid the joy of seeing Papa again, I had nearly forgotten that he was here too.

I stepped away from Papa, rotating until I saw him. He stood near the pianoforte. How had it only been a month since I had seen him? It felt like much longer than that. His gaze met mine, sending warmth through my chest and all the way to my fingertips. He wore a green waistcoat and dark jacket, his golden brown hair styled neatly. His blue eyes were filled with all the emotion I felt, deeper than the sea and warmer than the summer sun that beat through the nearby window.

We both drew a deep breath at the same moment, and I watched as a slow smile formed on his lips.

Neither of us moved, though I was tempted to run to him that very instant. He looked so polite and proper, standing rather stiffly, as if he were restraining just as much as I was. He turned toward Mrs. Sedgwick, then my parents. "May I request the privilege of speaking with Miss Sherbrooke alone?"

Mama and Papa smiled as they retreated into the hallway. Mrs. Sedgwick's brow furrowed with confusion, but she followed, her slow steps lasting an eternity.

With the click of the door, Mr. Hill filled the space between us in three long strides, stopping just in front of me. His hands cradled my face, warm and strong. "Tillie." He said my name in a quiet voice, and fresh tears pooled in my eyes. I never thought I would hear him say it.

My tears fell between his fingers. I laughed and sniffed at the same time, remembering my wet dress and boots and the state of my hair from being outside in the wind. Mr. Hill didn't seem to care at all, his gaze sweeping my face with raw adoration. "Did you receive my letter?"

I nodded, pressing my lips together. "Just minutes ago. I have been a watering pot ever since."

He chuckled, reminding me just how much I had missed the sound. His cheeks creased with his smile, his dark brows lifting. "Please assure me they are tears of joy."

"Yes." I laughed, a choked sound. "I daresay I have never been happier." I didn't have to explain to him the source of my happiness. The fact that he was here, that Papa was here, that he loved me enough to bring Papa home first. Jessie had been wrong—he hadn't come to me first. He had selflessly done all he could to save my father because he knew that was what I truly needed. "What you did for my father...my words are not enough to express the gratitude I feel."

He smiled down at me. "It was an honor to save an innocent man, and especially one who you love so dearly. I will ensure both your parents live comfortably for the rest of their days. Your father is ambitious and hard-working. There is no need to worry over his future. He is welcome to live in my home until he has found a new occupation."

It seemed impossible, but my love and gratitude expanded at his words. "How can you be so generous and kind?"

"I learned from you, you know." He smiled.

"Even after I deceived you." I shook my head. "How can you forgive me?"

"I know you well enough to know that you would never hurt anyone intentionally. The moment I discovered that you were Miss Sedgwick's maid, I knew you were not acting on your own will. It clearly explained why you were so insistent in your refusal of me." He brushed a strand of hair off of my forehead, tracing his finger over the side of my face. His smile grew lopsided. "You wouldn't have been able to resist my offer otherwise."

My smile grew to match his—I could not have scowled at his teasing even if I wanted to. "Surely you know me well enough to know I am determined. Perhaps I would have."

"Is that still your intention? Will you refuse me out of pride?" He leaned closer, one arm sliding around my waist, pulling me in.

"I suppose if you have set aside your pride for me, as you said in your letter, I ought to do the same for you." I rested my hands on his chest, feeling the beat of his heart against my palm, my hands rising and falling with his breathing.

"I spent the entire carriage ride planning my speech to you, but it seems you have already read it."

"I will not stop you from saying it again." I laughed, but it came out breathless. He was so close, his smiling lips just inches from my own.

He leaned his forehead against mine. "I think I would rather kiss you," he mumbled.

"I will not stop you from doing that either."

I watched his smile grow before his lips captured mine, his arms pulling me even closer. My hands slid over his chest and to the back of his neck, and I brought his head closer to ensure he knew without question that these kisses were willingly given, not stolen. His lips moved with certainty, and he kissed me as if he would never kiss me again, although I knew now that that wasn't true. All the doubt I had felt was banished from my heart with each second, each kiss, until all I felt was loved and cherished and utterly adored.

"I love you," I whispered against his lips. He tipped his forehead against mine. His chest rose and fell quickly beneath my palms, and he kissed my lips one last time, gentle and slow, before pulling back to look at my eyes.

"Does that mean you will marry me?"

I laughed, realizing I still hadn't given him a direct answer. He watched me as if he were still afraid I would run away or refuse his offer.

"Yes." I touched his cheek, tracing my thumb over the dimple that formed when he smiled. "But I do have two stipulations."

His eyebrows lifted. "And what might they be?"

"You must never make me sing for any guests, no matter how it will amuse you."

He tipped his head back with a laugh. "And the second?"

"You must never allow me near the tea tray until it is safely on the table."

He chuckled again. "Surely you will find a way to tip it onto one of the guests either way."

I smiled. "Only if Miss Downsfield pays us a call."

His eyes widened. "Hmm. You are not very amiable this afternoon, are you?"

We laughed until my stomach ached and tears streamed from my eyes. With Mr. Hill's arms wrapped around me and my head resting on his chest, I was safe, secure, and free to dream of a future of happiness, love, and contentment. As his laughter rumbled against me, he pressed a kiss into my hair, and I considered that perhaps Sophia's idea *had been* quite clever after all.

MORE IN THE SEASONS OF CHANGE SERIES

Don't miss the next book in the Seasons of Change series!
A Well-Trained Lady by Jess Heileman

Other books in the series:
The Road through Rushbury by Martha Keyes
A Forgiving Heart by Kasey Stockton
The Cottage by Coniston by Deborah M. Hathaway
A Haunting at Havenwood by Sally Britton
His Disinclined Bride by Jennie Goutet

JOIN THE NEWSLETTER!

SIGN UP HERE!

Stay tuned to receive updates about Ashtyn Newbold's latest works!

MORE BOOKS BY ASHTYN NEWBOLD

Larkhall Letters Series
The Ace of Hearts
More coming soon!

Brides of Brighton Series
A Convenient Engagement
Marrying Miss Milton
Romancing Lord Ramsbury
Miss Weston's Wager
An Unexpected Bride

Standalone novels
An Unwelcome Suitor
Mischief and Manors
Lies and Letters
Road to Rosewood

Novellas & Anthologies
The Earl's Mistletoe Match
The Midnight Heiress
Unexpected Love

ABOUT THE AUTHOR

Ashtyn Newbold grew up with a love of stories. When she discovered chick flicks and Jane Austen books in high school, she learned she was a sucker for romantic ones. When not indulging in sweet romantic comedies and regency period novels (and cookies), she writes romantic stories of her own across several genres. Ashtyn also enjoys baking, singing, sewing, and anything that involves creativity and imagination.

Connect with Ashtyn Newbold on these platforms!

ashtynnewbold.com

Made in the USA
Coppell, TX
05 October 2021